OBLUVIUM: SANCTUARY

Book One of the Obluvium Series

R. Dawn Hutchinson

This book is a work of fiction. The names, characters, places, and incidents are products of the writer's imagination or have been used fictitiously and are not to be construed as real. Any resemblance to persons, living or dead, actual events, locale or organizations is entirely coincidental.

Obluvium: Sanctuary

For Benjamin and Alyssa.

May you never outgrow your sense of wonder.

Contents

· Chapter One ·

Frankie held a piece of paper over the tombstone and rubbed his unwrapped crayon across it. Blue wax highlighted the chiseled lettering underneath, gradually revealing "Jeremiah St. John. Born September 17, 1764. Died Aug-"

Snap. His crayon broke in two.

"Stupid crayon," Frankie grumbled, throwing the broken crayon to the ground. Frustrated, he sat back on his heels and wiped perspiration from his face. It was a warm day in New York's oldest cemetery. Sunshine cast a golden glow on the graves and carefully manicured landscaping, making the cemetery seem a rather happy place. This annoyed Frankie even more. He had been excited about this school field trip to learn about some of the early citizens of the city. Visiting an old creepy cemetery could be awesome! What if they saw an actual ghost? But here he was, baking in the sunshine, with a broken crayon, and no ghosts in sight.

He looked around at his classmates. The nuns' sober warning about respecting the graveyard had fallen on deaf ears. Children ran over grave mounds and giggled loudly, gleeful to be away from the confines of the classroom walls. He saw his twin sister, Elise, who, in stark contrast to those around her, was making a solemn face at two gravestones with lambs on top of them. She put her hand on one as if to comfort it.

Frankie refocused on Jeremiah St. John's headstone. Dead people were boring; at least if they weren't ghosts, that is. He thought this tombstone might be more interesting because they shared the same last name, but it was still boring in the end. St. John wasn't Frankie's real last name anyway. He and Elise were only two years old when they had been found at the Catholic orphanage, left without any known history except their first names, which were scrawled on a torn section of the Sunday paper. They weren't even placed in a basket like he'd read about in stories. Nine years later, and he still had no clue where his last name derived. He guessed the nuns at the children's home gave them the name of St. John in honor of their favorite beheaded saint. At least he knew how *that* guy died. These tombstones didn't offer up any juicy information at all.

Sighing heavily, Frankie stood, deciding he'd rather sulk in the shade of the creepiest thing in the cemetery: a giant, old tree. As he walked toward it, he could see it was misshapen. The trunk grotesquely wrapped itself around a large stone that jutted out from the ground. Gnarled roots at the base of the tree roused his curiosity. He imagined finding a snarling predator hiding in the roots' hollows, its lips curled back from glistening teeth, with razor-sharp claws the size of human fingers, its body crouched and ready to pounce on its next hapless victim. Suddenly, the stone within the roots caught sunlight at just the right angle, blinding him for a second. As he blinked his eyesight back, he noticed it wasn't a grave marker. No hint of writing was on the stone, yet it looked tall and important amidst the twisted roots of the tree. Peering around the trunk, Frankie discovered more trees beyond this one, trees that looked even older. *Who knew New*

York had a forest? Frankie thought, intrigued. There was Central Park of course, but that didn't count.

Mesmerized, Frankie ambled toward the woods, its thick, quiet darkness seeming to call to him. Fallen twigs cracked under his feet as he walked through the dense forest, and more than once, low branches snagged locks of his curly hair. He had to take unusually high steps to clear some of the undergrowth, but Frankie hiked on, fascinated by the untouched land that edged so close to the city. He looked all around the sun-dappled landscape. There was no sign of any development. No apartments, no shacks, no roads. Trees muffled the constant drone of ever-present traffic, and the silence was unsettling.

He turned with a start as some hidden creature scurried under the leaf litter behind him. Startled, he instantly became aware that he couldn't see his classmates. How long had he walked? It seemed as if he had only taken a few steps, so he couldn't have ventured too far. Deciding that he needed to rejoin the group, Frankie retraced his steps along what he thought was the trail he had walked through earlier. Midway, he stopped and listened. Everything looked different from before. He thought to follow the noise of the other kids goofing around, but he heard nothing.

Not a sound could be heard, except his shallow breathing and the occasional rustle of leaves in the breeze.

"Ok. This is interesting." Confused and with panic gathering in his chest, Frankie hastened through the forest. As the sun crawled down between the tree branches, he realized it would be dark soon. How had that much time passed? It was mid-morning when they arrived at the cemetery.

This wasn't the first time Frankie had lost track of time. Once before, on a school outing to the seashore, he had been trying to dig crabs out from their hiding places in the rock jetty when he heard people shouting his name. The nuns ran up to him and said they had spent the past hour searching for him. They had even called the police. He swore that he had been near his class the entire time. No one believed him.

Now he was sure they would think he had run off again, and he'd be in deep trouble when they found him this time. That is if they actually did find him.

He came across a shallow cave, more of a hollow, at the base of a small cliff with tree roots clawing across its surface. Daylight was fading. Soon, he wouldn't be able to see where he was going. He decided to take shelter in the cave until someone found him. He hunkered down on the damp ground just inside the cave mouth. He figured that if he concentrated on the sunset, he might manage to ignore the fear spreading through his body. Though dread continued to creep over him, it still did not eclipse the thrill he felt from this new adventure.

Frankie tried to pinpoint the moment when the sun officially set, but the tree line hid the horizon. Night swept through the forest and replaced light with a thousand scurries, flutters, groans, and growls. Glancing around wide-eyed, he wondered how many creatures lurked in the black recesses, watching him, waiting. He leaned back against the cold wall of the cave and pulled his legs into his chest. Setting his chin on his knees, he peered blindly into the darkness. He felt the darkness return his stare.

· Chapter Two ·

"**Francis St. John!** Where have you been?"

Frankie's head snapped up. He stared dumbfounded at Sister Katherine while his brain put together the pieces of his present circumstances. Sister Katherine carried on, agitated after not getting an answer. Frankie could only manage to concentrate on half of what she was saying. He understood that she was angry at him. This wasn't unusual. His bum captured most of his attention. It was sore from sitting on the hard ground for so long. Sister Katherine's cheeks turned a vibrant shade of red, her booming voice certain to wake the dead in the cemetery just behind her.

Wait, he was back! It felt like he had just nodded off for a second, and now he was back in the cemetery. The question was, back from where?

"Yes, where have I been, Sister Kat?" Frankie demanded, standing. Twigs fell from his hair as he rose. The nun was speechless for a moment. She hastily regained composure.

"Frankie, I will not tolerate this behavior any longer! Running off to play hide and seek while we search high and low for you is not acceptable! You will have detention when you get back along with an office visit and further penitence."

"But," Frankie insisted, "I was here and—"

"Not another word!" Sister Katherine bellowed. "Now board the bus immediately before you incur further consequences!" She pointed a meaty finger toward the old, yellow school bus rumbling outside the cemetery gates. Frankie snapped his jaw shut and stamped off, brushing leaves from his t-shirt as he went.

Making his way through the narrow bus aisle, he squeezed past a mixture of perspiring faces, each looking curious about the unfolding events and angry from being cooped up on a bus waiting for him. Midway through, he saw Elise looking at him sympathetically. She was sitting with her friend Anika, who was showing one of her tombstone rubbings. He made his way past them and toward the back where he saw Luke and Steven, who were sometimes his friends and sometimes not. Today, they were not his friends. They laughed at him and pointed to the only open seat left; it was next to Aaron, a tow-headed, ruddy-cheeked, big-bellied bully who sat eagerly waiting to punch him in the arm or throw spit wads in his hair. Frankie sunk low in the seat and braced himself against the window, focusing his attention on the people and buildings passing by while trying to ignore Aaron's relentless jeers.

Frankie's thoughts bounced around in time with the bus as it lurched across New York's crowded streets. He wasn't too bothered by Aaron; he was just annoying and thick-headed. Besides, a good return jab in the ribs later usually kept Aaron away for a while. What really bothered him was being in trouble for something he didn't do. He wasn't a trouble maker.

Sure, there was that time that he toilet papered the statue of Saint Dominic and his little dog in the courtyard. And no one was likely to forget the time when he planted thumbtacks —points up— in Ms. Ternbird's library chair. The best part was when Sister Katherine sat in the chair instead. "Mother

Theresa in the morning!" she shouted, jumping up from the chair and earning a reproachful glare from the librarian. Frankie smiled remembering it.

But this situation was different. He was misunderstood, and the worst part was he didn't understand it himself.

· Chapter Three ·

Elise studied Frankie's face from her seat in the noisy school bus. He looked troubled, and out of nowhere, he smiled. But the smile faded quickly, and he looked troubled again. She was worried about him. Sister Bernadette wouldn't be merciful with his punishment this time. She'd probably make him kneel on pencils and scrub the scullery floor while saying a thousand Hail Marys.

"...and Sister Clark said this one was the owner of the first shipbuilding business in the colony!" Elise's friend, Anika, explained with excitement. Anika was a sweet girl with braces and olive skin. Her dark, wide eyes looked even bigger behind her pink wire-rimmed glasses. Her rubbings were thorough, as was all her school work. She probably used four whole crayons on this one rubbing alone.

Elise's rubbings were fair; she had only done two. The cemetery seemed such a sad place, and she didn't want to bring a memento back with her. The birds that lived there seemed happy enough though. She enjoyed watching as they cheerily sang, trying out the acoustics in one tree after the next, and she giggled at their occasional scuffles over territory.

"That's neat," Elise replied eventually. "What is your family having for dinner tonight, Anika?"

Anika sat back and pursed her lips in thought. "Well its Tuesday, so that means we will have Balti Fish tonight." Anika's parents were from Bangladesh and had immigrated to America where they opened up a successful dermatology clinic. Their life intrigued Elise; it was full of exotic foods and foreign holidays, not to mention an actual family like on TV, where they sat around a table and ate dinner together.

When they arrived at St. Dominic's, Anika exited the bus and then boarded a different bus, which took her home. Elise merely walked a few steps to her dormitory, an aging building located on the private Catholic school grounds. Later on, she sat down with about sixty other children at long white tables to eat dinner. She pondered that Anika was probably, at that moment, sitting down to dinner with her parents and her older brother. That night, when Elise finally slid between the coarse sheets of her rickety twin bed, which was surrounded by eleven other fifth grade girls, she thought of Anika, who had her own room. Elise wondered if Anika's mother was tucking her into bed and reading her a story, followed by a goodnight kiss on the forehead.

"Good night my darling girls. May God bless you with dreams of Heaven," Sister Claudette whispered, seeming to float past the long string of beds as she turned out the lights. Her bright eyes shone from underneath her habit as she closed the door behind her. Elise liked Sister Claudette a lot; she always smiled, and she remembered Elise's favorite candy, gummi bears, at Christmas time.

Elise laid her head down and lifted her long tresses from her neck, her hair making a fan on the thin pillow beneath her. The pillow was cool against the back of her neck. She took a deep breath and yawned out the day. The light through the panes of the long arched window left a warped grid on the ceiling above her bed. She began a mental game of tic-tac-toe with herself. Marian, a small girl with a cherub face that disguised her typical mischievous intentions, was tossing and turning in the adjacent bed, the ancient mattress springs squeaked loudly with each movement. The sounds of the traffic outside were still prominent, even though the dormitory was on the third floor. A siren sounded in the distance.

Suddenly, she heard it: a shuffle of teeny feet. Shuffle, shuffle pause. Shuffle, shuffle pause. It was coming closer to her bed. She looked down to see the flittering eyes and curious whiskers of Marty, her favorite mouse. He was coming to see if she had any cheese tonight. Elise saved bits of her dinner each evening to give to Marty if he showed up.

"Hello!" she whispered and reached under her mattress to retrieve the corner of bread she saved. "It's just bread tonight." She placed the crumb on the floor and Marty happily began gobbling it up. He was such a kind mouse. He always told her stories of his family and gave her a heads up about what dinner would be the next night. Elise would always warn him where Mr. Costa, the groundskeeper, had set his mousetraps so Marty could avoid them.

Mr. Costa was a cross man with bushy eyebrows who always smelled of diesel. His wife, the school nurse, wore copious amounts of rouge and blue eyeshadow that only seemed to make her look older. Beside Ms. Ternbird, the librarian, the Costas were the only laypeople working at the Catholic institution.

Marty continued to munch his bread crumb. No one else seemed to hear him, or any other animal Elise talked to. Well, she didn't really *hear* them. They communicated more in a series of pictures and sometimes feelings. If she concentrated hard enough, she could hear all the mice inside the walls, some of the bugs, and the family of pigeons that nested in the roof.

Once, she discussed Marty with Marian, who gave her a petrified look and walked away. Another time, she asked Anika whether she could talk to animals too. Anika said no, and that Elise probably shouldn't ask anyone else because they would think she was crazy. Now, she didn't talk about it with anyone but Frankie. Frankie never doubted Elise.

"Mushroom stroganoff tomorrow for dinner again? Bleh," Elise said. Marty continued to work on his crumb as he told her all about the new tunnel his father and his cousins were working on right now. It was enormous, and wound its way through the cracks in the old walls, up and over the archaic wooden rafters, and all the way from the music room to the playground. In her mind, Elise traveled with Marty in his flashes of memory through the darkness, actually feeling the tickle of straw beneath her feet, and brushing up against the cold stone of the sanctuary walls.

"No, I don't have the green thimble!" Another noisy roommate named Esther was talking in her sleep again a few beds down. Elise giggled to herself and looked down. Frightened by Esther's outburst, Marty had run for the safety of his home behind the walls.

Then she heard a different noise, one she hadn't heard before. It was a tapping sound coming from the window. The tic-tac-toe grid above her bed was shadowed by the hunched profile of a person. Elise slowly lifted her head and peered at the window. The hunched person morphed grotesquely into a tall figure with dark clothes and spiky hair. It pushed against the window, which shuddered and gave way with an abrupt groan. Elise gasped, plunged her head under the covers, and listened. The lengthening silence roared in her ears. Then, soft footsteps on the concrete floor padded closer to her bed, the sound stopping near her shoulder. Elise tried to muffle her breath, but it echoed in rapid gasps. An eternity went by with no sound. Slowly, she brought her hand up to move the sheet back just an inch. Ever so slightly, she peered out from the covers. Her eyes widened, and then her breathing stopped   altogether.

· **Chapter Four** ·

"**I saw the** Lady in White again," Elise said without looking up from her book. Multitasking had always been her talent. She could carry on a conversation while simultaneously absorbing information from a book, listening to an interchange across the room, and observing the weather outside. She seemed to soak in her whole environment like a sponge in water, picking out small details that no one else would have noticed. This ability was particularly annoying to Frankie at the moment because his plan to creep up behind her library desk was foiled. Her resulting shriek would have been hilarious, and Ms. Ternbird, the librarian, would surely have whisper-yelled some kind of reprimand.

But Frankie was too intrigued by her statement to be too disappointed. "Where? What happened?" he queried enthusiastically, pulling out the chair across from her. The floor was carpeted, but the wooden chair thudded hollowly as he dragged it backward. He plopped down into it, and his backpack slid off his shoulder and crashed onto the floor. Elise shushed him over the top of her book.

In the few hours between last class and dinner, most of the children at the orphanage spent time on the playground or in the recreational room. Elise, on the other hand, typically found comfort spending time with her animal friends, and when none could be found, she retreated to the library to read about them.

Elise gently closed the *Field Guide to North American Mammals* book and placed it on one of the two stacks at her elbow. A soft smile warmed her face. "It was different this time. She was actually inside! She stood by my bed!"

The Lady in White appeared infrequently, visiting Elise more often than Frankie who was privately jealous.

"She came inside?!!?" Frankie uttered in disbelief.

"Yes, she was standing right by my bed when I saw her. She must have opened the window and climbed in. She just stood there with her hands folded and smiled at me until I fell asleep. I think she's an angel!"

Only Frankie and Elise had ever seen the Lady in White. When asking about her around the orphanage, they were immediately teased for making up lame ghost stories, the ensuing mocking laughter shutting down any further questions. The last time Frankie had seen her was about four months ago, when he woke up to find her smiling at him from the window at the fire escape, her head gently tilted to one side. She never spoke, never touched them. Her white dress and head covering seemed to glow. Maybe she *was* an angel.

"Or maybe," Frankie said peering up through his brown curls, "she only comes at night because she's . . . a VAMPIRE!" He leapt up and ran to Elise's chair. Elise squeaked and bolted around to the other side. He almost caught one of her long strands of hair that streamed behind her as she ran, but instead, he knocked one of her towering piles of books onto the floor. The sound of destruction made them both freeze in their tracks. Ms. Ternbird marched toward them from the reference section, her square-heeled pumps making a muffled sound across the library floor.

"Francis and Elise St. John! I should have known!" she whispered fiercely. Frankie stood at mock attention and saluted. "Of course, I *did* know because I could hear the both of you talking from across the room!" Her clipped consonants echoed throughout the library despite her low tones.

"Ms. Turd- uh, I mean Ternbird, we are the only people here!" Frankie explained indignantly, standing at ease.

"This is a library and rules are rules, whether people are around to notice or not." Her narrowed eyes pierced both of them for a long second. Elise's face turned a shade of red deeper than her hair. "Now, reshelve all these books immediately. I will be watching, so don't try and dump everything into the Science Fiction section this time, Frankie."

Ms. Turdbird sure is a wet blanket, Frankie thought, slowly taking one book and dragging his feet to the Biology section. She was fun to get a rise out of though. She had a funny accent, like an English accent, but not quite. Maybe South African. During her stern whisper-lectures, her lips pursed so much that her accent all but disappeared. Sometimes, a few strands of her hair would come loose from her tightly pulled bun, and she would overlook fixing it for a while. Frankie found that amusing for some reason. If he was honest, he and all the rest of the boys at the school might admit they thought she was pretty. She had a way of walking that was a little bit hypnotic, and the fluorescent library lights somehow made her honey-colored hair shine. Of course, that was all tempered by the fact that she was an über-strict killjoy. That made putting garden slugs in her desk drawers still incredibly fun.

It was also incredibly fun to watch Elise as she struggled with her stack of books. Currently, she was trying to extract one from the middle of the stack to reshelve in the Reference section. She had nearly managed to finagle it out by using her chin to brace the top of the stack and her knee to brace the bottom when she lost her balance and the whole pile tumbled out of her arms. Frankie laughed heartily at the end of the row.

"Frankie, shush!" Ms. Ternbird hissed.

Elise angrily picked up the books and filed them away, nostrils flaring. Frankie followed closely behind her, still laughing. He had to walk while bent over because his sides hurt so much from laughing, but he stumbled along behind her nonetheless. Elise stopped at the table where she had been reading to pick up one last heavy volume. It was a book on whales and was suitably heavy. Frankie, with tears in his eyes, took the book from her. He was about to walk the book to the back of the library for his sister when the door opened.

A man entered. He was tall, had square-toed black boots, and wore a long, black duster that swayed dramatically with each step. What really got Frankie's attention was the man's hair. The sides of his head were shaved. What remained of his long, sandy locks was gelled straight up along the center line of his head into a tall Mohawk. He walked in confidently, obviously aware of the effect his looks had on people. His dark eyes peered at Frankie and Elise in turn.

"This is a private library, sir," Ms. Ternbird said, walking toward him and resting her hand on a chair. "If you are looking for the St. Dominic's Visitor's center, it is one building over to the west."

The strange man turned to her, the corner of his mouth crept up in an eerie smile. For a moment, the library was intensely quiet. Ms. Ternbird's expression was stone cold.

Frankie watched the scene with fascination. The man faced Frankie and Elise once again and said, "That won't be necessary. I have already found what I am looking for." His voice was coarse and cold. A chill swept through Frankie's veins.

He stepped toward the children, his long coat billowing slightly. The light reflected off something metallic at his waistband. Suddenly, the chair that Ms. Ternbird's hands had been resting on was in the air and splintering against the side of the man's head.

"Run, Frankie and Elise! Run now!"

· Chapter Five ·

S hocked, **Elise stood** stock still. Ms. Ternbird had just attacked a man with a chair and was now screaming in her library! The man stumbled, but withdrew the object that had caught the light; it was a curved blade, nearly circular. Elise had never seen anything like it before. He slashed downward at Ms. Ternbird's face, but she ducked and swept the man's legs out from under him.

"Run to Mother Superior's office immediately!" Ms. Ternbird shouted. Frankie darted for the door and Elise flew after him, Ms. Ternbird's lashing voice a motivating whip at her heels. Just before she cleared the door, she saw the slender man begin to rise.

The twins made a left at the corner of the library and ran down the breezeway. Elise kept up with her brother, but only for a little while. Soon, he made a right toward the Sanctuary when he should have gone straight. "Where are you going? Mother Superior's office is this way!" she yelled, thrusting a thumb in the opposite direction.

"Short cut!" he said breathlessly over his shoulder.

"We can't run through the Sanctuary! It's a Holy place!" Elise squawked.

Frankie silently rebutted, pointing toward Elise's suggested route. Two figures clad in black-hooded robes stood blocking the path. Their clothing was certainly out of place, but their utter stillness gave off a perceptible chill. Elise felt the hair rise on the back of her neck, and with renewed vigor, she sprinted with Frankie through the Sanctuary's side doors.

The doors closed with a clunk. A quiet enveloped them that can only be found in empty places of worship, as if the angels were holding their breath. Elise could not hold her breath, let alone catch it, but the soothing silence of the old stone Sanctuary reached out to her and she felt calmer.

Frankie was crossing in front of the altar on a beeline to the opposite side door when they heard a noise from the entry vestibule.

"Quick!" Frankie pulled on Elise's shirt sleeve, and she jogged clumsily after him to the seating area. "Get down!" he directed. He pulled her sleeve once more, and she dropped to all fours between two rows of pews. With her head so close to the ground, she could see under the pews down the Sanctuary's main aisle. The entry doors opened, and she saw two pairs of feet below flowing black robes enter and start down the aisle.

A glance to Frankie confirmed that he had seen the same thing. He turned himself around awkwardly in the small space and crawled toward the side door. As they approached the end of the row the side door swung open letting in a quick shaft of light along with two more hooded forms. Frankie frantically looked back at Elise. They were trapped. All they could do was stay quiet and still, and hope they weren't found

Terrified, Elise clasped a hand over her mouth to muffle her breath. She didn't know who these people were or what they wanted, but their ill intent hovered around them like a bad smell.

The dark figures did not speak, their tread was silent. The only sign of their approach was the faint rustle of robes. Somehow, the mysterious beings were honing in on the twins' position. The robed men made their way in pairs, gliding toward the twins, quickly closing in on them, until a black shoe showed plainly under the pew behind them.

Elise kept her hand at her mouth, though she had stopped breathing some time ago. The rustling of robes stopped. Looming over them was one of the men. His hood was drawn back to reveal pale, almost blue skin stretched tight over a bald head. His eyes were black and glistening in their deep sockets. He turned his sinister eyes onto the children and grinned.

Elise let out a frenzied, primordial scream.

Suddenly, the bald man's face altered into a grimace of pain. He quickly disappeared from view, hidden by the pews behind them. Elise heard a sharp exhale of breath, a loud crunch, and then nothing. Frankie peered above the pew to see what had happened.

"It's Ms. Ternbird!"

Elise peeked above the pew as well. It truly was Ms. Ternbird, clad in her smart black slacks and white chiffon blouse, delivering a powerful back kick that incapacitated a second robed man. Two more hooded figures ran at her from the center aisle, wielding long, thin blades from within the folds of their robes. She grabbed the wrist of her nearest assailant and spun into him, drawing the heel of her shoe down his left shin and hard onto his foot. Using his sword, she blocked another attack and sliced into the man's wrist. He dropped his weapon and recoiled. Ms. Ternbird cracked ribcages and shattered noses, and when she claimed the man's discarded sword, Elise buried her face in her brother's arm. A noise like the gardener's pruning shears clipped the air, followed by a deep sigh. Elise looked up to find the men had fallen together in a heap of robes. The Sanctuary was quiet again.

"Woohoo! Alright, Ms. T!" Frankie cheered.

Ms. Ternbird, her expression all business, shushed Frankie and gathered a large black backpack from the floor nearby.

"Let's go. Mother Superior's office," she ordered.

Elise felt a light, but firm, hand between her shoulder blades as Ms. Ternbird ushered them out of the Sanctuary.

They didn't waste time knocking at Mother Superior's door but burst in abruptly. Mother Hildegarde, a regal figure in a black habit, rose at the sudden entrance of the librarian and the twins.

"Mother Superior, call the police. There are violent men on campus and the children are in danger," Ms. Ternbird commanded. Mother Hildegarde's hawk-like eyes took in the scene before they focused at a point behind the group. Two more men in black cloaks entered the office.

Ms. Ternbird pivoted and pushed the kids behind the desk. Mother Hildegarde put a protective arm around them. The men drew their swords, but Ms. Ternbird swayed, avoiding the cutting blades. Mother Hildegarde gasped and squeezed Elise's shoulder tight. Ms. Ternbird swung her heavy backpack like a battering ram, taking one man out in the knees. Another sword swipe sent her ducking, but she came up with a kick that propelled her attacker into the fallen man. Both of them tumbled out the open door. She slammed the door with finality and dragged Mother Hildegarde's heavy desk to the door as a barricade. The nun gained composure and assisted pushing the monumental mahogany desk across the floor. Breathing heavily with exertion, she reached for the phone and dialed 911.

Realizing she had been holding her breath, Elise exhaled, her heart pounding in her chest. She gazed around Mother Superior's office, an ancient room with gothic ceilings and towering stained glass windows. Though she had been in this room a few times before, she had never noticed how the light shone through the windows, creating a carpet of color on the wood floor.

Noticing Elise's distraction, Ms. Ternbird cast a firm gaze on her. "We must keep moving," she urged.

"Why?" Frankie asked, befuddled. "She's calling the police now."

"This way," she instructed, not answering his question. She moved through the door to the adjoining copy room. Frankie shrugged and followed her. A kaleidoscope of color swept across his face as he passed the stained glass, an effect that soon faded to black when he stepped into the darkened room beyond. Elise took a quick glance at Mother Hildegarde, who was still on the phone explaining the brutal intrusion to the police. Reluctant to leave the nun, but anxious about staying, Elise bit her lip and hastened after her brother.

They ran as fast as they could through the copy room and down a utility hallway, which led to an outside door. No sooner had they spilled out onto the sidewalk when Ms. Ternbird flagged down a taxi. The sheer force of her strong will seemed to pull the cab toward them through the lanes of traffic. She threw the kids inside before sliding in herself. The driver was speaking to someone else on his cell phone earpiece in a Slavic language but paused his conversation just long enough to ask their destination.

"Bronx Zoo. Asia gate." Ms. Ternbird replied.

"Why in the world are we going to the zoo? What's going on? Who are those people?" Elise spewed frantically. For once, Frankie had nothing to add and stared expectantly at Ms. Ternbird.

Ms. Ternbird returned their stares and paused for a second before she said, "I know this is confusing, but for right now, I'm going to ask that you trust me to take care of you. I *will* keep you safe." She looked out the rear window as the cab zoomed ahead. Elise followed her gaze. The Mohawk man stood on the sidewalk in front of the school, scanning the street. He was looking for them.

The cab turned the corner, and the sinister man disappeared from view. Elise noticed that Frankie sat quietly, frowning while inspecting the back of the driver's seat in front of him. He probably didn't know what to think right now. Elise sure didn't. Twenty minutes ago, they were running around the library like silly kids. Now, they were running from bad guys in black cloaks.

Should they trust Ms. Ternbird? She had always regarded the librarian as a trusted adult and was definitely glad to be with her rather than those creeps with swords back at St. Dominic's. She didn't think they had much choice *but* to trust her.

The streets of the Bronx flew by, and soon she spied a thick canopy of trees ahead. The cab pulled up and stopped at a gateway marked BRONX ZOO in tall block letters. The driver, whose badge said Yosef, turned a dispassionate eye to Ms. Ternbird. She reached into her pocket, withdrew a fold of dollar bills, and handed them to Yosef. She was out of the car and pulling the kids with her before he was through counting.

Elise trotted toward the zoo's gate dubiously. Every couple of years, the school's science classes toured the zoo, something she always anticipated excitedly. The variety of animals, some even from different countries, was incredibly fascinating to her. Once, one of the mynahs in the World of Birds exhibit plucked a tiny white feather from his breast and gave it to her as a token of gratitude for being such pleasant company. She still had the feather in her pencil box at school.

However, this time, Elise was filled with dread. To her, the zoo had always meant safety and happiness. If her recent chaos entered the gates with her, it would taint the zoo forever.

"Elise, we're going this way!" Frankie's freckly face squinted under the bright sun. Ms. Ternbird waited expectantly a few steps ahead.

"We are not going to the zoo," Ms. Ternbird explained to Elise's relief. "I didn't want to raise any suspicion from the cab driver. The zoo is a normal place for a woman to take two children, so he wouldn't think to report us to the authorities," Ms. Ternbird motioned for the twins to move forward. "Please stay close."

Elise and Frankie barely kept up with Ms. Ternbird's commanding stride. Her typically impeccable attire was disheveled now and torn at the elbow. The back of her white blouse was stained red at the collar.

"Ms. Ternbird! You're bleeding!" Elise squealed. Mohawk Man must have cut her while Elise and Frankie were running from the library.

"It's a superficial wound," she replied dismissively. "We're here."

Taking in her surroundings, Elise realized they had arrived at a railyard. Dozens of tracks in rows before them were strewn with railcars of all types.

"Are we catching a train?" Frankie wondered.

"In a manner of speaking, yes," Ms. Ternbird answered.

· Chapter Six ·

"We must get to a safer place immediately," Ms. Ternbird said. Her indistinguishable accent was thicker when she spoke quickly. "We will need to be fast and stealthy while here. It is absolutely imperative that we are not caught by the authorities. I can't move you to a safe place if I'm in jail for kidnapping and train hopping."

"Won't the police help us get to a safe place, Ms. Ternbird?" Elise asked, puzzled. Frankie thought his sister's normally fair skin looked paler.

"In all other cases, yes," Ms. Ternbird responded, "but in this circumstance, we are on our own."

They walked for some time down a length of chain link fence, stopping near a squat metal building. A hole had been cut at the bottom of the fence. Ms. Ternbird gestured for Frankie to crawl through first. It was a tight squeeze, but he made it through. Elise wriggled in afterward, followed by Ms. Ternbird. With a few quick movements, she bent the chain link back to conceal the hole. About one foot of space separated the fence and the metal building, so they had to scoot sideways to the corner of the structure.

Once they reached the corner, Ms. Ternbird stopped and faced the twins. "Follow me closely and quickly. The faster we are, the less likely we'll be noticed on the security cameras. This is a dangerous place with moving trains. Be aware of your surroundings!" Ms. Ternbird did an about-turn and stepped around the corner of the building.

Frankie took a deep breath, looked a frightened Elise in the eye, and grabbed hold of her hand. Together they followed Ms. Ternbird's steady strides.

The railyard was expansive. He felt so small but exposed at the same time. His gut was telling him he definitely shouldn't be there; they could be discovered at any moment!

Whenever they spotted small groups of rail workers, in their thick leather gloves and hardhats, guiding engines and checking loads, the trio would wait until the workers' backs were turned so they could sneak past.

They ran across two sets of tracks before crouching down behind a boxcar that was completely loaded. Frankie thought the tracks were much wider than they appeared from high up in a school bus window.

"There's the police tower," Ms. Ternbird pointed out to Frankie. Elise froze with fear when Ms. Ternbird mentioned hiding from the police. "We need to keep the train cars between us and that tower. We're heading to that train." She pointed to a train a few tracks over that was longer than the rest. The train had tall metal cars with holes covering the sides. Frankie nodded in understanding.

"Let's go."

Ms. Ternbird darted for another boxcar. Frankie sped after her, pulling Elise behind him.

After thwarting a few close calls by workers who shunted away some of their hiding places, and after secreting behind a few more cars, they finally reached their intended train. Frankie figured that they were in the middle of the long string of cars, but he couldn't be sure. The train was so long he couldn't see its engine.

Ms. Ternbird made sure the children were hidden between the train cars before checking that the coast was clear. A policeman had driven by in his white truck earlier while they hid behind some rail equipment. Ms. Ternbird was certain he'd be driving by again at some point.

A train horn sounded from somewhere up ahead as she reached for the railcar's giant orange door. She flipped up a metal latch, and then pushed up on a vertical bar. The door cracked open slightly. She carefully inched it open in case the hinges let out a tell-tale groan that would alarm the workers. Once it had opened sufficiently, Frankie peered inside.

"Cars?"

There were two levels of SUVs and sedans filling the entire train car.

"Yes, cars. Get in." Ms. Ternbird lifted Elise from under her arms and sat her on the ledge. Just then, the train began to move. "Frankie, hurry! You could be pinched in the couplings!" She sprang up to the ledge. Elise scrambled to get her feet as far away from the couplings as possible. The train car moved forward and backward a bit, adjusting to the new momentum. Ms. Ternbird took hold of Frankie's arm and pulled him up. She peered around the corner of the train. The police officer in the white truck had turned around and was making his way back toward them.

"Get inside and get low!" she insisted. While the twins squeezed in, Ms. Ternbird shut the door behind them, making sure that the vertical rod didn't lock back into place. Frankie lifted his head and peeked through one of the many fist-sized holes in the railcar's wall. The train was now moving, but at a snail's pace. He watched as the white truck moved by slowly and without stopping.

The train gradually gained speed, and Ms. Ternbird finally signaled that it was safe to get up. "Pick a vehicle. We'll be here for a while," she instructed over the rattle and clunk of the train.

Frankie studied the line of cars. SUVs were on their level; Sedans were unreachable on the top level. He picked a blue Toyota Highlander. Elise walked along behind him apathetic to which car they chose. He tried the driver's side door, which unexpectedly opened. Elise sat in the back seat, and Ms. Ternbird took the front passenger seat.

The train's noise and commotion was vastly reduced after all the car doors were shut. Elise sighed in relief. Frankie immediately began playing with the Highlander's steering wheel and pedals. He had never been in the front seat of a car before, and he was entranced. He pushed all the buttons he could reach, while Ms. Ternbird inspected the glove box. After a while, the air inside the car became stuffy and hot. Elise fanned herself. Strands of red hair stuck in loops at her temples.

Ms. Ternbird produced a set of keys from the glovebox. "I'll turn the battery on and get the air circulating in here." Spellbound, Frankie stared at the shiny, jingling keys. He wondered what they might feel like turning the ignition.

Ms. Ternbird's eyes narrowed again. "We're switching seats," she said.

"Aw, man!" Frankie groaned.

They clamored through the tight space, the new leather squeaking and making farting noises that made Frankie snicker. Once each had settled, Ms. Ternbird clicked the key forward once and the air began to move through the car.

Elise sat up straight. "Ms. Ternbird, I don't understand what's happening," she said, voice shaking. The woman turned her harsh gaze on Elise. Trusted adult or not, Ms. Ternbird was still the scary librarian. Regardless, Elise was determined. "We need some answers."

"I agree!" Frankie shouted, and then asking in a lower tone, "Where do I go to the bathroom?"

· Chapter Seven ·

" "The coffee can is for number one; the paper bag is for number two. Throw the bag out one of the holes. Here are wet wipes," Ms. Ternbird said matter-of-factly.

Frankie giggled.

Elise and Ms. Ternbird sat in a thick silence together while Frankie exited the SUV and relieved himself in a coffee can somewhere out of sight. In a few moments, he opened the back passenger door and announced that he had left the can in the corner of the train car. Elise regarded him with mild disgust. She then glanced at Ms. Ternbird, summoning all her courage.

"Ms. Ternbird, why are we sneaking away like this? Where are you taking us? Who are those men at school? And why do you keep a backpack supplied with toilet paper?" Elise queried, the words spilling out in a rush.

"Where did you learn Kung Fu?" added Frankie, making chopping motions in the air with his hands.

Ms. Ternbird remained silent and stony. Whatever she was considering left no hint on her face.

"We are not originally from New York," she eventually replied. "I was sent here with you as protection. Those men are our enemies and want to hurt you. For a long time, I thought I had brought you to a place where they would never find you. Obviously they have, and now we have to flee to somewhere that is hopefully safer. If the police find us, so will those men, and it will be exponentially harder to protect you in that event, but I would find a way." She fixed both of the children with a piercing gaze.

"Why do they want to hurt us?" Elise pressed. "I don't even know who they are! What did we do to them?" Her hands began to tremble in her lap; she clasped them together in an effort to keep them still. Her grip was so tight that the tips of her fingers began to turn white.

"You brought us here so you must know where we came from, who our parents were," Frankie chimed in. He jerked his head up and gasped, "Are you our mother?"

"No, Frankie," Ms. Ternbird replied calmly. "We are on our way to Texas, Elise. There is a man there who may be able to help us. I believe that is all I can say at the moment."

She brought out the backpack and handed each of them a granola bar and a bottle of water. "I kept a bag ready in case of an emergency like this one. There is a few days' worth of food, some toiletries, and a change of clothes for both of you. Frankie, I know you will need to be entertained so I brought this book as well." She handed him a book titled, *The Great War: Pivotal Battles for the Allied Forces.* He ignored the book completely, more interested in devouring the snack bar. Elise was not interested in eating.

The evening sun cast a warm glow through the car, but it did nothing to chase away Elise's bad mood. She was tired and frustrated. Why wouldn't Ms. Ternbird tell them more? She felt as if her questions were important; they concerned their lives, their history, their future! Elise entertained the notion that perhaps Ms. Ternbird was making it all up, that she and her brother had just hopped onto a train with a crazy person.

She thought back to the bald men in cloaks, recalled their silence as they surrounded them in the church. She recoiled at the thought of their glinting swords, sinister leers, and their cold, dead eyes. She definitely had not made *them* up.

Elise shuddered. Her stomach rumbled. Reluctantly, she tore open the wrapper and attempted to bite into the dry granola bar. It was difficult to swallow.

Each sat with their own thoughts until it was too dark to see the countryside through the small holes in the railcar's walls. Ms. Ternbird exited the SUV and folded down the back seat. She fished in her backpack and brought out a thin blanket to serve as a bed, and set out the kids' extra set of clothes as pillows. Then, she climbed back into the front seat and sat still, one hand on the knife at her belt.

Elise hadn't realized how tired she was until she laid her head down. The rhythm of the train quickly rocked her to sleep, but she lapsed into fitful dreams about bloodhounds and monsters hidden in the dark.

· Chapter Eight ·

Frankie breathed in the stale air as he navigated through the trees. Despite the lack of undergrowth, there was no discernable path. Trees were covered in thick, black bark, their limbs shutting out life-giving sunlight, preventing growth on the forest floor. What little light that made it through was diffused by thick fog. Frankie didn't know where he was going, or how he got here but he knew he had to get away from this place. Stagnant mist hung in the air, making his breath quick and shallow. Though he stumbled over roots and knocked his head on low branches, Frankie never slowed his stride. Something was out there; he could feel it hunting him. The thought raised prickles on the back of his neck. He sensed its presence right behind him, but every time he looked, nothing was there.

"Frankie!" He heard a voice call out. It was Elise.

Where is she? He looked around frantically.

"Frankie!" she shouted again. He whirled around at the sound, which had come from a different direction this time. He couldn't see her! What if she was in trouble? How was he going to find her in this fog?

"Frankie! Wake up, Frankie!!"

"Huh?" Frankie's eyes fluttered open, and he glanced around, disoriented. He was laying in the back of an SUV, his sister shaking his shoulders. A strange light glowed from the front seat. He bolted up to see Ms. Ternbird, who was in the front seat, crouched and ready to spring any second, a dangerous-looking knife grasped in her hand. Directly in front of her was a ring of flickering gold light, radiating from where the dashboard and windshield should have been. In the center of the ring was an image of a dark, foggy forest.

"Hey, I was just there," Frankie groggily croaked, recognizing the trees.

"What? You've been right here all along, snoring!" cried Elise.

"I must have been dreaming it," he mused. "Am I still dreaming?"

"No Frankie, this is not a dream," Ms. Ternbird said in a cold tone. She climbed over the front seat and positioned herself between the forest and the children.

Frankie stared at the unnatural and stationary forest before him yet felt the rocking movement of the train all around. He began to feel a little sick. The shimmering gold ring wavered a little until it rapidly shrank and collapsed.

The forest was gone. The light was gone. The front of the SUV they were sitting in was also gone. Every part of the Highlander beyond the edge of the front seat had disappeared. Without the front wheels for support, the truck slammed down onto the floor of the train car. The steering wheel sat in the front seat because the steering column, which had supported it, had vanished. This was nearly as unnerving as the floating golden ring of nightmares.

Ms. Ternbird leapt over the seat and barked an order for them to stay put. Knife at the ready, she inspected what was left of the SUV, and then expanded her investigation to the perimeter of the train car. Elise and Frankie didn't move a muscle. Ms. Ternbird finally reappeared and opened the door by Elise.

"Whatever that was, it doesn't appear to have left anything dangerous behind. Frankie, you said you were dreaming of that place. Has this happened before?" The twins exchanged a blank glance. Frankie looked down and remained silent.

"I don't think so. But Frankie's had some other things happen to him," Elise answered for her brother.

Ms. Ternbird focused on Frankie. Her scrutinizing stare made his throat clench. He paused, unsure of how much to reveal. No one but Elise had believed him about his strange occurrences. Certainly, no adult had ever believed him; they thought he was lying. According to Sister Katherine, he was "concocting fantastical tales to gain attention." He looked at Elise, who nodded in encouragement.

"Well," he began hesitantly, "last week when we went to the cemetery, everyone was looking for me because they thought I was hiding. I wasn't. One minute, I was looking at a weird tree with a rock in it, and then suddenly I was…somewhere else." He glanced up to meet Ms. Ternbird's gaze.

"Go on," she urged.

"I was walking through the cemetery, saw a cool-looking tree, and had to check it out. All of a sudden, the cemetery was gone, and a forest was there instead. Not *that* forest," he said, pointing to the gaping hole where the front of the car once existed. "I didn't walk far, but I got lost. I couldn't find my way back, so I sat in a cave for a little while and must have fallen asleep. When I woke up, I was back at the cemetery. Everyone was mad at me."

Ms. Ternbird's brow furrowed.

"Oh come on Ms. Turdbird! You gotta believe me! I—"

"I believe you." Ms. Ternbird interrupted him flatly, ignoring his accidental insult. "You were back after you fell asleep, you say."

"Yes!" Frankie was immensely relieved that she hadn't dismissed his story.

"How many times have these strange things happened to you?"

"Just once more, when we were at the beach."

"Ah yes, I remember the Sisters talking about that in the lounge the next day. They couldn't figure out where you could possibly have hidden."

"I was just looking for fiddler crabs! Honest!"

Ms. Ternbird stared out the non-existent windshield and was quiet for a moment. Finally, she opened the door wider and offered a hand to help Elise exit the truck.

"Let's remove ourselves to a different car, and hope nothing out of the ordinary happens again."

They set up camp in another Toyota Highlander. Elise lay down, and Ms. Ternbird sat sentinel in the front seat like before. Frankie squished his extra t-shirt into a ball and tried to make himself comfortable, but he felt restless. He couldn't erase from his mind that dark forest and the fact that Ms. Ternbird and Elise saw it too. Worst of all was the thought that the horrifically scary place he dreamt of was real. Was he somehow responsible for bringing it to life? In that case, what other nightmares were waiting for him? For all of them? He shuddered, thinking about his other terrifying nightmares, like the one where Sister Katherine was half penguin and she started pecking him to death.

I just won't sleep! He thought, considering that the obvious solution. Satisfied that he had come up with a great plan, he inhaled deeply. The new car smell filled his lungs, acting like soothing aromatherapy, and he promptly fell asleep.

· Chapter Nine ·

Elise munched on the trail mix Ms. Ternbird had given her for breakfast. The pretzel parts were gross. She picked those out. There were chocolate candy pieces though, making her feel a bit mischievous. The Sisters at St. Dominic's would be appalled that she was eating candy for breakfast. Ms. Ternbird was sipping from her water bottle in the front seat, still in the same position Elise had seen her in before she fell asleep last night. Elise wondered if she had been up all night.

Frankie stirred. He looked around slowly and suspiciously.

"No penguins?" he asked, apprehensively.

Elise crinkled her eyebrows at him. "Penguins? No. But there are mountains!"

Trees blurred past the train car, and in the distance, off to the right, the morning sun glinted over the top of a mountain range. Elise marveled at how a grey mist hovered and obscured some of the peaks. There were mountains in upstate New York, but she had never seen one in real life; they were so much grander than they seemed on TV.

Frankie announced that he was going stir crazy, and left the Highlander to roam around the train car. Ms. Ternbird sat in the front seat, appearing to meditate, with her eyes closed and legs crossed under her. Elise had so many things she wanted to ask her, but Ms. Ternbird was too intimidating and mysterious. Truth be told, Elise had always been a little afraid of her. Ms. Ternbird had a daunting list of library rules. Terrified of what might happen if she broke one of the rules, Elise wrote them on her bookmark, double-checking the list each time she went into the library. Knowing now that Ms. Ternbird carried weapons made her seem even more formidable.

Elise thought that maybe if she tried to start a conversation, she could eventually steer it toward asking where she and her brother came from. After several minutes of steeling her nerves, she managed to squeak out, "Umm...Ms. Tern—"

Ms. Ternbird cleared her throat, but her eyes remained shut.

Elise thought it best to leave her alone, deciding instead to find her brother. She tried sneaking out of the car quietly, which was silly because the open door let in so much noise. She went to find Frankie, who was climbing on top of another car.

The rest of that day was spent racing Frankie down opposite sides of the train. It felt a little like flying when she ran in the same direction the train was going. Whenever they took a break from racing, she sat in the back seats of the other cars, pretending that she had a mom who was driving Elise to ballet lessons, occasionally glancing in the rear view mirror to ask what she had learned in school that day.

Elise took a moment to study the mutilated Highlander in which they began their journey yesterday. She wondered where the missing pieces of the vehicle had gone. It was as though a giant bread knife had sliced straight down between the dashboard and the front seat. Several possibilities entered her mind, each overwhelming her to the point where she had to give up and just ignore the whole thing.

At one point, Elise noticed that the sun had not only caught up with them on its own westward track but also that it had surpassed the train. It wasn't long after this realization, when Ms. Ternbird appeared in a fresh set of clothes, her hair in a single braid down her back.

"We will be in St. Louis soon. Both of you retrace your steps, and pick up after yourselves...please," she said, adding the last bit as if consciously reminding herself to be polite. "We must leave this place the way we found it. As much as possible anyway." She shot a disappointed glance at the Highlander with no front end.

"I thought we were going to Texas," Frankie said confused.

"We are, but we have to switch trains in St. Louis. We will have to wait a few hours before the next train leaves, however. It is still important that we remain unseen. When we stop, stay close and quiet."

Elise busied herself by picking up granola bar wrappers and apple cores. She became more nervous by the minute. Switching trains meant leaving the relative safety of their locomotive hotel. Several questions worried her mind: How many of those nasty, cloaked men were out there? How many bad guys with Mohawks and strange knives? What would these men do to them if they were caught? The train clunked over the tracks, keeping time with the heavy beating of her heart.

Frequent horn blasts signaled their approach to the city. Elise nervously watched as the train crossed over more and more urban streets, felt the train slowing, and then felt it stop.

Ms. Ternbird stood at the back door and peeked out to assess their surroundings. The children clustered behind her. Sunlight tapered in the western sky. Shouts of workers could be heard above the distant freeway traffic and the commotion of the railyard. Elise thought it was strange to not feel the constant movement of the train anymore.

Ms. Ternbird froze. She tucked her head back in and said, "There's a police officer with a dog up ahead. They are probably checking all shipments from New York for two missing children."

Elise's stomach churned nervously at the prospect of being caught.

"We have to get to the grassy field over there for cover," Ms. Ternbird directed. "The dog could still catch our scent, but we still have to try," she said, looking grim.

"Wait!" Elise exclaimed. "I might be able to convince the dog to not give us away!"

Ms. Ternbird looked at her as though she had grown a second head.

"She, umm, talks to animals," Frankie explained.

"And, they talk back?" Ms. Ternbird asked, unamused.

Elise flushed and stammered, "In a way."

Ms. Ternbird looked back at the Highlander, sliced apart from the night before, and then refocused on the twins. "Regardless," she said, "our best chance is to at least try and make it to the field."

A few rail workers walked by, bantering about a boxing match that was on TV the previous night. When they were a safe distance away, Ms. Ternbird jumped down and helped the twins off the train. Elise gripped her brother's hand tightly as he pulled her after Ms. Ternbird, who was sprinting silently. Elise wished she was a faster runner. She felt clumsy and like one of her legs was significantly longer than the other. The trio finally reached the field and knelt down in the chest-high grass.

Elise concentrated hard, reaching in her mind to connect with the dog. Her labored breathing made it difficult, but she could just sense an animal presence. The animal was low and searching for something. It became excited because it caught a scent...with its tongue.

Ah. Snake. Wrong animal, she thought, focusing harder. She sensed the dog as it rounded the corner of their train car and closed her eyes tight.

He was a German Shepherd, and was so happy to be at work! He was sniffing for people on the train, and he thought he had caught the scent of two small people.

"Hi, doggie!" Elise said in her mind. She visualized herself petting the dog's soft black fur. She could see his tail wag in her mind's eye. *"What is your name?"* she asked him.

"Shep" Elise heard the name in a man's voice, probably the policeman walking with him. Shep was confused. He could smell the children, but where was this girl who was talking to him? He looked up and around and walked in circles while sniffing the air. His handler followed closely, unsure.

"Shep, I know you are searching for us to help us," Elise thought. *"But we will be safer if you don't tell your man where we are. We have a friend who is guiding us to safety."*

Shep whined softly. Elise wasn't sure if she could hear him whine in her head, or with her physical ears. Images flowed into Elise's mind of a police team looking at pictures. She recognized herself and Frankie, and one yearbook picture of Ms. Ternbird. Then, Shep showed her images of people he had found in the past. Some were hurt or buried in rubble.

"No, Shep, we aren't hurt," she responded to him in her mind. The dog then pictured himself finding a person and receiving a piece of ham as a reward. There were also some moving images of his handler telling him he was a good boy. Shep licked his handler's whole face. Elise giggled out loud at the funny memory. Ms. Ternbird grasped her forearm firmly and squeezed a silent warning.

"Shep, we might get hurt if you find us. We have to stay hidden. Will you please tell your man that you can't smell us?" Elise thought in a mixture of pictures and words. Shep whined and once again walked in a wide circle. He showed her a glimpse of other train cars and walked on, his handler following.

"Thank you, Shep! Good boy!" she squealed internally. "He's going to pretend he can't smell us," she whispered to Ms. Ternbird.

Ms. Ternbird made sure the dog was well on its way before she led them out of the field.

· Chapter Ten ·

"**You could have** mentioned it sooner, Elise!" Frankie spoke indignantly around a mouthful of waffles. When they were leaving the field by the railyard they had to crawl on all fours to stay hidden beneath the grass line. Frankie had put his bare hand right on a snake.

"'*Oh yeah, there's a snake here*,' doesn't cut it," he said, resentfully.

"Don't be such a baby," Elise responded, rolling her eyes. "It was just a rat snake, and *you* scared it out of its mind!"

Frankie was miffed. He could still feel the disgusting sensation of slithering scales where ground should have been. It was a good thing this diner had delicious waffles because they were the only thing keeping him sane.

Before leaving the cover of the tall grass, Ms. Ternbird had reached into her backpack and pulled out black baseball caps for them both to wear. Elise tucked her eye-catching red hair into her hat, and Frankie crushed his over his curls. The curls fought back, springing out from beneath the brim wherever they could.

The kids followed the taciturn librarian past old brick buildings in an industrial area of town to a small diner a few blocks away. A red neon sign above slowly blinked out the name of the establishment, Slow-Mo's. The diner had sticky, black-and-white checkered tile and a long counter with bar stools in front of it. Ms. Ternbird picked a booth for them instead.

The twins were happy to fill up on real food and drink something besides tasteless, boring water. Stacks of waffles and tall glasses of orange juice were consumed in moments. Ms. Ternbird sat on the opposite side of the booth from the twins, facing the door. She ordered fruit, sausage links, and coffee. Currently, she was on her second cup. Frankie liked that she ordered breakfast for dinner like they had. Her eyes constantly flicked from the door to the large window beside them, to the old lady reading the paper at the counter and back again. She was scanning the diner for trouble.

She took a few more sips of coffee, scrutinized their surroundings once more, and then rested her gaze on the twins. Her stare unnerved Frankie. She seemed to see more than what was there, like she could see all his mistakes as well.

"What?" Frankie finally asked. "Why are you staring at us?"

"I apologize," Ms. Ternbird said, breaking her gaze. "Your eyes. They're," she hesitated, "a specific shade of blue. It runs in your family."

Frankie looked at Elise. Being fraternal twins, they didn't look much alike. The only physical trait they shared was their eye color. The color changed with the light, but on most days, it could be described as a dark blue. Sister Claudette once told him that God had taken extra time creating Frankie's eyes. She said the angels must have plucked sapphires straight out of the ocean to get just the right shade, and then she pinched his cheek and walked away singing to herself. Sister Claudette was a little weird.

"When you say our blue eyes run in the family, what do you mean?" Frankie asked.

Ms. Ternbird took another sip of coffee and set the cup down carefully. "Your father and brother both have the same color eyes," she explained.

"We have a *brother*? We have a family? Are they still alive?" The questions spewed out of Frankie's mouth along with some waffle crumbs.

"What color were our mom's eyes?" Elise wondered.

Ms. Ternbird eyed the window, and then the door. It was dark outside now. In the deserted lane, a few orange-hued street lights flickered on and off.

"Actually he is your half-brother, and you also have a half-sister. They are much older than you two. Their mother passed away when they were eleven…the same age you are now. Your father married your mother a few years before you were born." Her eyes passed over the diner again. The old lady was paying her tab with a handful of coins that clattered loudly on the counter.

"I am sorry I don't know the color of your mother's eyes. And, yes, they were all alive when we left. Though we have not been in contact since."

"Are we going to see them?" Frankie asked.

The waitress arrived to fill Ms. Ternbird's coffee cup. She had obsidian hair, fair skin, and lips like pink rose petals. The name tag pinned to her white apron said, "Leslie." Frankie had been too hungry to notice anything but the menu when Leslie took their order earlier. What a shame. She was enchanting.

"Would you like some more OJ, handsome?" she asked Frankie. Her eyes were kind, though there might have been some sadness in them too. Frankie's mouth remained open, but no words were brave enough to come out. He blushed up to his eyebrows.

"No thank you, ma'am," Ms. Ternbird answered for him. "We are ready for the check."

Leslie remained at the table with a pensive expression on her face. "You seem really familiar. Do y'all usually come to eat here in the mornings?" She touched her hand to her forehead as if concentrating, and then muttered, "I'll be right back." She hastily retreated to the kitchen.

"Move quickly!" Ms. Ternbird whispered while dropping a few dollar bills on the table. "Undoubtedly she has seen us on every news channel!"

Frankie was staring at the kitchen door, where the lovely Leslie disappeared. Elise, who was sitting on the inside of the booth, elbowed him in the ribs. "Come on, Frank. Time to go." The spell finally broken, Frankie scooted across the vinyl seat and followed Ms. Ternbird into the dark St. Louis night.

The air was warmer here than in New York, and it was much more humid. By the time they reached the railyard again, Frankie felt like he was breathing through a wet washcloth. The darkness made it more difficult to find a train car that was suitable for travel. There were no vehicle shipments on this run. This time, Ms. Ternbird investigated boxcars. Tank cars were the only other choices, and they were completely inaccessible, not to mention unventilated.

She ultimately settled on a boxcar that was half-full and contained enormous rolls of paper. The rolls were about five feet tall and strapped down at one end of the car to prevent them from tipping over. Ms. Ternbird gave the kids a boost to the top of the large rolls and fixed the door so it wouldn't close all the way and trap them inside. They huddled in the shadowed corner of the car, waiting for security to pass by or for the train to begin moving.

Frankie hated waiting. The silence, and the lack of anything fun to do, were driving him crazy. It was like sitting in the pews before Mass began with the nuns constantly shushing him. He threw his head back in exasperation, and it hit the boxcar's wall with a hollow thud. Ms. Ternbird reached out in warning and squeezed his shoulder hard.

Frankie rolled his eyes at her, immediately grateful that it was too dark for her to see him. Of all the people to be hiding on a train with, they were stuck with the librarian. Why was the Queen of Quiet being so secretive about this whole situation? He was grateful that she helped them escape those freaky guys in black, but what he really wanted was for someone to tell him the whole story. Great puzzle pieces of information were missing from his life. The person who could possibly fill them in was sitting right next to him, but she just wanted him to sit still and be quiet.

He stuck his tongue out at her in the dark. Ms. Ternbird squeezed his shoulder hard once more. For a moment, he thought she had seen him. Then he realized he had been tapping his foot, unaware, against the paper roll, and she was warning him to be quiet again.

After a few excruciatingly long minutes, he heard footsteps outside the car. Frankie could feel Ms. Ternbird tense beside him. Elise ducked low on his other side and he followed suit, his heart in his throat. The door to the railcar slid open, and a flashlight beam hastily shone around inside. Illuminating nothing of interest, the security man quickly slid the door closed before walking away. Soon after, the train began its turtle-like crawl forward.

Over the loud metallic screeching and clunking of the train, Elise gasped. Her sudden movement startled Frankie.

"What is it?" Ms. Ternbird asked.

"It's Shep! He's still outside. I was going to try to say goodbye to him, but he was distracted by a bald man wearing a black cloak."

· Chapter Eleven ·

"**Could you see** the man? Was he on the train?" Ms. Ternbird's hand was at the hilt of her long knife.

"I could see him through Shep's eyes. The man was standing in the grassy field where we were hiding earlier. Just standing there." Elise felt uneasy. Even Shep had sensed the oddness of this cloaked man. There was something unnatural about him that made the back of her neck prickle.

"He could only see one man though, correct?" Ms. Ternbird asked.

"Yes."

Ms. Ternbird slid off the group of tall paper rolls and landed silently on the boxcar floor. The train was well underway now. "Don't move from here," she ordered. She slid the heavy railcar door to the side and reached up to the top of the opening. She did a chin-up, kicked her feet out and up, and pulled herself onto the roof of the car.

The kids watched the empty doorway for several minutes, as the train's whistle blared into the night. Everything was much louder this time around without the comfort of an SUV to muffle the noise. Moonlight cascaded over the many hills and valleys stretching across the western plain. They passed serene-looking farms in the distance and small ponds that looked like glassy mirrors reflecting the moon's visage.

Elise leaned toward her brother and asked, "How did that man get here so fast?" Earlier, she worried that this might be a dumb question, so was afraid to ask Ms. Ternbird.

"I don't know," he said. "Maybe he hopped a train too."

"Frankie, are you scared? What's going to happen to us?"

"I wish I knew. Yeah, I guess I am scared. A little."

The lack of her brother's usual bravado made her own spirit lag.

"I'm not stuck anymore, though," he added.

"Stuck?" Elise queried. "You were stuck somewhere?"

"I felt stuck at St. Dom's, trapped inside the school walls, hardly going anywhere else, never doing anything new. I was sick of the Sisters watching me all the time like they were waiting for me to mess up so they could punish me for not following all their rules." He sighed heavily. "I think I'd rather be scared than stuck."

Elise thought about that. It was true that Frankie had always yearned for new experiences. He was constantly pushing the boundaries of mundane situations to make them more exciting. Elise believed this was why he always found himself in so much trouble. She privately thought it was to see how far he could go, to know what he was really made of. She had never felt trapped at St. Dominic's. She cherished the comforting familiarity of their routine and felt the most confident when behind its walls that she knew so well.

Just then, Ms. Ternbird's legs dangled above the railcar's doorway. She swung back into the boxcar like a practiced gymnast.

"There are only five other boxcars on this train and they are all unoccupied. The other cars are sealed shipping containers or are carrying liquid chemicals, so it's safe to assume those men are not on the train with us. Nevertheless, I'll keep watch tonight while you both rest."

"Did you just jump from car to car on a moving train?" Frankie asked, amazed.

Ms. Ternbird nodded. "It was the only way to be sure we were alone, minus the engineer, of course."

"Aw man, take me with you next time!" Frankie pleaded.

Ms. Ternbird helped Elise down from the paper rolls. Frankie jumped down dramatically like an action hero. Together, they spread the blanket out on the railcar's floor. Once the twins had settled onto the blanket, Ms. Ternbird established her position near the door. They all sat in silence for a while. Though the train's metallic rhythm threatened to lull her to sleep, Elise fought the urge. She had too many unanswered questions that she could no longer ignore. Luckily, Frankie was brave enough to ask them.

"Ms. Ternbird, why are—"

"My name is not really Ternbird," she interrupted him.

"Huh?" Frankie uttered, confused.

"My name is Onora Forgeron. I will tell you more about your circumstances in a bit. First, I need to ask: Do you trust me?" Her face was stern, and her eyes glistened in the moonlight as she waited for affirmation.

"I trust you," Frankie responded. "You took care of those bad guys back at the school. You brought food and a pee can. So yeah, I figure you're looking out for us."

"Thank you, Frankie," she said appreciatively. "And you, Elise?"

Elise nodded in assent.

"Very well." Thus the woman named Onora began her story.

· Chapter Twelve ·

"Back in our home country, a man tried to poison both of you. You were only two years old at the time."

"Why?" Frankie asked.

"He despised your father, and he poisoned you as a way to hurt him. You weren't affected, thankfully. We tracked him as far as we could, but never caught him. He was a highly skilled and powerful man, so we decided that the best way to protect you was to send you away and keep you hidden in a place he'd never find you."

"Couldn't the police find him?" Frankie wondered.

"This situation was far above the power of the police."

"Why didn't our parents come too? Why did they send you instead?" he queried.

"Your parents had to stay behind and run the country. I was sent with you because the Royal Family should always be accompanied by a member of the Royal Guard for their protection."

Frankie searched her face, expecting her to provide more explanation, but her expression remained stoic, as usual.

"So, our parents run a country."

"Yes."

"And, we're part of the Royal Family."

"Correct."

"Are our parents the king and queen?" he squeaked excitedly.

"Yes." Onora locked eyes with him as if to emphasize her seriousness.

"Of what country?" he asked, with excitement.

"The kingdom is called Stromboden," she answered.

Frankie was taken aback. He wasn't great at geography, but he was pretty sure there was no such place.

"It doesn't exist in this reality," Onora said, noticing his puzzled look.

Frankie caught sight of Elise in the dim light. She looked just as lost.

"We come from a country that's not real?" she asked.

"It is very real. But it isn't here, exactly. How it was explained to me was that there are different outcomes to every situation. For each different outcome, an entirely new universe is made that reflects its effects. When you ordered waffles at the diner tonight, another reality was also created in which you ordered pancakes. We are from a reality in which 'Earth' is called Anwynn. There is no 'America', but there is a country called Stromboden and you are both in line for the throne."

The train reeled and lurched around a curve. Frankie and Elise scrambled for something to hold on to as the car shifted on the rails. Onora seemed undisturbed. The tracks straightened again.

Frankie rubbed a bruised elbow and tried to wrap his mind around all this new information.

In a quiet voice, Elise said, "That sounds like make-believe."

"Says the girl who just had a conversation with a dog," Frankie retorted. Even though it was dark, he knew she was blushing.

"It does sound unbelievable, Elise," Onora agreed, "but, I assure you it is the truth. The man we are meeting in Texas will be able to explain all of this better than I can. He has a strong aptitude for science."

"How is he going to help us?" Frankie asked.

"He has a good security system in place, which will buy us time to figure out our next steps."

"We can't go back to our first reality, the place we came from?" Elise asked.

"You were sent away from Stromboden for a reason, and we can't be sure if it's safe there anymore. The kingdom might have been taken over. Keeping you hidden is the best tactic at this point," Onora explained.

"What are we going to do?" Frankie asked solemnly.

"Our friend in Texas may have some good options to consider. He is a clever man," she added. "It is my duty and honor to take care of you, and keep you safe," Onora said resolutely. She faced the large open door and crossed her legs under her. "Rest now," she quietly instructed.

Frankie felt the soft flannel blanket underneath him. He curled up some of it in his fist as he laid down. The blanket was real, and it was here, and he clung to it. A part of him felt relieved to finally have answers about where he came from. Pieces of his life were beginning to fall into place. That relief was dampened by the fact that his parents might be dead, and the home they shared could have been destroyed. Now, his own life was in danger. He glanced at his sister, who sat next to him, her head slumped over. Suddenly, he felt extremely tired.

The train horn blasted, rousing him from his gloomy thoughts.

Elise's head jerked up in alarm at the loud train horn. She sighed and then lay down upon the blanket. Frankie yawned as he turned over. "Here I am, a prince, and I haven't even slept on a real bed in days," he murmured.

Sleep descended on Frankie quickly that night. The last thing he saw before closing his eyes was Onora Forgeron sitting up straight as an arrow, her watchful eye on the countryside beyond.

· Chapter Thirteen ·

I t was hot. Brain-melting hot.

"Thank God for ice cream," Frankie mumbled over a heaping spoonful. The air conditioning at Dairy Queen was on full blast, but he still felt a few drops of sweat down his back.

They had arrived in Alpine, Texas earlier that afternoon, undramatically walking off the train in broad daylight. Security officers were nowhere in sight, and Frankie had a hunch that even if they were around, they wouldn't be bothered by a few hobos jumping off a train. It was too hot to be bothered by anything.

Alpine was a relaxed, small town that was nearly all brown: brown buildings, brown grass, brown hills on the horizon. It had a strange name for a town with hardly any trees. He was disappointed in the number of cars. He thought everyone in Texas wore cowboy hats and rode horses everywhere. So far, he had only seen one old guy in a cowboy hat, and he saw zero horses. Onora, Elise, and Frankie quickly learned the town's layout as they trekked through its streets, the sun beating down on their black ball caps. Frankie felt his lips cracking with each scorching second.

Onora seemed to have rehearsed and committed every detail of this escape route from New York to memory. She wanted to go to this particular restaurant because it had a pay phone out front. She was using it now. Frankie and Elise watched her through the window as they ate their ice cream. She faced them as she talked, breaking away every few seconds to look both ways down the front sidewalk.

Frankie briefly glanced across the red, laminate table at Elise, who ate her hot fudge sundae in relative quiet. He looked down, noticing his ice cream dribbles had made the table sticky in places. The soft serve was life-changing, but the fact that the restaurant served hamburgers called Hung'r Busters made this his new favorite place in the world.

His legs swung wildly under the table, and he barely missed kicking his sister in the shins. Grinning, he watched as she tucked her long, red hair under the hat again.

"Ha. You look like a boy with that hat on," he teased.

"I do not!" Elise yelled self-consciously, pulling the cap down lower on her forehead.

Waves of heat rushed in as Onora came back inside the door.

"I've spoken with Dr. Weyls. He should be here to pick us up in twenty minutes."

Frankie frowned. The sun had burned away last night's scary shadows, and his delicious meal made it easier to forget that they were being pursued by strange people. For a brief moment, he forgot the dark uncertainty of his original home and family. The mere mention of Dr. Weyls, their contact in Texas, was another reminder of their predicament. Uninterested in hearing any more about their hopeless situation, he stared into his empty ice cream cup, willing it to refill. Unsuccessful, he looked around the restaurant for another distraction.

Dairy Queen seemed to be a place for the older men of the community to read the paper and drink coffee. It also attracted small children trailing exhausted mothers who bought a window of quiet time with a soft-serve cone. Now that the schools were letting out, teenagers were celebrating their last week of classes by pushing three or four tables together and laughing wildly. One of the girls had blue hair and a nose ring. No cowboy hats. Frankie shook his head in disapproval.

The restaurant's background music took all their patrons into account by playing an odd mix of jazz standards and disco. Onora was ever so slightly mouthing along to Bobby Darin's rendition of "Beyond the Sea" that was currently playing. Elise stared at her in wonder.

"You know a song? This song?" Frankie corrected himself.

"Yes. It's one of my favorites," Onora answered, clearing her throat as she rose and ordered coffee at the counter.

Frankie sighed in boredom and began kicking his legs back and forth under the table again. He was trying to see if the momentum would raise him out of his seat. Then, a remarkable-looking man walked through the door. The man was tall and lanky, with a long, sharp nose and grey hair that came just below his shoulders. A modest, silver goatee hugged his smiling mouth. He wore a bandana at his neck, a faded plaid shirt with the sleeves rolled up, and long dark denim jeans, which ended in pointy, snakeskin boots. As he approached their table, his eyes twinkled. He tipped his tan, felt cowboy hat at them.

"Finally, a real Texan!" Frankie exclaimed.

"Howdy, Onora. Kids. I'm Dr. Julian Weyls."

· Chapter Fourteen ·

"Onora, you're looking well." Dr. Weyls offered her an arm up from the restaurant's booth.

"Dr. Weyls. You're looking…conspicuous. Children, it's time to go." She brushed passed his arm and herded the group out the door.

Elise didn't want to leave her half-finished cup of ice cream, but some were beginning to stare at the tall hippie rancher whose foreign accent carried across the room and advertised that he was, in fact, *not* a real Texan.

Dr. Weyls took quick steps for such a tall person. Elise had to trot to keep up with him as the group ventured out into the side parking lot. Frankie rushed ahead and found a long bed truck covered in a substantial layer of dust. He immediately went to work, writing "WASH ME" on the door with his finger.

"Will do, Francis, but let's get her home first," Dr. Weyls joked as he opened the quad cab's door. Frankie stepped aside with a sheepish grin, trying to avoid Onora's glare. Dr. Weyls offered a helping hand for Elise to climb into the seat. Even with the help, she had to look for other handholds. The truck was towering!

Dr. Weyls summited the front seat, tilted his hat back, and turned the ignition key. The truck awoke with an ominous growl. "Everyone buckled? Is the air reaching you?" he asked waving his hands in front of the vents. "Good thing Onora got us out of there so fast. The air conditioning is still cool! I was looking forward to an Oreo Blizzard though. Maybe next time," he flashed a smile in the rearview mirror and piloted the truck onto the open road.

"This thing is enormous! How do you keep it between the lines?" Frankie asked incredulously.

"It just takes some practice, Francis, and then it's like any other vehicle."

"Feel free to call me Frankie," Frankie said, pained, but good-naturedly.

"Absolutely, Frankie! And you can call me Julian," he grinned at the road. "I heard about St. Dominic's on the radio, and I knew you all would be here on the 1:30 from Missouri. I would have been here sooner, but one of my goats got his head stuck in the fence."

"You live on a real ranch?" Frankie asked in awe.

"Yes! We have goats, chickens, and of course the vegetable garden," Dr. Weyls smiled broadly.

"Wow, you really are a Texan."

"Far from it, Frankie. It took some experimenting to get a handle on farming out here. I'm still learning, of course. You should never stop learning," he smiled in the mirror again. Elise couldn't help but smile back.

"Dr. Weyls, did you come from...where we're from?" Elise asked, her curiosity overcoming her shyness.

"You mean, Stromboden?" Julian asked. When Elise nodded, he grinned. "Well, yes, ma'am, I did!" he responded enthusiastically.

"Did we all come to this, um, reality together?"

"Excellent question, Elise. I see Onora has filled you in with some of the details of your past. But if my theory is correct, you were hoping she would explain more." He didn't pause long enough for anyone to prove or disprove his theory. "Don't be too angry with her. It goes against her training to divulge information unless she is directed to. I gather you know you are the daughter and son of prominent people, and that an attempt was made on your lives, correct?"

"Yes." Elise and Frankie answered simultaneously.

"Well, Councilman Carvil—that was the name of the man who tried to poison you—he obtained an extremely rare substance, a metal actually, that was ground down into a fine powder. This powder was then put into two pieces of candy for you to eat. The metal was called obluvium and had an amazing but disturbing quality that made it programmable."

Elise and Frankie exchanged perplexed glances.

"For instance," Julian continued, "if you had some of this metal in your hand right now, you could merely *imagine* holding a knife and the molecules in the metal would begin to arrange themselves into a sharp pointed object."

Frankie's mouth dropped in awe. Elise remained perplexed. She struggled to pay attention; her inability to sit still on the smooth leather seat that made her slide all over the place whenever the truck moved, combined with Dr. Weyls' peculiar accent, made it difficult to follow the conversation at times.

"Carvil didn't want to stab you with a sharp object, however," Julian clarified. "His focus was on mind control. I was the scientist in charge of obluvium research. When the Councilman discovered its existence, he ordered me to conduct more experiments on how to program the metal to control the mind. His end goal was to use obluvium to warp your minds, eventually turning you away from your father."

The truck turned a corner, and Elise slid forward in her seat only to be jerked back by the seat belt. She huffed, annoyed that she barely understood a word Dr. Weyls was saying. She decided to just ask Frankie to explain later.

"We were never able to keep any of the test subjects alive for more than a few months," Dr. Weyls resumed. "Carvil grew impatient to carry out his plan, and he didn't care that it would kill you in the end. Controlling your minds was only one step of many in his plan to seize control of the kingdom. He was an affluent man, using his wealth and seat on the Council of Representatives to amass a small army of supporters for his efforts against the throne. His methods were…persuasive." Dr. Weyls wasn't smiling anymore.

While centering herself in her seat after being flung against the window, Elise wondered what it was about having power that made people act so crazy. She couldn't fathom why someone would want to run for president, let alone poison children to overthrow a kingdom. It was absolute madness.

"Councilman Carvil snuck into your bedroom one night, and gave you lollipops laced with obluvium," Julian continued. "Were it not for your loud complaints of belly aches following consumption of the candy, his plan might have worked. When the guards rushed into your room, they spotted Carvil fleeing from your bedroom window. They weren't quick enough, however, and Carvil escaped." Dr.

Weyls' eyes flickered momentarily at Onora, whose brows were knitted together.

Elise supposed Onora was one of the guards who were too late to capture their would-be poisoner. Onora must have felt terrible for failing her duty. Elise's heart sank in empathy.

"In a thorough search of Carvil's estate, the Royal Guard was, however, able to recover all the obluvium that he was experimenting with," Dr. Weyls explained. "Considering the discovery of his obluvium stockpile, and his strange fixation with you two, your parents decided that it was in your best interest to be taken away for your own protection. In addition, to keep the rest of the population safe, we had to get rid of the metal."

"What did you do?" Frankie asked, intrigued. "Did you melt it?

"Ah, a brilliant question, my young friend," Julian responded. "Obluvium can be cut, ground, and molded, but it cannot be destroyed; not by fire, pressure, or dissolution! Our best solution was to bring it with us, yet keep it far away from you. So, when Onora and I crossed through the portal to get here, she took you children, I took the obluvium, and we went our separate ways."

Elise saw Onora staring at the unremarkable scenery outside her window. Her stare was so fixed and heated that Elise felt — if she stared hard enough—she'd likely burn a hole right through the window. She wondered what sort of angry thoughts were swirling around in Onora's mind. Just then, Dr. Weyls stopped at an empty four-way stop. Elise slid forward in her seat, yanked the seat belt in frustration, and scooched back. She noticed Frankie was not having any trouble staying in his seat. She pursed her lips at the injustice.

"But why didn't we die?" Frankie asked. "The people in the experiments died after they had the metal. Why not us?"

That was a good question. Elise hadn't thought of that.

"Nobody knows, Frankie. It was completely unexpected." Dr. Weyls answered, staring at the road in front of him. He seemed lost in quiet thought for a while. Then, remembering himself, he grinned reassuringly at Frankie in the rearview mirror.

As they continued their journey in mutual silence, Elise noted they passed fewer and fewer cars. For some reason, Elise felt compelled to repeatedly look out the rear window. She didn't know what she was looking for but was glad not to see anything. The houses that had dotted the landscape disappeared from view, replaced with sparse vegetation that included scrubby, lone bushes, thorny grasses, and even a few spiky cacti. While in Alpine, Elise spotted what appeared to be small hills in the distance. As they traveled further into the desert, the hills grew taller, and she then decided they were mountains. These weren't the lush, green, mist-covered mountains that she saw while on the train. Rather, they were barren, brown and harsh. The mountains seemed to impose themselves upon the horizon, rocky monuments that stubbornly refused conformity with the flatland around them.

The truck slowed and turned onto a dirt road.

"Here is where it gets a little bumpy," the cowboy scientist said.

The truck rocked side to side, bouncing down and up as it navigated across potholes. Elise held onto her seatbelt's shoulder strap with both hands. After what seemed to be an eternity of being jolted around in their seats (Elise was secretly amused that even Frankie was jostled around), Dr. Weyls turned the truck north and off the road completely. Elise saw no signs or road markers of any kind.

Interestingly, this path was a lot smoother than what they had just traveled. The truck hit a few bumps, but it essentially sailed over the dusty, burlap-colored ground.

As they neared the base of one of the mountains, Elise was convinced they were going to continue to drive straight up its side, when the truck veered left and skirted its base. They rode around to the opposite side of the mountain, to a vantage point where Elise saw a vast array of craggy peaks stretching into the distance.

The truck rolled to a stop at a barbed wire fence, the powerful engine causing the truck to rumble and shake. Elise peered through the windshield. A few rooftops stood out in contrast to the mountain face beyond. Craning her neck around, she saw nothing else but bright blue sky. No houses, no roads, no cars. Nothing could be seen for miles and miles.

Dr. Weyls flipped his sun visor down and clicked a button on the remote control that was clipped to it. Elise heard a muffled buzz from outside the truck, and a gate swung open away from them. They pulled forward slowly, and the gate shut behind them. The truck continued its lethargic cruise, soon coming upon a few buildings that Elise was surprised to discover.

"We have to drive slowly now so the tires don't kick up a bunch of dirt and cover the whole town in dust!" Dr. Weyls said.

As they steadily moved forward, it became clearer to Elise that the town he referred to appeared to be a dilapidated old ghost town. They passed two faded brown, wood-planked buildings of undetermined historical purpose, one building with bars on the windows must have been a jail at some point, and another building that looked to be a small bank. The windows, all coated with years of dust and grime, made the buildings appear vacant, lifeless. Elise felt that the abandoned town would have been creepier if the afternoon sun wasn't splashing a joyful yellow hue on the buildings.

They turned the corner past a mercantile and then motored along for a few seconds. Along the way, Elise spotted an idyllic, white clapboard farmhouse. A picket fence surrounded the green yard, where crisp, white linens hung on a line. A handful of chickens scratched and pecked the grass beneath the clothesline. Goats and horses grazed languidly in large pastures beyond, and a stately red barn stood a short distance from the house.

A grey-spotted dog ran from one of the pastures and barked alongside the truck, kicking up dust as he went.

Dr. Weyls parked the truck outside the picket fence, and said, "Welcome home!" before opening his door. The four travelers spilled out of the truck.

A little boy of about five years old with a cap of brown hair ran out from the barn. "Daddy!" he squealed, leaping at the man. Dr. Weyls scooped him up and lifted him high in the air. Elise heard wind chimes tinkling from the house's front porch where a tall woman with waist-length, raven-colored tresses floated down the porch steps. She wore a long, cream-colored skirt, the fabric flowing around her legs as she moved. The woman offered a small, warm smile, and waited at the gate.

The grey dog barked incessantly at Onora, who didn't seem to take notice of him. Instead, she panned the horizon with her hawk-like gaze and adjusted her belt. Two short falchions now hung from it on either side of her hips, their sheathed blades curved slightly at the ends just before reaching her knees. Elise hadn't seen these swords before. Onora must have kept them in the backpack where they wouldn't draw the public's attention. The weapons certainly caught the dog's attention, however, because his barking had reached a fever pitch.

Finally, Dr. Weyls addressed his guard dog saying, "Good boy, Buddy. Enough now." Buddy broke into a grin and spun around in circles, his tongue flopping out of his mouth in the process.

Elise thought Buddy would jump up on her in all his excitement, but he somehow contained his bountiful energy into a polite sit.

"You have a family," Onora stated, giving the doctor a sidelong glance.

"Indeed, Onora. It's been a while since we've spoken."

· Chapter Fifteen ·

Dinner that night was served at a long-benched table on the Weyls' screened-in back porch. Above them, ceiling fans whirled on high, making it pleasant to be outside. The sun slowly dropped behind the mountains, while the hungry crew feasted on chopped summer salad, macaroni and cheese, pan seared chicken, and flatbread. Elise thought the salad particularly delicious, but that could have been because she chopped the corn and cucumbers herself. She also picked the cilantro and rosemary from the garden with Felix, the Weyls' son. He helped her identify what bushes to pick from.

Felix was an intriguing little boy. He was quiet and independent but had sporadic streaks of boisterousness that revealed the joyful inner workings of his growing mind. He was pensively eating his flatbread and silently sizing up the newcomers in between bites.

Lekana, Dr. Weyls' wife, wiped away a crumby smear of butter that had somehow found its way to Felix's forehead. He didn't notice her act of forced cleanliness. Elise had warmed to Lekana straight away. She didn't say much, but Elise felt completely at ease around her. It was her idea that Elise should help in the kitchen, a suggestion that Elise didn't hesitate to accept.

Dr. Weyls was truthful when saying that he had been expecting them to arrive. The Weyls had prepared a room upstairs for the twins to share that had twin beds, one on either side of a dormer window. Onora had her own, smaller room that usually belonged to Felix, who would sleep in his parents' room for the time being. Onora refused the room at first, saying she could sleep downstairs. She felt uncomfortable kicking Felix out of his own room, but his parents insisted that Felix usually wanted to sleep on their floor anyway. In the end, she reluctantly accepted the offer.

"The meal is delicious, Lekana," Dr. Weyls said, beaming at his wife, who sat across the table from him. She smiled and glanced down at Felix, who leaned against her and pretended his napkin was an airplane. Dr. Weyls dabbed at his mouth with a napkin and addressed Frankie and Elise.

"Onora and I corresponded infrequently throughout the years, but we had a plan in place for your safety." Elise tried to place his accent again. It made most of his Ds sound like Ts. "Lekana and I were sad to hear about Saint Dominic's, but I must confess, we were excited to see you."

"I'm sure no one would think to look for us way out here in the middle of nowhere, but what makes this place so safe?" Frankie queried. "No offense," he added.

"Excellent question!" Dr. Weyls exclaimed, blowing out some corn kernels in the process. "Tomorrow, I'll give you a tour of our security features, but for now I can tell you that we have an extremely powerful electric fence, surveillance cameras, and an alarm system. If someone does try the fence, we will all know right away."

"Coooool," Frankie grinned.

The crickets had begun their evening serenade, while a calm, warm breeze blew along the length of the table, touching all of them in turn. The valley around them was held in a violet glow, and the night's first star winked in and out from behind the patio screen.

"How long are we going to stay here?" Elise asked.

"We can't send you back to St. Dominic's; Onora will be arrested on the spot for kidnapping, and the people who are after you will surely find you again. We also can't send you back to Stromboden because the castle could be compromised. Until we can determine a more appropriate course, then you should live here with us," Julian said.

Castle? Elise hadn't pictured them living in a castle until then. It was every girl's dream to be a princess in a castle, wearing fancy dresses and jewels, and going to extravagant parties. As luxurious as it might seem, Elise was not excited. She was tired. She was homesick for St. Dominic's with its squeaky mattresses and familiar musty halls. Her heart felt small and shriveled like the last prune at the bottom of Sister Katherine's snack jar.

Elise began to cry, silently at first, until one uncontainable tear after another began flowing onto her face. She sniffed and then sobbed into her napkin.

Frankie belched. Onora gave him a withering stare worthy of the librarian that, up until two days ago, she had pretended to be.

"There, there now, Elise." Dr. Weyls stretched across the table and patted her shoulder. "We know it's not what you're used to, but in time you could grow to like it."

"No!" Elise wiped her eyes with her arm, which she then wiped on her jeans. "It's not that. You're all so kind, and this place is beautiful. I just miss Anika and Marty, and Sister Claudette." She turned her head to the side and laid her face down on the table. The whirling fan cooled her cheek where the tears flowed.

Lekana reached an arm around Elise's small shaking frame. She turned her crumby napkin inside out and wiped Elise's tears.

"You have had a long journey," she said, her voice smooth as melted chocolate. "Let us get you settled into bed."

Dr. Weyls and Felix did the washing up while Lekana showed the children their room and bathroom. She pulled a lavender nightgown out of a wooden drawer for Elise and went back downstairs to fetch a glass of milk. Elise examined the gown. It had lace around the sleeves. Elise thought it was so lovely, and for some reason, it made her cry even harder.

Frankie sat on his bed, blinking slowly in his Star Wars PJ set. Onora lurked in the doorway. She shifted her weight to her other leg. Elise wilted, ashamed for crying in front of such a fearless woman, one who offered as much comfort as a sheet of aluminum foil. Lekana returned from the kitchen with milk and handed it to Elise as she sat down next to her on the bed.

"Felix is brushing his teeth. I bet by the time we get in there, he'll be fast asleep!" Dr. Weyls poked his head in the door, gave a consoling smile, and then disappeared.

Elise sipped some milk and set the cup on the bedside dresser. She just couldn't stop thinking about her best friend, Anika, who she'd probably never see again. She never had the chance to say goodbye, but just suddenly disappeared. Elise wondered what Anika must think of her. The milk sat heavy and sour in her stomach. She flopped down onto her pillow.

The bed was comfy, but she still missed her squeaky bed back at St. Dominic's. Elise sobbed even more. Onora's eyes darted about the room as if she searched for something to fix the leak in Elise's face. She put her hand on her sword hilt in an instinctively protective manner, then took it off again. All of Onora's combat skills were useless against the invisible demons that plagued Elise. Having more experience with sobbing children, Lekana smoothed Elise's fiery hair back from her face until her sobs dwindled down to sniffles.

"Some much-needed rest will help ease your mind," Lekana reassured her, drawing the covers up around Elise, turning out the light, and then gently closing the door on Onora's intense gaze.

The room was dark and quiet for about half a second.

"Can you believe we're royalty?!!?" Frankie whisper-shouted from his side of the room. "I can't believe this is really happening! I mean, sure, Onora said we were royals, but then the doctor said it too! That means this is real!"

Elise groaned into her pillow. Her brain felt like tangled strings of thoughts. If she tried to pull one more string to think about their current situation, her brain was in danger of being a hopeless snarled knot forever.

"I don't really care," she mumbled into her pillow. "I just want to go home," she sniffed, "but I don't even know where that is!" Another new ravel in her ever-increasing brain tangle caused her to cry fresh tears.

"We're from a different reality? Can you believe it?!!? This is so amazing!" Frankie continued to babble on about portals and thrones as if Elise had not spoken at all. Elise moved her pillow over her face and ears to dull his chatter. She closed her eyes tight, trying to pretend this was all a dream, that she was in her old squeaky bed, that Frankie was just Marion, talking in her sleep again, and that the Lady in White was here, her angelic smile floating over her.

She sat up with a gasp. "Frankie!"

"Yeah?" Frankie said, happy that Elise was now excited with him.

"The Lady in White! She won't know where to find us now!"

Frankie sighed. "Aw man. She was cool."

Elise lay back down and widened her eyes, trying to find any light in the pitch black room. Without the street lights and traffic noise, it was unusually dark and quiet. She had apparently deflated Frankie's enthusiasm with her last notion about the Lady in White. He had hushed now, and she was left alone with visions of a lost angel.

· Chapter Sixteen ·

Frankie had decided that goats smelled a lot like camels. He had been to the Bronx Zoo enough to recognize that familiar scent hanging in the air when he entered the goat shed. After rising late, he wandered into the low-ceilinged wood building and found Felix cleaning out the stalls where the goats had slept the night before. Felix was about half the size of the rake, but he was still making quick work of the stalls. Frankie didn't know what else to do—he hadn't seen anyone else yet that day—so, he grabbed a rake and shovel, and went to work as well.

Sunlight streamed through cracks in the wood panels, making the air seem alive with tiny bits of airborne hay. The boys worked in silence for a few moments before Felix, seeing he had help with his chore, happily exclaimed, "You do this! I'm doing the chicken coop." He rushed to put his rake back on its rack and then ran off, his blue cowboy boots clomping on the hard-packed earth.

Frankie shrugged and went back to work. He hadn't slept well last night and was certain Elise hadn't, either. He lay awake thinking about the Lady in White for a while. At some point fatigue from the past few days must have caught up with him, because before he knew it, he woke up sometime in the afternoon to an empty house, apart from Elise who was still asleep. Someone had left a box of cereal on the kitchen table with two bowls and spoons. Frankie ate his brunch quickly and then went out the back door to find everyone else.

Heat had slapped him in the face the second he opened the door, and it still hovered over him as he raked the little BB's of goat poo on the ground. Though doors were open at both ends of the goat shed, air wasn't flowing through. Beads of perspiration trickled down his forehead, and dangled on the end of his nose, forming miniature snow globes of sweat and dust.

Frankie soon fell into a comfortable groove, repeating the tasks of raking, scooping, and dumping, until a flash of light interrupted his stupor. He glanced up and realized that the wheelbarrow was piled high with manure. Having absolutely no idea what to do with the pile, he replaced his rake and shovel on the rack. He slowly backed away from the pile, feeling as if Sister Katherine could appear at any moment and chide him for a job half done.

Frankie had almost made it to the door when he backed into Julian.

"Whoa-ho!" the scientist chuckled. "Little Felix told me you were working in here. Stalls look good! The goats will be very happy to sleep in here tonight." Julian removed a red bandana from his pocket and used it to mop his perspiring face. When he returned the hankie to his pocket, Frankie saw that Julian's jeans were spotted with peculiar brown stains. Frankie's face wrinkled in disgust as he imagined what could have created that particular shade of brown.

"It looks like your work here is finished," Julian announced, his accent coloring his words a happy melody. "Would you like to see more of our security system now?"

"Sweet!" Frankie exclaimed. He followed Julian out of the shed, through the picket fence, and across the hot, dusty farmyard toward the ghost town. "What was this place?" Frankie asked, his eyes taking in the eerie, ramshackle buildings, some of them leaning on each other for support.

"This was the beginning of a pioneer town built in the late 1840s. The people had a rough time of it, though. The native people were not happy about others settling permanently on land so close to their trade routes. Also, Mexican armies continually patrolled and raided the area. A few years later, Fort Davis was established close by to protect travelers on their way to California. It didn't take long before the townsfolk abandoned this place and headed there instead. After that, unfortunately, it seems most of them died of tuberculosis."

"Bummer," Frankie frowned.

Julian opened the door to the old bank and stepped inside. Surprised that the decaying door stayed on its hinges, Frankie hesitantly followed the rancher inside, wary that the floor might give way at any minute.

Some security measures, Frankie thought, disappointed and extremely insecure with the shoddy setup. The building's interior was dimly lit by its two grunge-covered windows, but Frankie could still make out a dusty wooden counter, a bank teller's cage, a doorway to a back room, and so many spider webs. He could barely breathe, the air was so stale and dusty. They went through the doorway—where a door had once been— into the counting room, where tellers would have counted and exchanged money through the window.

"Frankie, why don't you pretend you're a bank teller," Julian suggested with a little glimmer in his eye. "Go on now, step up to the window." Frankie did so, and Julian sidled up next to him.

Suddenly, the floor gave way. Frankie panicked and grasped at the counter.

Julian chuckled, "It's alright Frankie. We're safe." He helped Frankie steady himself while the floor slowly continued its descent like some sort of free-standing elevator.

The platform stopped with a sudden jerk, and Frankie tumbled off its side onto the ground a few inches below. Embarrassed, he played it off with a gymnast's dismounting flourish and bow. Julian chuckled again. Frankie squinted in the darkness and concluded they were in a dark hallway. The air was much cooler down here. He turned his face into the direction of the air flow. It was like cool water running over his hot, dusty face. Frankie could have stayed there forever, except he was too curious about the room immediately in front of them. The door was open, a bright light emitting from inside. Julian went in first.

"This is our surveillance room," he announced, beaming.

Frankie was blown away. He wished his eyes where bigger so he could look at the whole room at once. The entire wall in front of him was covered in multiple screens, showing different parts of the property above. In the center of the room was a long desk with what looked like a control panel built into it.

"From here we can see a great deal of the ranch," Julian explained. "Seventy-five cameras are set up around key areas, like entry points or areas we frequent." He pointed to a series of buttons on the panel. "Here is where we control the electric fence. It's powerful enough to send a one hundred and sixty pound person flying! I won't discuss how I know that." He cleared his throat, his cheeks colored slightly. "We can also control the EM and RF shields."

Julian flipped a switch and pushed a few buttons. The screens began to switch between cameras more rapidly.

Frankie recognized images of the barn, the gate, and the house. He saw that Elise was awake now, and currently taking laundry off the line in the yard. Some of the screens showed views of the plain outside of the fence, while others displayed different perspectives of the main road through the ghost town. Some views seemed to come from cameras that must have been in the mountains behind them.

"What's an EM shield?" Frankie asked.

"Ah, yes. It's a kind of wave frequency that masks information coming from inside it. For example, the emails I sent to Onora and the phone calls I received from her will be untraceable and protected," Julian said satisfactorily.

"Where *is* Onora? I haven't seen her all day." Frankie squinted at each screen in turn trying to catch a glimpse of their nimble guardian.

Julian pushed a button, and the screen directly in front of them switched to show a room with a cowboy and short, sweaty kid, staring at a bunch of computer screens.

"Oh, hey, that's us!" Frankie exclaimed, waving dumbly at the screen.

Julian rotated a knob, and the camera panned out. "I think you'll find that Onora is never far away," he said grinning.

Looking closer at the screen Frankie could barely make out a figure standing just outside the door behind them. It was Onora, her black shirt blending in with the dark hallway behind her.

"Geez!" Frankie flailed and spun around, his heart racing in his chest. "How did you get down here?"

"I jumped," Onora stated flatly, joining them in the room.

Having regained his composure, Frankie turned his attention back to the computer screens. "St. Dominic's had a computer lab upstairs. It had about eight computers and really slow Wi-Fi. The school couldn't afford anything like this!" he said, mesmerized. He reached toward the screens to see if he could feel their glow on his fingertips.

"Yes. Well, the king…er…your father made sure we had sufficient funds before we left. He gave each of us several gold bars, more than enough to provide for the land and the materials needed to build this system," Julian confessed

"You built this?" Frankie asked, incredulous.

"Yes. It took some time to learn about computers, and once I got the hang of the Internet—incredible invention—the assembly was a breeze. After that, I ordered the parts and assembled a system to fit our needs." Julian said proudly.

Frankie was fascinated. He had never considered building his own computer before, let alone an entire security system for a compound. He felt at home here amongst the soft whir of processing computers, their lights blinking a predictable rhythm, the clean smell of electricity and new plastic; it soothed him. He liked the idea that he could control so much with just a touch of a button, if he ever figured out which button did what.

An image flashed on the screen. It was a room with piles of barrels and lined with shelves.

"Where is that?" Frankie asked.

"That's the mercantile. We can stop by on our way out of town if you'd like," Julian offered.

"Sure, yeah," Frankie agreed, excited to explore another part of town. He followed Julian as he exited the security room. A sudden gust of cool air fanned Frankie's face.

"Where is that breeze coming from?" He squinted, scanning the darkness.

"The settlers thought they would make it rich mining for gold. They dug a few tunnels here, but I don't think they ever found any gold," Julian answered. "The tunnels go only a few hundred yards out and down. This one caved in not far from where we are standing. However, air currents still maneuver through any crevice in the mountain caves and cycle through here. It's quite refreshing!" He said, inhaling deeply. "Do you want to see the coolest part?"

Frankie sensed Julian's eyebrows wiggling, even in the darkness. "Well, yeah!"

"Then please join me on the platform again!"

Frankie hopped up to the platform after Julian, and though he didn't see or hear her, he knew Onora had stepped on as well.

"Do keep all limbs and appendages away from the platform perimeter," Julian cautioned. Onora forcibly pushed Frankie toward the center of the square. Something made a clicking noise, and the platform was lit by a hazy red light. A powerfully loud buzzer sounded once, and then a metal cage sprang up around them. A thunking movement knocked them all off balance, and they began to descend.

"Whoa, cool!" Frankie exclaimed.

The elevator rumbled and shook as it took them further underground than Frankie expected. A few minutes passed, and then Julian, his face lit red by the elevator light, shouted over the mechanical noise.

"Did you realize that the entire universe is built on top of an invisible foundation?"

"I thought the universe was floating," Frankie answered, his dubious expression illuminated by the rouge light.

"Floating in or around what though?" Julian prompted. When Frankie didn't offer an answer, Julian continued, "You see, the amount of stuff that's in the universe now, moving at the speed it's moving, would have flown apart long ago had there not been this other invisible stuff holding it together." His hands, flying wide apart to illustrate his point, hit the elevator cage. "The invisible stuff is called dark matter because it's so mysterious and, well, dark."

Frankie nodded, still feeling confused.

"It's the web upon which all other matter of the universe sits." He raised an eyebrow at Frankie, and wagged a finger in the air, "However, no one has ever proven its existence!"

"Uh huh." Frankie backed away from Julian's crazed excitement and bumped into Onora, who stood motionless.

"Dark matter is all around us, Frankie, but we can't see it because it doesn't interact with light. It doesn't interact with anything at all, except gravity." He studied Frankie a moment and then smiled. "I know what you're thinking. You're thinking 'if it had enough mass to hold the universe together, then we would be able to feel it around us!'"

"That is *exactly* what I was thinking!" Frankie's sarcasm went unnoticed.

"You see, it has weight," the doctor continued, "but it would pass right through the scale before you could weigh it. Dark matter is utterly fascinating! And so, I have built an underground laboratory to capture it!"

"If this is all about space, shouldn't we be going up, instead of down, and looking outside? You know, at space?"

"Ah, you'd think so, wouldn't you?" Julian chuckled. "We don't need to go into space to seek dark matter because it is theoretically everywhere, falling through the earth. I have built special machines to detect it. Living out here has brought two welcome surprises."

"Me and Elise!" Frankie interrupted pompously.

"Yes, yes, of course. The other surprise is that the sky is clean out here. There is not a lot of, I guess you could say, *junk* in the air that might interfere with my readings. This handy mine shaft also helps keep my machines at a regulated temperature, safe from the heat above."

The elevator finally stopped and the cage door shook open. They disembarked into a small space with only one exit: an institutional-looking white door with cold, bright light spilling out from its tiny, rectangular window. Julian entered the door and beckoned the others to another small room.

Everything in the room was white. Frankie squinted as he was greeted by glaringly bright, white walls. Crisp white coats hung from hooks, which were situated directly above white benches that lined the walls. The white, linoleum floor gleamed in the fluorescent light, reflecting another white metal door on the opposite wall.

"The next area is a clean room," Julian explained. "This means that we have to be clean when we enter it."

Frankie tried to remember when he last had a shower. Julian handed him a white coat and something that resembled a cloth shower cap. Following the doctor's lead, Frankie put the white coat on over his clothes and struggled to put the cap over his wild hair. Julian put covers over his boots, and Onora and Frankie did likewise. After everyone finished donning protective clothing, Frankie laughed inwardly at how they all looked like Sister Gladys from St. Dominic's cafeteria.

Julian opened the second white door. It occurred to Frankie that the room didn't really *feel* clean, but rather seemed more crowded than anything... and freezing! Three, tall, boxy machines—about the size of wardrobes—towered close together along the dark walls, blinking intermittently.

"If a dark matter particle passes through the ground and through these machines, it will strike a specially-designed receptor that will change temperature slightly. When that happens, I'll go back through the data and confirm that it actually was dark matter and not some other anomaly."

"So, you're just waiting around for this particle to fall on you. On the machine," Frankie clarified.

"Yes! Nothing has happened yet, but it's so exciting to be on the edge of scientific discovery!"

Frankie took in the cold, cramped room with its machines, which did nothing but blink. "Yep, it's real…exciting."

Onora reached for the door. "We've lingered here long enough," she said.

"Yeah!" Frankie exclaimed, then checking himself, feeling bad that his boredom might have hurt Julian's feelings. "I mean…let's go see that mercantile up top!"

They shed their white garments and then boarded the elevator, ascending to the decrepit bank above. After exiting the bank, the trio made a right and passed two small, empty buildings before reaching the mercantile. The first thing Frankie noticed when entering the old shop was the glass cabinet at the end of the room.

"This is where I keep all the paraphernalia I've found around the ghost town over the years," Julian explained, picking up small objects from shelves lining the walls, and then carefully putting them back down. Frankie followed in Julian's wake, picking up the same objects he had just discarded.

"There you are! I've been looking all over for you!" Elise huffed from the doorway. "Lekana says it's time to get cleaned up for dinner." She glanced around the room, her flushed face donning a curious expression. She stepped into the mercantile, mesmerized, as she waved at a cloud of dust that had plumed up in a beam of light. "Oh, wow, look at all these old things!"

Frankie heard Elise turn the crank a few times on a refurbished flour mill. He had wanted to do that too. First, he had to see what was in the glass case. Julian followed him to it and stood beside Frankie as his eyes poured over all of the case's contents. He marveled over the antique forks and spoons, tiny rusted metal tools, and wooden spools, fragments of string and faded pictures. He wondered if the people in the pictures held these very tools in their hands, and what function the tools might have served.

Elise eventually made her way through the store, leaving Onora standing alone by the door. Elise glanced to the glass case next to her and gasped.

"How beautiful! Look at this watch, Frankie!" Elise pointed to an object on its own pedestal on the right side of the case. The fob watch, its dark pewter finish ornately engraved with swirls, leaves, and small animals, was left open to reveal that it was still ticking dutifully. "Did you find the watch here, Dr. Weyls?" she asked, her blue eyes widened as she wondered to whom it could have belonged.

"Actually, I made this watch," he said, gently lifting the glass case's lid to remove the watch from its pedestal. "I attempted to build it with tools that would have been used during the time this town was founded. The metal I chose proved difficult to work with. The watchmakers from that time would have put me to shame!" He wound the crown a couple of times, then replaced the watch in the glass case. "Personally, I think it turned out nicely," he said smiling.

"What metal did you choose, exactly?" Onora questioned, seeming to materialize in front of the case. She leaned toward Julian, her fingertips pressed lightly on the glass lid. Her demeanor was calm, but the menace running beneath the current of her voice made Frankie shiver despite the heat.

Julian blushed. "It's perfectly safe, Onora, I assure you." The scientist walked around the case toward her with his hands up. "I've done multiple experiments and tests on the metal. The results show that the obluvium, while not performing saintly miracles, is now benign. I admit, my experiments were intended to change the obluvium from its seemingly evil, natural inclinations to positive tendencies.

That didn't happen, but it now seems to have no tendencies at all." Julian shrugged defensively.

"Wait. This is *the* metal? The metal that guy used to poison us with?!!?" Frankie yelled in disbelief. "You just keep it out in the open?"

Onora arched an eyebrow in agreement with Frankie. "Yes. Why *do* you keep it out in the open?"

"Well…now," Julian stammered, "if anyone happened across this place and found a mysterious metal buried in a locked box underground, don't you think they'd be more interested in that than in a fob watch just laying out in the open? Of course they would! It only follows that tests would be performed on it, and with its true nature revealed, would ultimately start another war! That was the reason I fled with it to Anwynn in the first place, Onora! Please understand!" Julian pleaded.

Frankie and Elise stood silently by the case.

If Julian isn't from this reality or Onora's reality, where is he from? Frankie wondered, his head feeling as if it was going to explode from information overload.

Onora still faced Julian, her expression inscrutable.

Julian took a deep breath. "At its worst, it is an evil substance. At its best, it's a little fob watch in an old mercantile shop. I remain in control of it and have programmed it to do nothing but keep time, a job it performs well, I might add," Julian said calmly. "Let's go prepare for dinner now, shall we?" He gestured toward the door. "After you."

Onora stared daggers at him a moment longer, and then slowly turned to leave. Julian followed her, ushering the kids out. Frankie gave the case one last long look before he closed the mercantile door.

It really was a cool watch, he thought, rounding the corner of the store, his high-top shoes making soft crunching noises in the dirt. The sun had already begun to set. A muffled chirping sound came from overhead. Whatever it was breezed by, then faded, and then swooped low just above his head. He instinctively ducked as the fluttering and the chirping sounded again.

"Holy cow! What was that?"

"Bats!" Elise replied in astonishment. She clapped and giggled with delight.

"Bats! Uh-uh! No, no, no, no, no! Is it on me? Is it in my hair?" Panic-stricken, Frankie raked his hands through his hair repeatedly while running, crouched, toward the mercantile's protective eaves. He froze in place, realizing that Julian and Onora had stopped and were now staring at him with blank faces. Elise looked as if she was going to burst, she was holding in such a boisterous laugh.

"So I'm the only person worried about flying creatures with teeth?" Frankie asked angrily.

"They don't bite, Frankie. They eat bugs! They're good!" Elise assured him, smiling a little too excessively for his taste.

Frankie looked to Julian for confirmation. Although his nerdy sister knew more about animals than anyone he knew, he decided that because Julian lived here, and would have experienced a bat attack first hand, his information was more reliable. Besides, Elise looked too amused to be trustworthy right now.

"Yes, she's right," Julian confirmed. "Bats come out by the millions during the warm months of the year, and they eat an extraordinary amount of insects. We are grateful for them! We've not had one vampire sighting…yet," he teased, with a wink.

Frankie reluctantly believed Julian, though he didn't appreciate the little jab about vampires. Who knew what was out there in the dark? If alternate realities existed, then vampires could also. Vampires or not, the bats were still creepy, and they could fly at his face at any second without warning. He just wanted to get inside as quickly as possible.

As they continued their walk to the house, Frankie constantly cast distrusting glances at the sky. Elise paused occasionally, face up and eyes closed, no doubt hoping to stop a bat long enough so she could talk to it in her own unique way. During these pauses, she steadied herself on Frankie's shoulder, and though his brain screamed at him to sprint to the house to get away from these sinister bats with their sharp, pointed teeth and wings made of skin, he stayed with Elise. After all, she never did laugh at him.

· Chapter Seventeen ·

Lekana removed the freshly-risen flatbread dough from a bowl and set it on the counter. With practiced hands, she pinched and rolled the dough into little balls and then used a long stick similar to a rolling pin to roll each one into thin pancakes. While rolling out the dough, she sprinkled more flour across its smooth surface so the dough didn't stick to the pin. Her hands seemed to move of their own will, familiar movements born of daily repetition. Lekana made short work of the dough, and before Elise knew it, she was looking at several perfectly round, thin pieces of uncooked flatbread before her. Lekana placed a well-used cast iron pan on top of the stove and lit the gas burner.

"Elise, would you help me cook the flatbread?" Lekana flashed a wide smile.

Stunned, Elise suddenly stopped. Apart from the salad that she helped prepare last night, her only kitchen duties had been to wash dishes for Sister Gladys and pour glasses of milk or orange juice.

What if I mess up? she thought, panicking. *I could ruin all the dough that Lekana made. I could burn the house down!*

"I will show you how, and I will be right here if you need help," Lekana reassured her. Though wary, Elise nodded in agreement. Lekana placed one piece of flatbread on the skillet and waited. A few seconds ticked by before the bread puffed up in places. Lekana lifted the flatbread, out of the skillet with her bare fingers, quickly flipping the dough to cook its other side. Pockets in the bread filled with steam, expanding to form a round pillow in the pan. Lekana took the newly-cooked bread from the skillet and set it under a napkin to keep warm.

"Now you try," Lekana encouraged, beaming at Elise.

"How did you not burn your fingers?" Elise asked, intimidated.

"I have done it so much I do not feel the heat anymore." Regardless of the fact that Lekana's voice sounded obviously American, she spoke slowly, seeming to measure each word twice before speaking it aloud. "Here, you can use a fork instead," she suggested, retrieving a fork from a nearby drawer. She placed another piece of flatbread in the skillet. Gently, she guided Elise toward the skillet and placed the fork in her hand.

Elise noticed that Lekana's right thumb had strange geometric shapes drawn in blue ink that ran up the middle toward the thumbnail. On the outside of the shapes were different leaves, and Elise thought she saw a rabbit. Her gaze didn't linger long; it wasn't polite to stare. She knew what Sister Marguerite had said about tattoos being evil, but that was something from the Old Testament. Elise wasn't even sure that God read the Old Testament anymore.

She stepped closer to the skillet. The bread started to puff into a pillow. Elise's breath came quickly. *What am I supposed to do again?*

Thankfully, Lekana saved her by instructing, "You can turn it now."

Elise hastily stabbed the edge of the flatbread with the fork. She had to hurry; it could burn to a crisp at any second! She twisted her wrist around, and the bread flapped into the pan, its uncooked side sizzling at the touch of heat. Once the bread puffed up again, Lekana said it was time to take it out of the skillet. Elise used the fork once more to pick it up, and then set the warm bread under the linen napkin, as Lekana had done.

I did it! I cooked something and didn't burn it, and everyone lived! Elise thought, smiling triumphantly at Lekana.

"That looks delicious, Elise! Good job! You should take a bite now. Flatbread is best fresh from the fire." Lekana grinned knowingly.

Elise removed the freshly-made flatbread from under the napkin, and then took her first bite. She closed her eyes, savoring its warm fluffiness, which soothed the raw edges of nervousness that had stirred at the unexpected challenge of cooking. Now more sure of herself, she took a second bite before tossing another piece of raw flatbread into the skillet. Lekana's expression softened at Elise's newfound confidence. A gentle smile played on her face as she began chopping the vegetables for dinner. Soon, both quietly settled into their tasks, enveloped in the comforting aroma of herbs and bread.

❓

It was taco night at the Weyls' house. Instead of tortillas, they used Lekana's flatbread, which was like a really puffy tortilla, anyway. St. Dominic's had taco night too, but it wasn't nearly as tasty as this. Sister Gladys had a big heart under her ample apron, but Elise believed her skills were put to better use during her weekly Canasta games rather than in the kitchen.

Tomato juice ran slowly down Elise's hand. She was in the midst of deciding between taking another bite of her taco or capturing the wayward tomato juice with a napkin first when Dr. Weyls interrupted.

"Lekana and I trust that you all are settling in well here and that you slept well last night."

Slept. The truth was that Elise hadn't slept one wink. She was still awake to watch the sunrise color the room pink that morning. Bad men were after them, they were ripped from the only life they had ever known, she had to leave her friend Anika and the Lady in White, and nothing was ever going to be normal again. It was just...a lot. Her heart had felt raw and hypersensitive like a scratchy ball of electrostatic fuzz. Sleeping wasn't easy with a scratchy ball of fuzz in your chest.

Buddy the Dog slept outside their door for a while last night, which made her feel a bit better. She was thankful for her ability to peer into the minds of animals because Buddy's dreams were a welcomed distraction. They were full of chases and leaps and often featured the bubbly laugh of his favorite little boy, Felix. Elise knew it wasn't nice to spy on others' dreams, but she figured Buddy wouldn't mind.

Currently, he lay at Felix's feet, gratefully glopping up the five-year-old's jettisoned taco bits. Elise smiled.

"We hope that you treat this place as your home," Dr. Weyls continued, disrupting Elise's thoughts. "We would also like to ask for your help."

"What's the matter?" Elise asked, worried.

"Oh, nothing's wrong," Dr. Weyls responded, waving dismissively. "As you can probably see, there is a lot of work to do on a farm. With your help, our days could be a lot shorter, and we would be free to do fun things."

"Okay. What do you want us to do?" Frankie asked.

"Frankie, we thought that you might want to feed the horses and help in the vegetable garden. Because you did such a great job in the goat shed this morning, perhaps you'd like to take on that responsibility too."

"Okey-dokey," Frankie agreed, giving him a thumbs up.

Dr. Weyls beamed approvingly at Frankie, then focused on his sister. "Elise, we thought you would be interested in collecting eggs from the hens every day, cleaning the coop, and feeding the chickens."

"Do you think I could also help fold the laundry?" Elise whispered, color rising to her cheeks. Frankie stared at her like she smelled bad. She stuck her tongue out defiantly at her brother and then glanced at Dr. Weyls. "I did it today, and I liked it," she explained.

"Of course! I think that would be a great way to help. Thank you, Elise," Dr. Weyls answered, looking pleasantly surprised. He turned to face his son. "Felix, your chores have changed now as well."

Felix lifted his eyes from the small LEGO action figure he was playing with. Amused, Elise had been watching him, believing that Felix had positioned his fork into the yellow LEGO man's hand, intending it as an imaginary, magical trident that conjured waves of sour cream to engulf a town of tiny diced tomatoes.

"You will now be in charge of feeding Buddy and pulling weeds from the garden," Julian explained. Felix shrugged and went back to his plate of destruction.

"That's settled, then. Thank you all for your willingness to contribute." Dr. Weyls stood and took his plate into the kitchen. Elise watched as he disappeared through the doorway, and then reappeared again in the pass-through from the kitchen to the dining room. As he bent to scrape the remains of his meal into the scrap bin, he went out of view, only to return to view when he bobbed back up.

Elise couldn't help wondering if going through a portal was as easy and similar as Dr. Weyls' walking between the kitchen and dining room. She struggled to remember anything about the time that she and her brother had made that journey, but her mind was a blank. She pondered about what crossing through a portal involved. She wondered if they just disappeared and reappeared on the other side. Perhaps it hurt. Maybe they had to say a magic word.

As if reading her thoughts, Frankie asked, "How does a portal work?"

"Great question, Frankie," Dr. Weyls responded, seeming pleased at the interest. "A portal is a doorway between two realities or parallel universes. Have you ever heard the term 'parallel universe'?"

"Maybe on TV once," Frankie said.

Elise shook her head no.

"Hmm. I'll try drawing it for you. I need a pencil and paper." Dr. Weyls picked up a notepad off the counter, and then searched around for a pencil. Suddenly, he stopped and shook his head. "No, it's better to show you."

Everyone at the table sat quietly watching as Dr. Weyls stood in the kitchen, thinking, while drumming his fingertips on the counter.

"Aha!" He shouted, startling his quiet audience. "Come with me, kids!" Dr. Weyls motioned for them to follow. The twins rose from their chairs and followed him through the living room. "Where I am originally from, I was a physicist. I studied portals. Like I said before, they are doorways to another reality. We might also call this other reality a 'parallel universe,' which is a place that exists outside of our universe, unreachable by space travel."

Elise felt her thoughts becoming fuzzy. She tried picturing his description in her head but found it difficult to grasp.

"Parallel universes can be drastically different from each other, or they can be similar except for some minor differences," Dr. Weyls explained. "Your original reality is similar to this universe that we are in now. They are similar in many ways, but have a few marked differences."

They stopped in the sunroom—a medium-sized area adjacent to the living room—that had floor to ceiling windows and a few potted plants scattered about.

"We planned this sunroom here so we can grow our vegetables indoors during the winter months. This room faces west, so the plants can thrive in longer sunlight. In the summer, though, we needed a way to block out the light efficiently, so I installed vertical blinds. You just pull the string like so, and voila!" The blinds flipped shut. "The effects of the hot sun are now mitigated. Easy peasy, as you say."

"We don't say that. No one says that," Frankie said dryly.

"Well someone said it, and I liked the sound of it, so I adopted it into my lexicon." Realizing he had ventured off topic, Dr. Weyls snapped his fingers. "That's not why you're here!" He pulled the string to reopen the vertical blinds, which hung down from the ceiling like tall, skinny dominoes lined up and waiting for a push.

"Let's imagine," Dr. Weyls resumed, "that each one of these plastic blinds represents one reality. This one in the middle here can be the reality we are all in right now. This one hanging next to it is the reality we all left together nine years ago. Realities actually exist like this—side by side, parallel to each other—never crossing or intersecting."

Elise brightened, thinking that maybe she was actually following this now.

"However, every now and then, something extraordinary happens and they touch!" To demonstrate this, Dr. Weyls grasped either side of the two reality blinds and closed his fingers until the blinds touched. "When this happens, portals can form, and when portals are formed, people like you and me can leave one reality and go into another."

"What's the extraordinary thing that happens that makes them touch?" Frankie asked.

"Portals are formed during each full moon. Now, we aren't foolish enough to think the full moon *causes* parallel universes to touch. One small moon inside an unimaginably large universe could never cause that big of an effect. We haven't yet discovered what makes it happen. What we do know is that you can time this event by watching the moon phases, and when the moon is full, the portals can be opened," Julian explained.

"It has also come to my awareness that those originating outside of a particular reality will tend to gravitate toward each other over time. So, people from Anwynn who are now on Earth will find themselves bumping into other people from Anwynn while they're here. We don't understand why this happens. It's as if an invisible force is drawing together anyone alien to the reality that they are currently in. Parallel universes were a new scientific field of research in my reality, but here, people who talk about traveling through portals aren't taken seriously. Thanks to the Internet, however, I have found that certain message boards create a safe place to discuss ideas and theories. We're still outside the mainstream acceptance, of course, but perhaps one day portal travel will be worthy of scientific attention."

Finished with his demonstration, Dr. Weyls led them back into the dining room. Frankie made a beeline to the table and helped himself to another taco.

"Mmm! Still good, even when it's cold!" Frankie managed to say through a bite of taco. Elise was thankful he swallowed before speaking again. "So, the moon gets full and a portal opens. What does a portal look like, a swirling tunnel of lightning?!!?"

"You've actually seen one before. Quite recently, in fact," Onora stated flatly from across the table. Elise had forgotten she was even in the room. Everyone at the table turned to face her, waiting for her to elaborate. "A portal appeared in the middle of the night on the train from New York to St. Louis. From what I can tell, Frankie has been encountering them frequently."

"That shiny, gold ring with the forest inside was a portal?" Frankie asked, shocked.

"Yes," Onora answered, her tone cool, pragmatic.

"It certainly sounds like one," Dr. Weyls added. "All of the portals I have experienced had a rim of wavy golden light around their perimeter. We believe this is the Chen Space-Time Horizon. It looks like it could be golden water. Does that sound right?"

"That's it!" Frankie exclaimed. "You think I went through a portal in the cemetery?" Frankie asked Onora, who nodded affirmatively. "On the beach too?"

She nodded again.

"But there was no ring for those times. I was just somewhere else all the sudden," Frankie added.

"Sometimes, portals open and close rapidly," Dr. Weyls explained. "Perhaps you didn't notice the ring because you were focused on something else. In fact, that is precisely the way they open; the person opening them must be completely calm and focused. Ancient peoples would fast and bring themselves into a trance to open their portals. You must have been in the perfect state of mind!" He frowned, then seemed to think aloud, "Why would they open during a time when the moon wasn't full...and on a moving train?"

Dr. Weyls grasped the hair at his scalp, large chunks of hair sticking out through his fingers. He rested his elbows on the table apparently weighted down with this new information. After a pause, he exclaimed, "I have never encountered this before. This is astounding!"

Elise was amused by his wild, open-handed gestures and his mussed hair that stuck up in places. She thought he resembled one of those troll dolls. Then, she had a moment of insight.

"Why do these portals only open around Frankie?" Elise looked at Frankie, puzzled. "Are you opening the portals?"

Dr. Weyls' widened in astonishment at the magnitude of this possibility.

"How could I open something if I don't even know what it is?" Frankie asked defensively. He shoved his plate away from him and crossed his arms over his chest.

"Perhaps you are somehow influencing the portals, Frankie. Stranger things have happened," Dr. Weyls said looking at the boy with fascination. "Particularly to you two."

Elise couldn't disagree. Incredibly strange things had happened to them in the past few days alone.

"That last portal, the one on the train, I was asleep," Frankie said, looking terrified, his face so pale that his freckles stood out in sharp contrast. "If I am opening portals, I could open another one in my sleep, and something could come through and get us!" he shouted.

"Oh lad," Dr. Weyls soothed. "Please don't worry about that for one more millisecond. It is physically impossible for anything to come through from the other side. The energy flow through portals is one direction only. Even soundwaves cannot come back through. If you open a portal—on purpose or otherwise—only objects from this side can go through to the other. Nothing can enter from another reality unless a portal is opened *from* that reality. So no one need fear a spontaneous portal from you."

"Ok," Frankie responded dubiously, looking slightly relieved.

Onora rose and began clearing the table. Dr. Weyls patted Frankie on the shoulder and then left to continue his kitchen cleanup. Lekana called Buddy to her and went outside. Felix followed closely behind his mother, holding the back door open, and then beckoning the twins.

"Wanna play?"

Elise thought they could all do with a bit of playtime right about now, especially Frankie, who sat still in his chair, looking glum. She decided to make him go outside and play whether he wanted to or not. She rose from her seat, and then pulled his chair back with all her might. The chair moved too easily, and she fell backward onto her rump. Frankie cackled. Elise laughed until she couldn't breathe.

They giggled as they made their way outside, Elise rubbing her hind end where she had landed. Getting Frankie back to his chipper self again was worth the pain. The screen door creaked and slammed behind them. Cicadas called back and forth to each other from the two ancient mesquite trees in the side yard. They sounded like miniature machines whirring and rattling somewhere among the leaves. Their songs overlapped each other and faded away in waves.

Lekana and Felix were playing fetch with Buddy using an old tennis ball. Felix had thrown the ball into a pile of hay, and Buddy dived in enthusiastically, his nub of a tail wiggling wildly. He emerged moments later with the ball and a mouthful of straw. Felix belly-laughed and tried to catch Buddy, who was now playing keep-away with all the humans. Lekana made a move to stop him, but he pivoted like a cutting horse and sprinted between Elise and Frankie. The two nearly knocked their heads together trying to catch him. Felix squealed with laughter.

The screen door slammed again. Onora and Dr. Weyls came down the steps with after-dinner coffee in hand. Dr. Weyls contentedly surveyed the humorous chase scene playing out before him and blinked into the setting sun.

Onora looked farther, to the mountains, scanning the horizon.

Elise smiled at the gentle scientist and their sober guardian as Buddy zoomed past, nearly taking out her legs. She resumed the chase.

The sun slowly set to the tune of a cicada lullaby, playful dog barks, and children's happy laughter.

· Chapter Eighteen ·

Frankie woke with a start. Something had grabbed his leg. He kicked violently at his attacker, and then sat straight up, ready to fight. The street lights cast a dim grey haze around the room, and he could just make out the lively features of Dr. Julian Weyls.

"Sheesh! What the heck, man?!!?"

"It's time to go feed the horses, Frankie. I made you some coffee." Julian grinned.

"Feed the horses? It's the middle of the night!"

"I'm afraid not. Come on downstairs, and I'll walk you through the feeding process."

Frankie looked out the dormer window. There were no street lights; the light was coming from the new morning sun. He wondered how Elise could be handling all this. She was gone and her bed was made…of course.

Julian tapped Frankie's foot. "You have a solid right kick," he said. "I wouldn't want to tangle with you!" He gave Frankie an amiable smile and then left the room. Frankie could hear his solid boots clunk on the wooden stairs as he descended.

Frankie sat still a moment and adjusted to consciousness. He flopped his legs over the side of the bed and yawned. Bringing his hands up to either side of his face, he lightly slapped his cheeks a few times. He wiggled his toes and flexed his feet, trying to bring life to sleepy limbs that didn't feel keen on ambulating at this hour of the morning—not that he blamed them. In his attempt to walk to the dresser, he stumbled instead and had to catch himself on the bedpost. He steadied himself there before grabbing his red-striped shirt and blue jeans. He put one leg into his jeans, immediately lost balance, and fell back onto the bed, where he lay for a while, thinking that the horses might be better off without him.

Frankie counted to three, and then sprang to a standing position, wavering back and forth for a few seconds before regaining his balance and heading for the door. He tromped heavily down the stairs before his tired, mutinous legs gave out from under him. He missed a step and slid down four more as he grappled for the handrail. Coming to a stop at the bottom of the stairs, he landed perfectly balanced on both feet, adrenaline pumping through his body. He finally felt wide awake.

"Nice landing," Julian said, handing Frankie a cup of coffee.

Frankie took a sip. The coffee tasted bitter, and it burned his tongue, but he sipped it anyway. He and Julian headed out into the early morning light, walking together in an easy silence toward the red barn. Frankie, wanting to appear manly, but not wanting to drink the foul liquid, conveniently spilled most of his coffee along the way. The air was still, and Frankie was surprised at how cool it was outside given yesterday's insufferable heat.

The horses nickered and stamped in their stalls. On each side of the barn's main aisle were two stalls; the end of the aisle had a tack room and a feed room that stood opposite each other. Julian grabbed a large, red bucket from the feed room, and instructed Frankie to fill it with four plastic cups' worth of the feed.

"Is that all they get?" Frankie asked, his own belly beginning to stir.

"They will be turned out today to eat some grass and hay in the back pasture," Julian responded. "Though, Blister and I will go count goats together in a little while. That's why we need to feed them so early; they need time to digest properly before getting worked. Otherwise, they will get sick."

Frankie regarded the horses' long faces that poked out of the stalls. He tried imagining which one could be Blister. "Is that Blister?" he asked referring to a palomino horse on the left nodding its head up and down impatiently.

"You're correct!" Julian said.

Frankie dumped a cup full of pellets into the stall of a bay mare, who instantly began chowing down. The wooden nameplate above her stall read "Tin Roof."

"Blister has been with me nearly as long as I've been in this reality," Julian explained, as he topped off a long trough of water with a garden hose. "When I first brought him home and unloaded him from the trailer, he pulled the lead rope from my hands and ran full speed into the field. It took me hours to catch him. Both of my hands were covered in one big blister from the rope burn. We worked out our differences over time. Now, I depend on him for a lot of jobs here." Julian patted the palomino's golden neck, but the horse ignored him, intently focused on the red bucket that Frankie held.

Frankie scooped out food for a bay gelding named Rocky Road, and then and a black-and-white paint horse named Shadow. When he dropped food into Blister's bucket, the palomino dove into his bucket so quickly that Frankie jerked his hand back so it didn't become part of Blister's breakfast as well. The sound of muffled chewing filled the wood barn as the horses munched contentedly on their meals.

As each horse finished its breakfast, Julian opened their stalls. At the opposite end of the barn, by the feed and tack rooms, the large door opened onto an alleyway between two long fences broken up by gates. The gate at the far end of the alley was open, and the horses trotted down the lane, through the gate, and into the grassy pasture beyond.

Frankie had always liked the horses he saw on TV. He had never been close to one, however, and was shocked at how much bigger they were in real life. Julian opened Tin Roof's stall last and she bolted out, bucking and neighing loudly as she galloped down the alleyway.

"Whoa!" Frankie exclaimed, taken back. "What got into her?"

"Tinny rules the roost here. She's the second youngest, but highest in the herd's pecking order. She doesn't like to be last," Julian said with a smile. "I like to keep her humble by letting the other horses out first to stake their claim on the grazing field. It's also a good reminder for her that I'm the one who's in charge." He winked.

"Go ahead and put the feed bucket back where you found it, and then lock the door; the horses will go in and have a buffet if you don't," Julian instructed. Frankie jogged to the feed room. "We'll go to the goat shed next. It doesn't seem like you need much instruction there, but I will show you where the compost pile is located so you can dump the wheelbarrow there this time."

Frankie wrinkled his nose at the thought of another pile of goat poo.

"Can I come count the goats with you?" Frankie asked, afraid of the impending boredom after he was finished cleaning the goat shed.

"If you get the goat shed cleaned out in a reasonable amount of time, yes," Julian answered.

"Why don't you just count the goats while they're in the goat shed?" Frankie asked, not fully comprehending Julian's previous response.

Julian chuckled lightly. "We have seventy-eight goats across twenty acres of land. I ride out every morning to count them and make sure they are in good health. The shed is just for injured goats or goats that have lambed out of season from the rest of the herd. Three nanny goats and four kids are in there now. They can't keep up with the rest of the herd so we separate them for a while. Until they are strong enough to be released, they will spend their nights in the goat shed and have their own small pasture to play in during the day."

Frankie nodded in understanding, starting to see how a goat ranch worked.

"If you come with me, I'll put you on Shadow. She is gentle and will follow Blister."

"Okay," Frankie said absently while latching the feed door. Then, he stopped, realization slowly dawning on him. He would be riding an *actual* horse, like in the movies! "Sweet!" he shouted excitedly, running full speed to the goat shed, the sound of Julian's amused chortle echoing through the barnyard.

· Chapter Nineteen ·

E lise tenderly cradled the egg in her hand as she reached for another in the adjacent nest box. Folding up the bottom of her T-shirt, she created a soft hammock to hold the eggs in place. As she picked two more eggs, she was surprised at how they came in so many different colors. Of course, there were the regular white ones, but they also came in brown and green. She thought the green eggs were especially pretty. She wondered if these were what the famous rhyme was about, why "Sam-I-Am" was so adamant about not eating green eggs.

Six nesting boxes were in the hen house—one for each hen—each containing one egg. Elise thought it was like a small-scale Easter egg hunt, but if one fell out of your basket, you certainly didn't get any chocolate.

Elise recalled the Easter egg hunts at the children's home. St. Dominic's received a large amount of funds from the families of students who didn't live at the orphanage. A private school education cost a lot of money, but most of those funds went toward the upkeep of the ancient church building and to food and clothing of the Sisters' orphaned charges. Ordinarily, the Easter eggs the children found were filled with slips of paper containing Bible verses, rather than costly candy.

She set the colorful eggs safely aside and used a nearby broom to sweep the soiled hay out from the nesting boxes. A rectangular hay bale sat outside the coop. Its baling wires had been cut, and Elise assumed the hens' hay came from here. She tried to grab a handful, but it portioned itself off easily into a big square that she carried into the hen house and parceled out among the boxes. She emerged the henhouse feeling confident and a little itchy from where the hay had touched her arms.

One chicken, a plump black one with a short spiky crown, waited for her at the door. "Well, hello there," Elise greeted the hen, its beady black eyes looking at her expectantly. The other hens began to gather around her feet now. Some pecked at her shoelaces.

"Oh, yes, you're hungry," Elise said, watching as the other chickens joined in attacking her shoelaces. When they had managed to untie a string on Elise's right shoe, she figured this would turn into a full-scale riot if she didn't act soon. "Now ladies," she said calmly, "if I knew where the food was I could feed you."

The pecking continued in earnest, so much that Elise feared they'd break through soon and get a toe. She took a deep breath and closed her eyes. Now more relaxed, Elise could feel the presence of the chickens, a stronger feeling than the jabs of their little beaks. The sensation was like a warm nearness; a feeling similar to the one she'd had when someone stood behind her, and she knew they were there, but couldn't see them. She felt the hens' presence in her heart and at her feet at the same time. The warm nearness quickly dissolved into six separate sparks, each with their own buzzing thoughts. With a small amount of concentration, Elise managed to hone in on one spark in particular: the plump, black chicken. This particular hen seemed continuously confused about why this long, white worm wasn't squishy like worms should be, but was determined that this next peck would break its skin and release the juicy nourishment inside.

Tangy bile rose in Elise's throat. She took another deep breath and came back to her purpose. *"Mrs. Chicken,"* she said in her mind, *"where do they keep your food?"* Elise felt the chicken stop pecking her shoe, and she saw the image of a garbage can flash in her thoughts. That didn't make any sense. She must have asked the question the wrong way.

Distracted, she opened her eyes. The black hen had left the others and was briskly strutting toward the back of the coop, behind the hen house. Elise knew the chicken was heading somewhere important. She glanced down at her feet. Some of the hens were still feverishly pecking at her right shoelace, while others had untied her left shoe. Not wanting to step on or accidentally kick them, Elise made a slow shuffle toward the back of the henhouse where the black hen had disappeared.

The five remaining chickens continued pecking at her shoes, regardless of Elise's deliberate movements. After several long minutes of walking like a penguin stuck in molasses, Elise finally reached the end of the little wooden building. She turned the corner and saw the black chicken pecking repeatedly at a shiny, metal trash can with a heavy brick on its lid. Heaving off the brick and lid, she found a large bag of feed with a drawing of a chicken on the side.

"Oh thank you, Mrs. Chicken!" Elise picked up the square scoop by the handle and asked, "How many scoops do you get?" The sound of the metal trash can lid being removed alerted all of the hens. Mrs. Chicken, and the rest of the hens, forgot all about Elise's shoelaces and began darting about the area, clucking madly with the belief that she had already scattered the food. Knowing she wouldn't get any answer out of them now, Elise shook out one scoop, hoping it was the right amount. She decided to check with Lekana later and make sure.

Elise found the chickens fascinating. Most birds that she communicated with tended to share a grander perspective on life. Perhaps it was because they didn't use their wings as much, but the chickens were more homespun and preferred their own patch of land. They seemed to like people more than other birds did. Even the pigeons she met in the city, who got many of their meals from human hands, were mostly indifferent to their fellow city dwellers. Chickens seemed to genuinely like people; they welcomed them and expected more from them. She pondered all this while watching the hens dash from one grassy patch to the next, pecking at anything round and grain colored.

Lekana walked around the corner, her deep, brown eyes shining. "I am sorry I did not come to help you sooner," she said with a smile. "I did not know you were awake already. I saw you from the house. The chickens are not used to shoelaces," she said, kicking out a boot from under her long skirt.

"You saw me?" Elise blushed.

Lekana giggled, a girlish sound that belied her maternal demeanor. "You did a good job, even without instructions! I can see the chickens are happy. Will you get a wheelbarrow and a pitchfork? The old hay should go to the compost heap."

"Sure!" Elated by the compliment, Elise ran to get the wheelbarrow.

？

Elise wheeled the ancient, rusty wheelbarrow through the picket fence gate. Lekana's instructions were to find the compost pile by going through the second metal fence, past the goat shed, and behind the garden. The rickety wheelbarrow felt unsteady under Elise's guidance, as though it was leading her around instead. She was about to turn the corner around the goat shed when she heard a strange squeaking noise. Tilting her head to inspect the wheel's looseness she nearly collided with Frankie, who was turning the same corner with his wheelbarrow from the opposite direction.

"Compost?" Elise asked, jerking the wheelbarrow to an abrupt stop.

"Compost," Frankie answered.

"It's over there," she said leading the way across the rocky earth toward what appeared to be a hill of straw and dirt behind the fenced garden. As they drew closer, Elise's nose confirmed that it was not dirt. Frankie pulled the neck of his T-shirt over his nose until all that was visible was freckles, curly brown hair, and a pair of blue eyes.

"I thought the goat shed smelled bad. Shew!" he said. His shirt muffled his sentiment.

"It is pretty stinky," Elise grunted while tilting the wheelbarrow up, adding the old coop hay to the pile of decaying scraps and elimination from various farm animals. "Lekana said it makes a really healthy garden, though." She waved a hand at the large garden in front of them, its rows of lush green vegetables standing in great contrast to the arid brown world around them.

"Um-hmm," Frankie shrugged, his mind elsewhere. He followed Elise's lead and dumped his wheelbarrow too.

"Lekana said that the biscuits should be ready now. She also has fresh-squeezed orange juice." Elise elbowed her brother in the ribs. "I'm so hungry, I can't wait!" She steered the rusty wheelbarrow back down the path, but Frankie didn't follow her as expected. She turned to her brother, frowning. "Aren't you coming?"

Frankie put a hand to his belly, "Ah, no, I'm going out with Julian. We're going to ride the horses out to the pasture to count goats!" He sprinted off, recklessly pushing his wheelbarrow back to the goat shed.

Elise stared after her brother's rapidly disappearing form. That was the first time she could recall that Frankie had ever missed a meal on purpose.

R. DAWN HUTCHINSON

· Chapter Twenty ·

Frankie bounced around on the saddle like a popcorn kernel in a hot pan. Earlier, when he climbed the fence to mount Shadow (because he wasn't tall enough to reach the stirrups from the ground), he was excited to finally ride a horse. Now, he wasn't so sure. Julian had held Blister at a walk for a while, but Blister's walk was extremely brisk, so Shadow had to trot just to keep pace. Afraid that Shadow might bolt and cause him to careen to his doom, Frankie overreacted to every move the black-and-white mare made. Periodically, Julian called out instructions, adding to Frankie's frustration.

"Grip with your knees more! Not that tight! Keep your feet in the stirrups, Frankie!"

Eventually, Blister's speed walk became a trot, and Shadow broke into a lope to catch him. Frankie yanked back on the reins and held them high and tight in the air.

"You're confusing her now, Frankie." Julian's vague European accent made the word confusing sound like 'confuseenk', and then it was Frankie who was confused for a second. "Loosen your reins. You're telling her to come to a full stop, but she knows you want to keep up with us." Julian wheeled Blister back around in a wide arc to come alongside them. The palomino, resenting having to retrace his steps, made his impatience known with a head toss and a snort.

Frankie dropped the reins altogether, deciding instead to hold on to the saddle for dear life. Shadow found a miniscule patch of greenery and began to nibble.

"You're doing well, especially for your first time riding, Frankie," Julian reassured him, clipping Frankie's shoulder with his fist. "Try to relax a little bit more. Shadow is almost twice your age and has been down this trail many times over the years. She knows where we are going. Sit up straight and tall, grip lightly with your knees, avoid yanking on the reins, and you will be fine."

"Okay," Frankie exhaled, feeling overwhelmed. "Okay. Let's go."

They started out slowly, but Blister couldn't keep that pace for long. Both horses were soon at a trot. Frankie cringed, thinking it was a long way down with nothing but rocks to break his fall. He inhaled deeply, sat up straighter, and forced himself to relax.

"That's the way!" Julian shouted. "A little looser with the reins! Very nice!"

Frankie was starting to get the hang of it. Sitting up higher on the horse offered him a strange new view of the world. The commanding view gave him a glimpse into what it must be like to be a prince. Sometimes, Frankie rifled through his brain to try and remember anything about their lives before he and Elise arrived at the orphanage. Elise said she could remember some things, like a big window, a red wagon, candy apples, and an orange cat. All Frankie could recall was a horse. His only memory was of trying to reach up high to pet the big nose bowing down over a stable door.

Saint Dominic's didn't have horses, so the memory must have come from his life before the orphanage.

"Julian, what is Anwynn like? You said that parallel universes can be either similar or different. Is ours different from this?" Frankie queried.

"There are some marked differences," Julian said, thinking.

"What, is the sky on Anwynn green or something?" Frankie almost hoped this was true.

"No, no, no," Julian responded, chuckling. "I would say the biggest difference is that Anwynn has a lot more water; it's more of a series of large islands than major continents."

"Weird," Frankie muttered, not expecting that answer.

"With all that water, there are very, *very* big fish. Also, civilization in Stromboden is not as advanced as it is here."

"You said you had to learn about the internet when you got here, so I figured they didn't have computers. Are we talking the Stone Age here?" Frankie felt a trickle of sweat run down his face. The sun had turned its setting to broil. Being a cave dweller sounded like a nice shady option.

Julian laughed. "No. The times, at least in the kingdom of Stromboden, are like America and England were at the end of the Regency Era."

Frankie raised his eyebrows. Did Julian expect him to know what that meant?

"What did they teach you in that school? I'm referring to the early 1800s."

Frankie shrugged his shoulders and gave Julian a sheepish grin.

"Napoleon, Jane Austen, the first occurrence of electricity in the home? Though I must admit, they didn't have electricity before I got there." Julian tipped his cowboy hat at Frankie.

"Are you saying you invented electricity?" Frankie asked, dubiously.

"Well, no. They had discovered it, but they hadn't yet engineered a way to harness it for practical use. That's where I helped." He smiled. "Yes, Stromboden is poised on the brink of an industrial revolution." Julian reined Blister back in again from an unexpected canter, and the two horses trotted side-by-side once more.

"Does Stromboden have horses?" Frankie asked, patting Shadow's smooth neck, worried that his mind might have invented that early memory of home.

"Oh, yes. The only form of land transportation is by horseback or horse-drawn carriage."

Frankie sighed in relief, glad to know that something familiar existed in his original reality.

They trotted near the base of the hills. Elise called them mountains, but Frankie disagreed. From far away, the plants along the hillside resembled scrub brush; but up close they were actually a swath of pine trees. The patch of dark green snaked up the steep slope and disappeared around the bend. They followed the hill's curve for a while and came to a wider area of pasture sprinkled with white and brown goats.

"Here they are," Julian said and began counting the floppy-eared goats out loud.

"Why don't you invent something to count the goats for you? Ooh! You could also invent a machine that cleans out the goat shed and the barn too. Why don't we just count the goats using the surveillance cameras?" Frankie thought his ideas were genius. Julian had cameras set up everywhere on the ranch, they might as well use them.

Julian had stopped counting and was staring at Frankie from underneath creased eyebrows.

"Sorry," Frankie apologized, realizing that he had interrupted Julian mid-count. "You were on twenty-four." Frankie sat silently astride Shadow and followed Blister while Julian continued his count. When Julian reached seventy-eight, he started over again. Satisfied that all goats were accounted for, he turned Blister around and addressed Frankie at last.

"To answer your questions, there are a few areas of the property that are out of camera range. Plus, with so many different angles, it's difficult to know whether I have counted a goat more than once."

"Oh. Well, that makes sense."

"I *could* create a device to clean the barn for us or to count the goats, sure. Hard work has its own merit, though. In any case, it's not as if we're suffering. Being on horseback isn't too shabby," he said with a smile.

Frankie couldn't disagree with that logic. If he was on foot, he would have probably roasted alive out here in the blazing sun before he made it back to the house.

They rode back to the barn along the fence line. There were actually two fences; one was the perimeter electric fence that went around the entire ranch, and the second, about eight feet inward, was a wire panel fence that outlined the goat pasture.

"It's always good to check the fences to see if they need any repairs," Julian said explaining their alternate path home.

Blister veered around a substantial prickly pear cactus that looked ready to assault anyone who dared venture too close. Shadow wisely followed. Julian reined Blister to a stop at a leaning fence post on the panel fence. He dismounted and tried to straighten the post. Frankie sat in the hot sun and took in the surrounding desert. The hot air danced in shimmering waves on the horizon. Ocotillo and yucca plants, as Julian called them, protruded stubbornly from the scaly earth.

"How do the goats even survive out here?" Frankie questioned.

"Goats will eat just about anything, but we also lightly seed and irrigate the pastures. They have picked this one nearly clean. In a few days, we will move them to a new pasture with fresh grass," Julian answered while fiddling with the base of the fence post.

Frankie's eyes wandered from Julian, then along the parched ground to the other fence. There, just outside the electric fence, was a set of bootprints, the square toes and heels clearly marked in the thick dust accumulated next to a post.

That's weird. Who would be walking out here in the middle of nowhere?

"Whose are those?" Frankie pointed to the prints.

Julian stood and squinted at them. "Hmm. They must be mine. I was out here not long ago testing the voltage." Julian stared awhile at the spot where the prints were before squatting and returning to his work.

After adjusting the post, Julian stood, removed a bandana from his pocket, and wiped his sweaty brow. "It looks like I will have to come back out later with some concrete and reset this post. It will hold for now." He mounted his horse again, coaxing him to a trot along the fence line. Frankie and Shadow followed close behind. They rode quietly back to the barn, where Julian taught him how to put the tack away and brush down the horses.

Shadow seemed to enjoy her brushing session, and Frankie was relieved to be back in the barn's protective shade. As he turned Shadow loose to join the rest of the horses, an uneasy feeling settled in the back of his brain. Something wasn't right. He just couldn't get his mind off of those bootprints in the sand.

· Chapter Twenty-One ·

It felt like Lekana had just finished hanging the laundry on the line to dry when Elise was already taking it down. The scorching Texas sun had sucked all the moisture out of the laundry in minutes. Elise moved her wooden stepstool down the line every few feet. Barely able to reach the line on her tiptoes, she couldn't get a grip on the clothespins without a boost. She folded as she went along, dropping perfectly smooth, crisp sheets and towels into the basket below her. Sometimes, she held the fabric to her nose, taking a long whiff of detergent and summer air, before she let go.

Lekana was in the side yard under the mesquite trees cutting back a few branches that had grown too close to the house. Elise watched as she appeared to dance in and out of the old, shady branches. Sunlight stole every opportunity to weave golden strands into her night-colored tresses.

Elise took a small, Man of Iron-themed T-shirt off the line. The super hero's automated helmet stared at her with wide, lifeless eyes. She hurriedly folded the tiny garment, carefully tucking away any frightening memories of the bald, cloaked men and their dead eyes. She moved onto another miniature, blue shirt. Both shirts obviously belonged to Felix, whom she hadn't seen much of today. She wondered what days on the ranch where like for a five-year-old boy.

As if to answer her query, a high-pitched cry sounded from around the goat shed.

"Felix!" Elise gasped, knowing. Thinking he must have fallen or cut himself in the shed, Elise looked to Lekana, who had already thrown her shears down and was sprinting toward the goat shed. Elise leapt from her step stool perch and ran after Lekana. She passed the squat, white building, stopped and then gazed across the field. The cry still came, a plaintive, frantic expression of pain.

"Felix?!!?" Lekana shouted into the pasture. Elise caught up to her and looked into the shed. The boy was nowhere in sight.

"Felix!" Lekana cried, her brows furrowed as she scanned the horizon.

"Over there!" Elise yelled, pointing toward the barren pasture where a small, white goat lay on its side. A larger goat, presumably its mother, stood near it at attention, challenging anything that came near. The kid lay still, then struggled and cried out once more. Elise noticed that it sounded remarkably like a child.

Lekana skillfully climbed over the fence and rushed to aid the baby goat. Elise chased after her to help. The nanny goat, seeing a potential threat running toward her baby, squared off to face Lekana. It shook its head and brandished a pair of sickle-shaped horns. Earlier, Elise had thought the horns were cute. She thought differently now. Lekana had just moved in front of Elise as the nanny prepared to charge when Onora emerged from the shed and vaulted over the fence. Her abrupt entrance distracted the goat. It charged at Onora, who side-stepped at the last second. The nanny circled around. Lekana moved toward the baby goat, but the nanny caught her movement and refocused her attention on the persistent woman. Onora pounced from behind, grappling the nanny's horns and wrestling her to the ground. The kid screamed and tried to right itself. Its mother kicked at the ground, and Onora wrapped her legs around its torso, trying to disarm her further.

Confused, angry, and desperate, the nanny cried for her baby. The resonance of her turmoil deeply affected Elise. A wail erupted from the baby as Lekana approached. Its cry rang in Elise's ears, echoing painfully in her heart. Distressed, Elise covered her ears and yelled, "Stop it!"

Lekana jumped back at her outburst as if something had burned her. Onora held resolutely onto the nanny.

"Sorry," Elise murmured, remembering herself.

Elise took a deep breath and then approached the nanny with caution. Her anxiety was replaced as she invited a sense of calm and peace to wash over her, and when she felt the tranquility flooding her heart, she imagined extending it to the goats.

"We are here to help you and your baby," she soothed, holding a hand out toward the panicked animal. *We will not harm either of you. Please don't hurt us,* she thought, sending the goat mental images of gentle hands stroking fur and a healthy baby goat.

The nanny surrendered and stopped struggling against Onora.

"You can let her go, Onora," Elise instructed. "She's agreed to let us help."

Skeptical, Onora hesitated, and then finally relented. She released its horns, and the goat rolled to its feet.

Elise knelt by Lekana, who cradled the baby goat in her lap. Its leg had been caught in a hole formed in the dry ground. The woman ran her tattooed thumb down its forehead, across its ribs, and along its swollen leg, while whispering strange words. Elise couldn't place the language; it sounded choppy and unlike any she'd ever heard. Lekana finally looked up and asked Onora to bring the medical supply kit, which was in the barn's tack room. Onora gave the nanny goat one more suspicious glance before jogging to the barn, her long braid bouncing on her back.

"The leg is not broken," Lekana told Elise, "it is pulled. Sprained," she corrected herself, while absentmindedly rocking the little bundle of fluff in her lap. Her bronze skin stood out in sharp contrast to the kid's white fur. The nanny goat sniffed the baby's face, making sure it was safe.

"You can talk to the animals," Lekana observed after a pause. Elise nodded shyly, looking at the ground. "The sister of my father could talk to them also." She grinned nostalgically.

"Do you talk to them too?" Elise asked, relieved that her sanity wasn't questioned.

"I talk to the spirits," Lekana answered, her expression falling.

A creaky hinge announced Onora's arrival with the medical kit. Felix was at her side.

"I found them both in the tack room," Onora said, referring to the boy and the box.

The lines on Lekana's brow eased upon seeing the brown-haired boy clopping along in his tall, blue boots.

"Is the baby gonna be okay, Mama?" Felix crouched down to look at the floppy-eared goat in his mother's arms. His brown eyes were pools of tenderness.

"He will be fine in a few weeks," she said, removing bandages from the box. She wrapped the leg tightly and then carried the fuzzy bundle to a stall in the goat shed. The nanny followed closely. "He will stay in here until his leg is better," she said. After a few falls, the baby stood and hobbled around on his three good legs. Elise grinned and stroked his velvety ears.

Onora grabbed a shovel and then left to fill the hole where the baby had fallen. When she returned, she helped Lekana fill the goats' buckets with food and fresh water. The mother goat butted Lekana's thigh lightly, and she returned the thank you with a handful of food. The nanny turned to Onora next, butting her in the hip much harder, knocking her sideways a step.

"Understood," said Onora with a miniscule lift of an eyebrow. "I won't do it again."

Felix followed the women out of the shed, but Elise stayed and watched the baby goat suckle for a little while. She couldn't imagine a life where she couldn't communicate with animals; it was how her life had always been. She wondered why she could do it, yet no one else could. Lekana's aunt was the only other person she had heard of who shared this gift.

Even if she never met the lady, it was nice to know she wasn't alone.

Elise walked back to the half-empty clothesline, thinking about Lekana's sullen face when she revealed that she could communicate with the spirits. Elise was certain Lekana was not alluding to the Holy Ghost. She wondered who these spirits were, and what could they be saying to make Lekana so sad. Elise glanced around, wondering if the spirits were around her. A light breeze wafted through the lane, stirring the flames of her red hair, and sending a shiver up her spine.

· Chapter Twenty-Two ·

"Frankie. **Wake up**, Frankie."

Frankie heard Julian's voice speaking to him.

It felt too early to open his eyes, and he wasn't altogether certain that the body attached to the voice wasn't merely part of a dream. He squeezed his eyes tighter, hoping the voice would drift away.

"Frankie." A calloused hand touched his arm and lightly shook.

Frankie raised a heavy eyelid and peeked. Yep, it was Julian all right. Heaving a sigh, he slowly sat up. "What?" he asked, attempting to keep his eyes open without letting any light in them. This was difficult and resulted in a squinting sneer.

Julian looked unamused. "Did you forget to set your alarm?"

"No. It's Saturday." Frankie answered slowly, deliberately.

"You can take a nap this afternoon. There are no days off when you have animals depending on you for their meals. Let's get to it now, lad!" Julian patted Frankie's exposed foot and left the room.

Frankie stared after him, barely comprehending what had just happened. What kind of place was this? Even the nuns let all the kids sleep in on Saturdays!

He thrust his legs into a pair of jeans and stepped into his sneakers without bothering to tie the laces. He trudged downstairs, walked out the door, and marched down the lane, grumbling to himself. Every morning, for the past four days, he had woken up early to feed the horses and clean the goat shed. Surely, that had earned him a break! He glared at the early morning sun, knowing it would be glaring back down on him in a few hours.

The horses heard his quick footfalls and neighed their disapproval from afar. "Yeah, yeah, yeah," he muttered under his breath. Entering the barn, he saw four long, angry faces snorting at him impatiently. "I'm sorry I'm late," he uttered through clenched teeth while making his way to the feed room. Tinny drove her point home by repeatedly kicking the stable wall with her front hoof.

He scooped out food for each and then waited for them to finish their meals. Their satisfied chomping took the edge off of his frustration. Only Tinny held on to the grudge, somehow managing to eat angrily as she kicked the stall wall between bites. On her way out the stall, Shadow nuzzled Frankie, leaving a thick smear of oat-laden slobber on his T-shirt.

"Eww! Yuck!" Frankie grabbed a cloth from the tack room and tried to wipe off the slime while making his way to the goat shed. He flung the rag in the corner of the shed and snatched up a rake. He was eager to finish this job so he could head straight back upstairs to his soft, relaxing bed. They had been parted too soon.

The rake had nearly touched the ground when he heard a whisper. Frankie stopped. It was coming from behind the goat shed. Creeping closer to the back wall, he could make out two voices in quiet debate. He could only catch a few words, but then clearly heard the word "bootprints". Frankie pushed the entire side of his face against the wall so he could hear what was being said.

"I'm forced to believe that security is not as good as you made it out to be."

It was Onora talking. Frankie could recognize the librarian's hushed, clipped consonants anywhere. Obviously, she had seen the same prints in the sand that Frankie had a few days earlier, and she was now suspicious.

"If people are drawn to others who have traveled through, then it's only a matter of time until we are found. Seeing as you can't confirm where those prints are from . . ."

"Onora, please, calm yourself. Those prints are-"

"This living situation can only be temporary," Onora interrupted. "We *must* have a backup plan, Dr. Weyls, especially considering someone here is not who I thought they were."

Frankie heard Onora's accusing tone through her whispers. He was stunned at what he was hearing. He thought this *was* their backup plan. Now it wasn't working? Julian had said the bootprints were his. Why didn't Onora believe him? Frankie pressed his ear against the wall once more, straining to hear the hushed conversation.

"That is ludicrous! We—" Julian was cut off again by a noise inside the goat shed.

Frankie's heart raced. He had let the rake slip from his hand, and it crashed down on top of an empty bucket. Mortified that he'd be caught, he tiptoed back to the first stall and began casually raking it out, pausing occasionally to listen. The discussion never resumed.

Frankie's heart continued to thunder in his chest, and it didn't settle until he had showered and laid down for his long-awaited nap. Though now he couldn't sleep.

⏸

That evening he joined everyone around the large, round, oak table for a spaghetti dinner. The table always reminded him of King Arthur's round table. Tonight it occurred to him that there was more in common between the Arthurian legend and the story in this room than just the shape of the table. Royalty sat at this table too. Of course, King Arthur had created a round table so that there would be no head, and everyone would sit as equals. All the knights were aware of who was *really* king, though. Frankie wondered if everyone at the dinner table was aware that he was their prince and Elise their princess.

He surveyed his companions around the table as he repeatedly stabbed a meatball with his fork. Normally, he could overlook their individual idiosyncrasies. Tonight, however, he couldn't help but be annoyed by even the most benign habit. Elise was contentedly chewing away, dabbing at her mouth with a napkin between every bite. Next to her was her polar opposite, Felix, who had spaghetti sauce all over his face and every surface within his reach.

That kid is a mess, Frankie thought to himself.

Lekana was on Felix's other side. Periodically, she tried to wipe her son's messy face or hands, but her effort was pointless—she might as well have been putting a napkin to Old Faithful. It never seemed to frustrate her though, she just continued on her fruitless quest for cleanliness.

Frankie glanced at Julian. The early riser. The chore-monger. He had a funny way of eating that made his mouth go sideways when he chewed. It reminded Frankie of a turtle. With Julian's cowboy hat hanging off the back of his chair like a shell, the look was complete.

Onora sat between Julian and Frankie. It was bizarre to Frankie how her soft features could seem so hardened merely by the cold personality within. She was already finished eating and was also stealing surreptitious glances at their table mates. Frankie wondered what she knew about all of them that he didn't know. He was sure that King Arthur's knights didn't whisper and keep secrets behind the king's back. Certainly, that kind of behavior was met with dismemberment or a hanging.

Or at least a meatball in the face, he thought. Frankie imagined himself flinging a meatball right at Onora's nose. A self-satisfied smirk spread across his face.

Frankie spent the rest of the meal lobbing imaginary meatballs at everyone's noses. He envisioned the pure satisfaction of hitting the target, the shocked faces of his victims dripping red with sauce. During his reverie, a real meatball fell from his fork and landed with a squishy thud on top of his noodles. He stared at it with contempt.

When he finished his meal, he was sequestered into the kitchen. It was the twins' night to wash dishes, another incredibly un-kingly chore, and Frankie grumbled to himself in resentment. Perhaps the temporary nature of these living conditions wasn't such a bad idea.

He felt Elise's eyes on him as she dried a plate. Peeved about being scrutinized by his judgmental twin, he stuck out his tongue at her before leaving the kitchen. She pursed her lips when he stomped by. He headed up the stairs to their shared room, threw his shoes at the corner of the room, and then belly-flopped into bed.

Elise entered the room shortly after, studying her brother. Finally, she asked, "What's the matter, Frankie? You seem…bothered."

Frankie heaved a sigh. He turned his head to face the wall and fell into an uneasy sleep.

· Chapter Twenty-Three ·

Holding the radiant golden processional cross high before her, Elise marched forward and hummed along with the Gloria. She knelt at the altar and turned to the congregation, her forehead glistening with holy water. When the song ended, she knelt in prayer, giving thanks for God's sacrifice. Sunlight shone through the stained glass windows, warming her shoulders, making her feel the sacredness of the lofty cathedral around her. She was safe.

She broke the bread and offered it to the women gathered around the altar. They took it from her greedily. Sister Henrietta clucked.

The clucking continued, startling Elise from her daydream. Sister Henrietta was, in fact, a chicken that had clucked, and Elise felt deflated as the cathedral around her melted from her imagination. The interior walls of the hen house materialized in its stead, and six pairs of beady, black eyes stared at what remained of the host in her hand. She scattered the remnants of her breakfast roll on the floor and took up a collection of eggs. Grabbing the rake which she had used as a processional cross, she headed out to the garden.

It was Sunday and she missed Mass terribly. No one else here seemed to notice that they weren't attending church. Elise was certain that Frankie didn't miss it one bit. She knew he found it dull, and he had constantly received negative marks from the nuns for falling asleep during Father Patrick's monotone, canned sermons.

This was their second week of missing Mass. Elise was beginning to feel like a stringless balloon, drifting farther into the wild winds of the atmosphere. Mass kept her grounded, with its predictable rituals and hymns. She looked forward to contemplating the mysteries of the Holy Trinity and sitting among people from every walk of life. She loved the glowing candles, the heady smell of incense, and even the disjointed resonance of Sister Monica's bungled organ playing.

She closed the squeaky garden gate behind her and gazed at the little white farmhouse, then the goat shed and the barn. Elise smiled. Mass was the only thing she would add to this place so that it felt more like home.

Elise rummaged through her basket and found her pruning shears. She began snipping the ripe pods of okra off the tall, knobby stalks. Gardening wasn't on her list of chores, but she had nothing else to do. Earlier, she thought of reading a book, but the Weyls' library only included books about Thomas the Train or about neutron detection. Her interest level lay somewhere between these two subjects.

Elise sat back on her feet and plucked a splintery okra hair from her finger. The offending hair removed, she knelt to search for okra pods further down on the plant. While contentedly occupied with her task, she heard the garden gate squeak open and then shut. She recognized Frankie's familiar shuffle, his sneakers crunching on the gravel between the long, rectangular, raised beds. Elise didn't let her presence be known; if he was as grumpy as he was last night, she'd rather not be found.

"Elise, there you are," Frankie said, his tone somber. "I thought you'd be in the hen house or with the baby goat."

She clipped one more pod and looked up. Frankie looked downtrodden. "I *was* in the hen house, but I finished early," she said wryly. The morning sun was beginning its transition to afternoon blaze. She adjusted her baseball cap to shade her eyes and then looked up at her brother. He squinted, the freckles on his nose more pronounced in the assaulting UV rays.

Frankie drew a deep breath and then exhaled. "I'm tired of running." He looked down at his sister expectantly. Elise only frowned at him. Frankie reached for an overturned bucket to sit on, but he wasn't paying attention and grabbed Elise's basket instead. When he began his descent, Elise snatched the basket from its impending destruction and curled protectively around it.

"My eggs!" she shouted, producing an empty bucket beside her.

"Oops, sorry," Frankie replied. He positioned himself on the bucket and looked at his sister thoughtfully. "I meant that I'm tired of running away from whoever it is that's after us."

"We did stop running. We're safe here, Frankie," Elise said setting her basket down a safe distance from Frankie.

"That's just it. When I was out with Julian, I found a set of bootprints outside the electric fence. Julian said they were his, and I believed him. Yesterday, when I was working in the goat shed, I heard Onora and Julian whispering about something. Onora said she saw the bootprints too, but she didn't believe they were Julian's. Onora said they had to prepare a backup plan because it's only a matter of time until 'they' find us." He stared at his sister.

Elise placed the shears back in the basket and sat pensively. "Onora does seem on edge, but she's a Royal Guard; it's her job to be a bit paranoid."

Frankie stood up, knocking the bucket over in the process. "We came from a whole different reality just to get away from this guy. Then, his henchmen found us, so we ran. Now, it sounds like we're getting ready to run away *again*. When will it end?"

Elise examined her brother towering above her, all fire and freckles. "I don't see what other choice we have," she replied.

"I'm going to open a portal."

"On purpose?"

"Yes. We can use it to go back and deal with this head-on."

"You don't know how to open a portal on purpose, Frankie, and the portals you have opened led to some weird places. What if Councilman Carvil finds us there?" Frankie's idea was too outlandish to even be considered, but she was becoming agitated. "He could kill us on the spot."

"He tried to *poison our minds*. He never intended to *kill* us," Frankie stated as if he knew the councilman personally. "Besides, they wouldn't expect us there. They're all looking for us here, right?"

Elise stood up. She knew the uncertainty showed in her eyes, but it was impossible to hide. "Do you know how to open a portal, Frankie?"

"No," he huffed. "I don't know *how* it's done, but I know I can do it. Julian said that people in olden times went into trances to open portals. I figure that if I want to open one on purpose, I just need to go into a trance too."

Elise realized that Frankie gestured with his hands the way Dr. Weyls did when he was excited. She grinned despite her insecurity. "So you're going to learn how to meditate?" she asked crossing her arms.

"Is that what meditation is, focusing and trances?"

"I know meditation helps focus your mind. I guess you could go into a trance." She shrugged. "I don't know."

"You'll teach me how to meditate, then?"

"I don't know how, exactly, but Onora does." Elise smiled mischievously.

"Oh great!" Frankie rolled his eyes. "I can picture how that's gonna go. 'Onora, will you teach me how to meditate?'" Frankie squared his shoulders back, squinted his eyes and pursed his lips tightly, mimicking Onora. "The answer to anything you ask will always be no!" he said, in a tone that nearly matched Onora's accent.

Elise threw her head back in laughter.

Pleased that he had entertained his sister, he grinned. He glanced around the garden and then began walking up and down the rows as if he was looking for something. He stopped at the end of a row and gave Elise and irritated look. "Hey, did you pick my potatoes? Lekana said to wait another week!"

"I didn't pull any potatoes," Elise answered defensively, walking over to investigate the area where Frankie stood. The earth was indeed disturbed, and one potato plant was missing. There were other potato plants standing whole and untouched around the freshly churned dirt. "Hmm," Elise muttered and twirled a lock of hair around her index finger, a habitual movement she made when in deep thought. "I wonder who did this. Lekana hasn't been in the garden this week, and Felix knows the plants too well to mistakenly pull a potato plant while he was weeding. Dr. Weyls usually doesn't do much gardening other than spreading fertilizer."

Frankie frowned and shook his head. "What about rabbits? I know they can't get through the garden fence, but can they dig up from underneath to take vegetables?" Frankie asked.

"No," Elise answered slowly. "Dr. Weyls said that he lined the whole garden with chicken wire, and then put soil on top of that, so no rabbits or mice could get at the roots.

"Well, if you didn't pull them, and I didn't pull them, and we know no one else did, then what got my potatoes?"

A hot breeze blew past and rustled the spiky leaves of the okra plants.

Elise twirled a lock of her hair. "Maybe it was the spirits," she said under her breath. Frankie gave her an incredulous look. "Lekana told me the other day that she talks to the spirits," Elise explained.

"What spirits?"

"I don't know. We didn't talk about it in detail. Maybe she can ask them, and they will know who took the potatoes."

Frankie crossed his arms over his chest and kicked a small rock. "Maybe that's what Onora meant when she whispered to Julian that not everyone here is who they seem to be," he said, glancing at his sister, whose face crumpled in confusion. "Maybe these aren't just any spirits she's talking to. Maybe they're the bald men in black."

"What? Frankie, what are you saying?" Elise couldn't believe what she was hearing.

"Look, Onora is suspicious of somebody here. Lekana could be the one she was talking about. What if Lekana is secretly talking to these guys and telling them how to get to us?" Frankie asked adamantly. "Julian couldn't have put chicken wire underneath the whole ranch! Maybe they're digging under the electric fence somewhere."

"Wait a second. I said Lekana talked to the spirits, not evil men in black coats." Elise refused to ally her friend Lekana to those foul beings.

"Think about it, Elise. Those guys, those . . . things in black hardly seemed like people, did they? They were more like evil spirits."

Elise scowled. She had to agree with him on that point, but she didn't have to like it.

"Lekana is nice and all, but what if she's just trying to buy time so they can dig outside the range of the surveillance cameras?"

Elise stared at her shadow on the gravel-covered ground. The afternoon sun felt like it was threatening to burn a hole straight through the back of her shirt. Could he be right? Could Lekana be working against them? It was hard to fathom that Lekana—the same woman who taught her how to make flatbread, the one who made a healing salve for Frankie's scraped knee—was conversing with people who wanted to harm them. She didn't want to believe it. Deciding not to think about that possibility anymore, she stalked back to her basket and continued searching for more okra pods.

Unfinished with the discussion, Frankie followed her. "Do you see why I want to try and start opening portals?"

Elise didn't answer.

"Onora is right," he said, "it is only a matter of time before they find us again, if they're not here already."

Elise found a pod, clipped it from the stalk, and tossed it in the basket.

"I feel so helpless just sitting here waiting for them. All I do around here is scoop goat poop and feed horses! I have to do something that might help us, and maybe that something is learning how to open portals. Don't you think?" Frankie righted the bucket and dropped down onto it.

"I think you should talk to Onora," Elise stated flatly, dropping another pod in her basket.

· Chapter Twenty-Four ·

I n, two-three-four. Out, two-three-four. In, two-three-four.

Frankie's back began to ache from sitting up straight for so long, so he slouched forward. He, Elise, and Onora were sitting cross-legged in a loft area above the horse barn. Frankie had begged Elise to help him ask their taciturn bodyguard if she would teach them how to meditate. Onora had been sharpening one of her swords when they arrived, which made Frankie more nervous. Onora carried what she called dragonfly blades. The falchions and two daggers were forged by a master swordsmith from the same piece of steel.

Apparently, they required a lot of care. That, or she just liked touching them a lot.

To Frankie's surprise, Onora enthusiastically agreed to his request. Perhaps enthusiastic was the wrong word for her response, but she didn't furrow her brow when she said yes. That was a good sign. Of course, he didn't mention *why* he wanted to learn how to meditate. Admitting he wanted to purposely open portals would have guaranteed that Onora would not only put a stop to his plans but also follow his every move. If she knew Frankie was planning on going back to Stromboden to face their problems once and for all, her eyebrows would have furrowed for sure.

Frankie realized he was thinking about Onora's brow instead of focusing on his breathing, as she had instructed them. Ignoring his aching back, he sat up straight and began again. He breathed in to the count of four, and then out to the count of four. In, two-three-four, out, two-three-four.

"Become aware of your body, the feeling of air expanding your lungs, the beating of your heart," Onora had instructed during their first meditation session. "Be conscious of any emotions that arise, and how they affect your body."

Frankie thought that part was funny. Meditation must be extremely easy for Onora, considering she only had one emotion: dead seriousness.

Bah! His thoughts had drifted from his breath again. He recomposed himself. In, two-three-

How am I supposed to pay attention to my breath and emotions at the same time? he thought, then checked himself. *Good grief, I've done it again.*

He jerked his body up straight, squeezed his eyes shut, and began again. He would do it this time for real.

In, two-three-four. Out, two-three-four.

In, two-three-four. Out, two-three-four.

The darkness was suffocating. The silence, excruciating. The nothingness, unbearable. He risked peeping an eye open.

No glowing wavy circle of light. No portal. It was just Elise and Onora sitting quietly, breathing in slow rhythm. This was their third day of meditation practice. Each day after their morning chores were finished, Frankie and Elise would meet Onora in the hayloft to meditate. He still had nothing to show for it except a squished bum from sitting so long.

Frankie slouched again in defeat and threw his head back quietly. His eyes rolled back, and his tongue lolled out of his mouth. This is how they would find his body. Frankie St. John: Dead from boredom.

A warm drop of drool traced from the tip of his hanging tongue down his cheek. He dragged his face across his shoulder to dry it. When he brought his head up again, he was startled to see Onora's steely eyes staring back at him. Unsure of how much she had seen, he decided to play it cool.

"How is your practice progressing, Frankie?" Onora asked stoically.

"Uh, good! Real good. I'm definitely not getting anywhere, but that's the point, right? To just sort of sit there, not going anywhere. So, it's great!" He stretched his arms up and began to rise. Elise had opened her eyes and was looking around.

"Is the time up already?" she asked.

"I think so!" Frankie said, standing and trying in vain to avoid Onora's gaze.

"We have a few minutes left, but this is a good stopping point," Onora responded from her seated position.

"Remember, it takes time to quiet a restless mind. A person must become king of himself first before expanding his dominion." Her eyes took on the color of black coffee in the dim light.

Frankie gave Onora a thumbs up and descended the loft ladder with haste. If he was going to be king of anything, he'd have to get back to his own stupid castle.

Elise caught up with him but struggled to keep pace with his brisk walk back to the house. "That felt good," she said, bright-eyed. "It's like a little cat nap. I feel refreshed!"

"How? It's the most mind-numbing experience ever!" Frankie complained.

"That's the goal, to numb your mind a little."

"Well, I can't do it. It's a special kind of torture that only you seem to enjoy for some reason."

"I guess it's because I've been doing it all along, and I didn't know it."

Frankie frowned, confused and indignant.

"When I talk to animals, I have to make my thoughts quiet so I can hear them. That's basically what we're doing when we're meditating, but we're staying in that quiet place for longer than I normally do. I never knew I was doing mini-meditations! Though I have to be honest, I do end up hearing the chickens, or Buddy, or the goats, or something while I'm up there. It's hard to shut them out, but I have to if I want to keep my mind quiet. That's the part I'm working on."

Frankie rolled his eyes. He turned on his heel and stomped off in the opposite direction, eager to be alone.

Exiting the picket fence he followed his feet to the old ghost town. His sneakers made soft stamping noises as they padded over the sandy earth. Wispy clouds smeared the sky, doing nothing to hide the scorching sun. He reached the shade of the mercantile's porch and began pacing over the aging plank foundation.

Opening portals couldn't be that difficult if he could do it while he was sleeping. Agitated, he paced faster, the wood plank porch groaning loudly under his weight. He didn't understand how he could open portals in his sleep, but he couldn't do it on purpose. All he needed to do was open one more, measly portal, and then he and Elise could get out of here, back to Anwynn and their own kingdom. But he couldn't even manage to sit still on purpose. Why was that so difficult?

He stopped pacing and stood in front of the mercantile's window, looking at his reflection. He sighed, and let his forehead hit the grimy window pane with a hollow plunk. Gazing into the window, his eyes wandered around the interior of the old building and settled at the far end of the shop. The black pocket watch sat silent and still in its glass case, seeming to mock him with its rhythmic tranquility. A flame of jealousy ignited in Frankie's belly. It flickered and then grew into anger. He was overcome with the urge to punch through the window, break the glass case, and crush the watch and its black metal casing in his fist.

A movement in the corner of his eye caught his attention. He glanced at the reflection in the windowpane by his forehead. Someone had appeared in the window of the building behind him, in the saloon. He whirled around, but the saloon windows were empty.

Frankie stood stock still. He was certain he saw a figure walk past the window. Why would anyone be in the saloon? Julian said he hadn't done anything with that building except clean it. No secret surveillance rooms or laboratories were built beneath it. It was just a plain, old saloon that at one time probably hosted drunken card games and maybe some cancan dancing.

Perhaps the original inhabitants of this town had not all vacated. Maybe some people left their spirits behind to carry on romping about the saloon. If there was a cancan dancing ghost, Frankie had to see it.

He took a step off the porch, but then halted. He considered his warning to Elise about Lekana: the spirits she spoke to might not be good spirits. Something evil could be in the saloon. A sense of dread cascaded over Frankie at the thought.

Slowly, he walked across the street toward the saloon, his curiosity overpowering the nearly paralyzing fear of whatever lurked within.

The saloon porch creaked with each footstep, ruining any sort of stealth Frankie had attempted. He peered into the window, his hands on either side of his face to block out the afternoon sun. A thick slab of wood ran the length of the wall to his left. That must have been the bar. Toward the back of the room was a slightly elevated area of floor that could have served as a stage. Ragged remnants of faded, purple cloth hung from the ceiling above it. Everything bore the dull grey sheen of dust. No tables or chairs. Frankie wondered if the townspeople took those with them when they relocated.

No one appeared to be inside the building.

Julian had long ago replaced the old-time, swinging saloon doors with a plain wooden door. With a sweaty palm, Frankie pushed down on the brass latch. The door didn't give right away, and he had to shove it with his shoulder to get it open. The door scraped against its frame with a piercing wail, then swung open wildly. Frankie stumbled over the threshold and took a few more steps into the room. He breathed in the hot stagnant air, catching a whiff of decay coming from somewhere. A few flies buzzed curiously around his head. He shooed them away, and they found their way out the open door.

In his periphery, Frankie saw something large and white take shape in front of one of the windows. It faded away and then reformed itself. He turned to face it, heart racing. Nothing was there. After staring wide-eyed at the empty space, he realized that the mysterious form was just dust particles riding the currents of air brought in by the open door. The dust motes spun and rose in great masses, in and out of the sunbeams, creating the illusion of an apparition. He drew a shaky breath and turned to inspect the room again. A muffled knocking sound came from somewhere around the bar area.

Knock-knock-knock.

Pause.

Knock-knock-knock.

It repeated again and again. Frankie's breath grew shallower as the seconds ticked by. Flies returned to the saloon, unable to resist the scent of rot. They followed an invisible trail around the room, and landed on the bar, scurrying across its splintered surface.

Frankie took a silent, slow step closer to the bar, as though quick movements would anger whatever lived there. The knocking continued unabated. He dared to take another step forward when a long shadow spilled over his shoulders and across the floor in front of him. Frankie uttered a small, terrified whimper. He brought his hands up in his best Kung Fu hand strike positions and spun around.

It was Julian.

"There you are, Frankie. Is everything okay in here?" He stood in the doorway, the sunlight glinting off the scales of his snakeskin boots.

Finally, it hit Frankie; the toes of Julian's boots were pointy, not square like the bootprints in the sand were. Julian had lied.

"I was hoping you would help me repair a leaky pipe from the spring," the lanky man said. His eyes darted about the room, following the flies. "There's a lot of digging involved, and I could use an extra hand."

Frankie kept his hands up and didn't move. His heart still beat at full tilt.

"I'm sorry if I scared you," Julian apologized. He stepped forward into the saloon and reached toward the boy. Buddy appeared at the door, panting. His ears perked up, and he cocked his head at the sight of Frankie with his arms up.

"Guess I got a little spooked," Frankie said, laughing nervously. He slowly lowered his hands, staring at Julian's boots. "Yeah, I'll help you."

Frankie shimmied carefully passed Julian and exited the saloon into the bright daylight. If Julian had lied about the bootprints being his, what else was he lying to them about? Perhaps he was the person who Onora was whispering about behind the goat shed the other day. Perhaps Julian was the person who was not who he seemed to be.

Buddy barked, trying to entice Frankie into a game of chase. He patted the bouncy pup on the head but didn't feel much like playing. Frankie didn't really know what he felt like anymore.

· Chapter Twenty-Five ·

Elise was startled awake by a high-pitched, other-worldly call that was immediately followed by thundering footsteps across her bedroom floor. Her eyelids sprang open and she discovered Frankie standing at the bedroom window. Between the two of them, they had forgotten to turn the ceiling fan on before they went to bed. She had been sweating so much that the sheets clung to her. She peeled the sheets away from her, and the strange call rang out again.

She joined Frankie next to the window and searched the darkness outside. It sounded like a group of toddlers having a party, yelling and carrying on. Frankie looked frantic. His breathing was heavy and he craned his neck in all directions, trying to catch a glimpse of the sound's source.

"They're coyotes."

The twins turned to see Onora standing behind them. The hollow and squeaky floorboards in their bedroom typically announced the presence of all who walked over them, but neither of the kids had heard Onora's approach.

"Geez! Don't sneak up on people!" Frankie yelled. Catching his breath, he faced the window again, mumbling complaints to himself. Elise managed to pick out, "wandering around" and "giving people heart attacks" from his whispered verbal tirade.

Onora glanced down at Frankie and then gazed out into the night. The sky was pitch and glistened with countless sparkles of stars. The moon was a mere sliver of light hidden among them. Crickets sang their sweet melody, while the coyotes resumed their chattering farther away.

"You can go back to sleep," Onora softly advised, her eyes still drinking in the night sky.

Frankie grumbled his way back to bed, but Elise stayed a moment, entranced by the stars' glittering white light. She wanted to reach out and touch them, to see them glimmer and shine in her hands. Onora shifted behind her and briefly touched Elise's shoulder as she turned to leave the room. Regretfully, Elise withdrew from the window and walked to her bed. She paused to take one last look at the magical sky before climbing in. That's when she saw a shadowy figure dashing across the front lawn. The wisp of moonlight glinted on long, black hair as it streamed past.

Elise turned to Onora, wondering if she had seen the woman too.

"To bed, Elise," Onora commanded, switching on the ceiling fan before closing the bedroom door.

Elise got in bed like she was told. Maybe Onora had missed Lekana running in the front lawn. What was she doing out there in the middle of the night? Elise threw back the sheets and stood on her mattress to get a better view of the front yard.

Onora can't get mad. I'm still in bed like she told me to be, Elise thought with a grin.

Rolling onto her tiptoes, Elise balanced on the wobbly mattress, peering into the darkness for a sign of the raven-haired woman. Finally, another shape moved to the left, a shadow chasing a shadow. It quickly flew past the window, but Elise could still clearly make out the silhouette of a woman with a braid trailing behind her.

Onora, she thought knowingly, a sickening feeling rising in her stomach.

The shadow merged into the darkness again. For the briefest second, Elise thought she saw the sickle-shaped moon mirrored on a smooth, steel blade below.

"What are you doing?" Frankie asked sleepily propping himself up on his elbows.

Elise realized how strange she must look standing on her bed. Not wishing to encourage Frankie's negative assumptions about Lekana, she chose not to explain what she had seen outside. She knew he would jump to conclusions and pronounce Lekana guilty of being secretly in cahoots with the bad guys. Though she had to admit, this didn't look good.

"Oh, nothing, just looking at the stars," Elise tried answering casually. Hoping Frankie was convinced, she settled back into bed. She stared at the ceiling for an eternity trying to think of the glittery stars, and not the secret comings and goings of the two women outside.

❓

After two hours of being wide awake, Elise gave up thinking of plausible explanations for Lekana's midnight excursion, and finally dozed off. She slept restlessly, roused by the faintest of sounds. Was that a dog barking? Was that the sound of a door latching? She opened one eye, unsure if she heard soft footfalls on the stairs or simply the sound of her heartbeat echoing in her ear.

All at once, everything was wrong. An explosive noise split the air as if a train had blasted its horn in their bedroom. Elise sat bolt upright. The blast sounded again, shaking the floor and rattling Elise's teeth.

Frankie jolted out of bed, ran to the door and flung it open. Elise could see into the hallway where Dr. Weyls flipped on the hall light and fumbled with his smartwatch. Onora was already there, shouting at him. Dr. Weyls yelled back, but neither could be heard over the noise. Buddy appeared to bark, but then retreated somewhere into the master bedroom, his tiny tail tucked away in fear. The siren blared, repeating its warning cry every few seconds. Frankie ran back into the bedroom and scrambled to put his shoes on with shaking hands.

Elise was terrified. She clasped her hands to her ears, desperate for the siren to stop. Lekana appeared in the hallway, fully dressed and clutching Felix on her hip. The boy held his ears and buried his face in his mother's shoulder. Lekana's face was calm, an eye in the midst of the chaotic storm; Elise latched her gaze onto it.

Dr. Weyls finally pressed the right code on his watch face, and the siren ceased. Elise exhaled slowly in relief.

Wasting no time, Onora shouted, "Where?"

"South perimeter of the east pasture," Dr. Weyls replied.

Onora glanced at Frankie and Elise, checking their current status, and then thrust a knife—handle first—at Dr. Weyls. "If the need arises, use it," she ordered before charging down the stairs.

Though frazzled, Elise ventured into the hallway. Everything appeared normal, though it didn't feel that way. She walked over to Onora's bedroom and leaned against the doorjamb, braving a peek inside. Her bedroom window was open, making Elise wonder if that was her way in and out of the house when tailing Lekana earlier.

Dr. Weyls sighed. "I tried to tell her it was probably just the coyotes."

Elise glanced back at Dr. Weyls, who stood in the hallway in his thin, white t-shirt and blue-and-white striped shorts. His hair stuck out at all angles, and silver stubble sprouted from his cheeks. The sight was mildly amusing, though Elise couldn't bring herself to laugh; an ominous feeling still hung in the air.

"A large pack of coyotes lives in the area, and they try the fence every now and again. The goats look tasty," he said to Frankie, wiggling his eyebrows. Frankie merely nodded and swallowed hard.

Dr. Weyls swiped his watch's screen, which displayed scenes from the various cameras around the farm. Intrigued, Elise joined Dr. Weyls and stood on her tiptoes to get a better look at the footage. He flipped from one scene to the next: the dark and quiet chicken coop, the eerie rooftops of the old town, a group of goats huddled together in a pasture. Elise thought it was creepy that the goats' eyes glowed green in the night vision cameras. Dr. Weyls swiped to a view of the perimeter fence line and stopped. Onora appeared into view.

"She got there fast," he observed.

Onora approached the fence and crouched low. After a second or two, she rose and peered out over the fence and into the nothingness beyond. Then, she jogged out of camera range.

Buddy came out of the bedroom. He leaned against Dr. Weyls' skinny legs and panted heavily. Elise bent forward and stroked his multicolored head. She glanced to the side, noticing that Dr. Weyls didn't have any socks on his feet. More remarkable than that, his pinky toes were both absent. Looking further she saw that all of his remaining toes were missing toenails. In their place was lumpy, pink scar tissue. Elise stared agape at the doctor's mangled feet. Suddenly aware of herself, she snapped her jaw shut and then looked at Frankie, whose face was ashen. He was looking at them too.

Dr. Weyls swiped through multiple screens on his watch. "No sign of any intruders," he murmured to himself. "I don't see Onora either."

As if on cue, Onora jogged up the stairs and joined them in the hall.

"Did you find anything? We saw nothing from the cameras," Dr. Weyls said, dangling the knife toward her as if it was something filthy.

Annoyed, Onora snatched the knife out of his hand and slid it smoothly back in its sheath on her forearm. "I found upturned earth on the other side of the fence. Someone or something had been digging," she reported.

Elise glanced at Frankie again, who glared at the floor.

"Uh-huh," Dr. Weyls nodded knowingly. "I'm sure it was the coyotes yet again. They dug too close and set off the proximity alarm." He smiled and stretched. "Nothing to worry about, kids." He kissed the top of Felix's head. The tired boy rested his head on Lekana's shoulder, staring blankly at nothing as his mom swayed soothingly back and forth.

"It's three o'clock," the doctor continued. "We have a few more hours until the sunrise. Let's all try to get as much sleep as we can, shall we?" He grinned and put a hand on the small of Lekana's back, gently leading her back into the bedroom.

Frankie's face took on a scowl as he tromped back into the room. Elise knew he was worried. Surely, he had his doubts about coyotes actually setting off the alarm. Of course, he already had his doubts about Lekana too.

Elise followed him to the room, feeling like a rag doll. The evening's chaos had completely drained her. As she closed the bedroom door, Elise peered through the crack, watching Onora as she took one last glance down the stairwell before entering her bedroom. Elise noted that she laid on top of her covers, and she didn't bother closing the door. She wondered if Onora slept at all.

Dr. Weyls put an arm out of his bedroom door and switched off the hall light. "Goodnight," he said through the darkness at Elise. She shut the door quietly behind her and dragged herself to bed.

· Chapter Twenty-Six ·

The goat shed was particularly fragrant that morning. Frankie had just scraped the last of the manure into the biggest pile yet. He grabbed a shovel to begin scooping it into the wheelbarrow.

The injured baby goat seemed better to Frankie, but it was still recovering in its stall. It ran circles around its mother and bleated impatiently at Frankie.

"I hear ya, little guy," Frankie said to the goat. "I want to get out of here too."

After last night's alarm fiasco, he didn't get much sleep. He woke up late to find that Julian had already fed and turned out the horses. Frankie wondered if Julian was mad at him for sleeping in; he hadn't seen him all day. It was well past noon by the time Frankie reached the goat shed in a rush, worrying that Julian would be fuming about how this job was started so late.

Maybe I wouldn't be in this mess if a stupid alarm hadn't woken me up in the middle of the night! he thought, grumbling, his anxiety turning to grouchiness the hotter and sweatier he became.

Perhaps the alarm had been set off by coyotes. Perhaps not. He and Elise were still all right; nothing got past the fence, but that didn't mean it wouldn't happen sometime soon. That looming possibility increased Frankie's urge to figure out how to open a portal. He didn't feel like he was even close to solving that puzzle, despite the hours of meditation he had subjected himself to. The more time he wasted, the more he wondered what would happen to them if he was never able to open a portal on his own. Would they end up staying here forever, scooping out stalls and checking security cameras? Worst, was the thought of the bald men finding them and doing God knows what to them.

He *had* to open a portal soon, he just had to. Why wasn't it working?

He scooped the last of the pile into the wheelbarrow, which was heavily loaded with a mound of manure he could barely see over. He carefully leaned it up so he could roll it out to the compost heap. A bit of the pile fell away here and there, but he could come back and scoop it up later.

Frankie slowly steered the wheelbarrow out of the barn. The air was heavy, stagnant, and still. No birds or bugs flew about. He found that odd; swatting at flies had become second-nature to him now. A shadow unexpectedly passed over the sun, and Frankie looked up to see a gargantuan, billowing cloud sailing overhead. It must have been the size of a city block with enough room to fit half a dozen skyscrapers inside. He had never seen a cloud that size before.

Careful not to spill his precariously-piled load, Frankie rounded the corner of the goat shed, where he spotted an even bigger cloud approaching above. This one was an ominous grey and streaked black in places. He might have been more nervous at the sight of such a threatening-looking cloud, had he not been distracted by the sound of hushed voices.

The voices belonged to Onora and Julian. They were meeting again in their secret place behind the goat shed for telling more secrety-secrets. Fed up with the adults around him quietly scheming, Frankie scowled and strained to hear what they were saying.

"You're jumping to conclusions!" Julian whispered adamantly.

"I need your assurance that you're taking this seriously," demanded Onora.

"Absolutely!" the doctor responded. "Preparations have begun! However, I do urge you not to make any rash decisions."

A dam of pent up frustration burst inside of Frankie. He careened around the corner toward them, determined to break up their covert plans. The unwieldy wheelbarrow got away from him and fell sideways. Its reeking contents were dumped all over the ground and spilled on top of, and inside of, Frankie's shoes.

Onora and Julian stared in mild astonishment. Frankie saw their faces and then looked down at his shoes, which were buried in muck. He roared with anger.

"What is going on here? What is with this place?" he bellowed. Thunder growled long and low overhead. Julian moved to restore the wheelbarrow to its upright position, but Frankie stepped in front of him.

"Why did you lie to me about the bootprints? They aren't yours, and you know it! Why do you keep saying there is nothing to worry about when there obviously is?"

"And you," Frankie turned to Onora, "stop sneaking around and hiding things from us! We have a right to know what's going on!" Onora regarded him as an explosive weapon she had never encountered before.

Elise came running from the backyard to see what the commotion was about. She reached out to touch Frankie's shoulder, and he rounded on her. "Oh, look! It's the Golden Child! Princess Perfect who can talk to all the animals and meditate perfectly without even trying!" he shouted in a mocking tone.

"I didn't mean to—"

"Why don't you just go be perfect somewhere else!" Frankie stood rigid, his hands clenched and nostrils flaring, seething with anger and glaring at all of them. Tears welled in Elise's eyes, and she ran off, stumbling along the way.

A bright flash, followed by an ear-splitting thunder clap almost shook Frankie out of his skin.

Julian turned the wheelbarrow upright. "Onora, I'll need your help getting the horses inside." She gave him one quick nod and jogged off toward the pasture. Giant raindrops pelted down on them with stinging ferocity. "You had better head inside, Frankie," he advised, pulling his hat down low over his eyes.

Another strobe-like lightning strike was all the encouragement that Frankie needed.

He ran through a wall of rain to the back porch. He opened the screen door, and a sudden, fierce wind slammed it shut behind him. Water poured from his clothes onto the concrete porch floor. He glanced down at his feet, noticing the rain had washed all traces of the manure away.

At least I won't have to clean poop off my shoes, he thought as he kicked them off and removed his water-logged socks.

He walked back to the door, wringing out the corner of his t-shirt while watching the storm build. In his periphery, he saw a small form streaking in from the pastures. Suddenly, Buddy leapt the picket fence and scooted in under the eaves of the house. Frankie opened the screen door for him.

"Buddy! Here, boy!"

The dog came bounding through the door. He took a few steps inside and promptly shook the water from his coat, spraying Frankie in the process. Frankie snickered and wrung out his shirt again.

The door to the house opened with a creak and Lekana poked her face out. "Oh! You are soaked! I will bring towels." She disappeared without another word. The boy and the dog stood side-by-side, dripping wet, and listening to the wind howl through the screens around the porch.

Lekana materialized with an arm-load of towels and handed a few to Frankie. She then attempted to dry Buddy, who apparently thought a game of tug with the towel would be more fun. Twice, Lekana grabbed the towel, and twice Buddy yanked it away, his short tail wagging excitedly. Ultimately, she dropped the towel on his hindquarters and watched him run in circles to catch it. "He will dry himself off this way," she said smiling.

Lekana regarded Frankie for a moment. "Frankie, Elise has been crying. Do you know why she is upset?"

Frankie scowled and then huffed. "I'm going to go change clothes."

· Chapter Twenty-Seven ·

Frankie changed into dry clothes and towel-dried his hair, which poofed out comically. He retreated to the bedroom, where he found an old, ragged tennis ball of Buddy's on the floor. He sat against the foot of his bed and bounced the ball off the wall in front of him. He caught it and threw it again. He continued to catch and throw the ball, while the rain battered the metal roof above him. The sound practically drowned out his thoughts, which was just fine with him.

He tried to forget the mean things he said to Elise and to erase from his mind the past two weeks of running from phantoms and endless heat. He wanted his life to go back to the way it was before when the only thing remotely cruel in their lives was Sister Katherine and Aaron, the bully. He wanted to go back to the time when Onora was just a librarian, rather than a blade-wielding bodyguard following their every move.

What am I thinking? he wondered, shaking his head in disbelief. He didn't really want to go back to the children's home. Even if he did want to return, the bald men in black would find them.

Frankie threw the tennis ball hard in frustration but didn't bother trying to catch it this time. It bounced across the wood floor, then rolled out of sight somewhere under his bed. He sighed and hung his head. He knew that whether the bald men found them or not, he would disappear. He would either be taken away by evil men or he would waste away in a life of hiding until, finally, he would simply vanish altogether.

Thunder exploded right above the house, and the wind screamed at the window. He thought about the tornado shelter, the two doors at the side of the house near the mesquite trees. Surely someone would come get him if a tornado appeared from the storm.

Wouldn't they?

Doubt and fear compelled him to leave his bedroom. He padded downstairs. At the bottom of the stairs, Frankie looked out the window. The sky was dark, rain poured in sideways torrents, and a fierce wind shook the window panes as the storm raged outside the house. Nervous, he walked down the hall, his socked-feet slipping in places on the smooth wood floor. The living room lamps were on, giving off an inviting, calming glow. He drew in a breath, inhaling an enticing smell from the kitchen.

His anxiety melted away. The whole experience was somewhat cozy.

Frankie walked past the kitchen, breathing in the sweet, buttery aromas. He wondered what Lekana was cooking. He wanted to go into the kitchen, snoop around, and maybe sneak samples of the goodies. However, his uncertainty about the mysterious, dark-eyed woman's motives gave him pause. Wanting to avoid a direct conversation with her, he decided not to go inside. He reluctantly slid away from the kitchen and ducked around the corner.

"Frankie!" she called out cheerfully.

He'd been caught. Frankie cringed and slowly turned around.

"Would you take this to Elise, please?" Lekana handed him a square pan of what looked like brownies with a dark, red swirl in them. "She is in the sunroom. You might like some too." She grinned.

Frankie took the pan and stared at it blankly. "What is it?" he asked.

"It is a recipe from the sister of my mother. She called it *walganko*." She chuckled, noticing Frankie's puzzled expression. "It is delicious, you will see." She handed him a knife and a few napkins.

Thunder shook the house again as Frankie crossed the threshold into the sunroom. Elise sat at an old card table, watching the storm through the tall windows with her chin propped up in her hands. She jumped when the thunder cracked. She was so easily frightened. Frankie felt like a real monster for making her cry. He thought of the gargoyles on top of St. Dominic's Cathedral, whose only job was to hulk around overhead and frighten little girls. He was a gargoyle.

Frankie glanced down at the pan in his hands. He wasn't sure what he was more afraid of, apologizing or trying a food he couldn't pronounce. Frankie gently laid the pan on the table in front of his sister, who didn't look up at him but merely sniffled a few times.

"Lekana said you would want this," he uttered.

"Are they brownies?" Elise asked glumly, peering at the dessert.

"Wall Geckos," Frankie announced. Elise slowly met his gaze, checking to see if he had gone insane. "That's what she called it. I think," he said defensively, cutting piece, and handing it to her on a napkin.

Tentatively, she nibbled the corner. "Yum!" she said, her expression brightening slightly. She closed her eyes to savor the taste.

Frankie cut himself a piece but held onto it a while to see if Elise would live or not. He glanced around the room. "Where is Felix?" he asked.

"He's under the dining room table, playing checkers against himself. I asked if I could play, and he said no." Elise sniffled again.

Frankie frowned at his square confection and took a bite. It was like fudge and maple-covered pancakes all together in one. Before he finished chewing the first bite, he cut a second piece for himself. He sat down next to Elise, a brownie in each hand.

"Look," he smacked his lips, "I'm sorry about what I said earlier."

Lightning spread like a vein across the dark sky, and for a second, it illuminated every detail of the scrubby landscape all the way out to the hills.

"Ooh," Elise said in awe.

Ignoring her, Frankie continued. "It's just this place, and not knowing what's going to happen to us, and the fact that I can't make a portal on purpose. It's annoying. Everything seems so easy for you." He gulped down his first piece, taking care to not look Elise in the eye. He really wanted an enormous glass of milk but didn't want to go into the kitchen.

"It's ok." Elise gave him a timid smile and patted his freckled arm.

Frankie flashed her a chocolatey smile and then started on his second piece, even without the milk.

Rain lashed at the floor-length windows, forming rivers on their surface. It gave Frankie the feeling of being under water. Lightning struck back-to-back, piercing the land and setting off ear-splitting bursts of thunder in the sky. The twins experienced the spectacle in silence, except for Elise's random and involuntary cries of "Ooh" when the light show was particularly impressive.

Eventually, the rush of rain became a sprinkle, and the thunder tamed to a dull rumble in the distance. The storm had concealed the transition into night. Clouds covered the stars, and because the moon was new, the sky was intensely black. Frankie and Elise sat together, staring at reflections of themselves in the windows, beyond which hung a backdrop of darkness.

Elise shivered. She rose and began to clean crumbs from the table. "This gecko cake was good," she giggled. "It was nice of Lekana to let us have the first pieces."

"What I really don't get," Frankie said, cleaning his teeth with his tongue, "is why no one is bowing to us. I'm a prince aren't I?" Elise shrugged. Frankie stood up and walked toward the long wall of windows. "If we're really royalty, then why do they have us cleaning barns and chicken coops?" He put a hand on his hip.

"Future leaders are to know the particulars of their subjects' daily lives," answered a jovial voice from the doorway. Julian chuckled and stepped inside the sunroom. He had changed into a pair of dry jeans and a fresh plaid shirt.

Frankie wondered how long Julian had been standing there, listening. Heat rushed to Frankie's cheeks in embarrassment. He hadn't meant anyone but Elise to hear that comment.

"Leaders must know how to do many things, which ensures that they are reliable to make wise decisions based on experience," Julian continued. "This is what separates a reckless despot from a great king. Cornelius Carvil wants to rule, but he uses intimidation to rise above people. And so, he will never be a great king. The type of ruler you will be is still up to you."

Thunder rumbled over the hills and across the plain.

"This would have been a great place to watch the storm," Julian commented, changing the subject. Elise walked past him on her way to the kitchen. Julian's face lit up when he saw the pan in her hands. "Ooh! Maple nut fudge!" he exclaimed, reaching for a piece, while Elise held the pan steady.

"Is that how you say it in English?" Frankie asked and picked up their napkins.

"I don't know. That's just what I call it because I can't pronounce the real name," Julian responded with a wink.

When they reached the dining room, Lekana came out of the kitchen and stopped Elise with a hand gesture. She put a piece of maple nut fudge on a napkin and waved it alluringly under the table toward Felix. When she brought her hand back up, the piece was gone.

Onora entered the dining room, wearing her usual uniform of a black, long-sleeved t-shirt, denim jeans, and a hardened expression. Her hair hung in a loose, damp braid over her shoulder, but her clothes were dry.

"Onora! Have some maple nut fudge!" Julian offered amiably.

Onora eyed the dish with deep suspicion, then turned the same gaze on Lekana. The tall, dark woman smiled broadly, handed her a piece, and took the pan back in the kitchen. Julian followed her. Onora watched the couple until they disappeared around the corner, and then took a bite of the fudge.

Maybe Frankie imagined it, but he could have sworn that he saw her face soften ever so slightly as she chewed.

· Chapter Twenty-Eight ·

Frankie still had a paper towel bib tucked into the neck of his shirt when he climbed into the saddle. He didn't have time to remove it. Julian had burst into the kitchen during breakfast and asked for everyone's help. Two goats were missing from this morning's count, and he needed all eyes to help spot them. After last night's brutal storm, Frankie hoped they were still alive.

He snatched the napkin from his collar and stuffed it in his pocket. Julian was cinching the saddle on Tinny when Elise came into the barn and started to pet Rocky's nose.

"Elise, you should ride with Frankie on Shadow," Julian instructed. "Rocky is young and has not been ridden much."

Elise wasn't listening. Caught up in her own private conversation with Rocky, she giggled. The lofty bay horse walked serenely to a fence, where Elise climbed up and onto his back.

Stunned, Julian looked to Onora. "Talk some sense into that girl."

Onora peered down from her perch on Tinny. "She's fine. We should be going."

Julian shook his head, fetched a halter and rope, and fitted these to Rocky's head. He handed the rope up to Elise to serve as reins. "I cannot believe that your guardian is content with you riding an inexperienced horse without a saddle. I, for one, will not let you leave without a halter at least. You will need it to control Rocky."

Elise giggled again. "His name isn't Rocky," she said covering her smile with her hand. "It's Kisses."

Julian gaped. "That's what Felix named him when he was three. Did Felix tell you this?"

"No, Kisses just told me."

At that, the lanky horse trotted forward and followed Tinny who, under the direction of Onora, had started out to the pastures.

Shadow walked at a more moderate pace after them, which suited Frankie just fine. Julian mounted Blister and caught up quickly. Buddy scampered around the group of horses, eager for an adventure. Julian followed Rocky closely, Frankie assumed, in case Elise had trouble with him. Frankie knew, of course, that she wouldn't.

When they were several paces into the pasture, Frankie heard the sound of a small engine. He swiveled in his saddle to see Lekana barreling toward them on a four-wheeler, her long hair whipping behind her. Felix sat in front of her, his tiny hands gripping the handlebars.

"Aw, cool!" Frankie exclaimed, slightly jealous. Shadow snorted. "No offense, girl," he apologized, stroking her neck. "You're pretty cool too."

The group fanned out and searched the wide, flat pasture. Frankie was surprised to see large cracks still snaking across the ground after all the rain. They caught up with the main herd of goats, their long, brown ears flapping and stocky tails wagging pleasantly. Until Buddy showed up, that is. He rounded them up, and Julian counted them again, but they were still two short.

About fifteen minutes after passing the goats, the sun began to rage. Frankie fanned his face and flapped his shirt, but there was no escaping the heat. What little breeze there was pushed dust into his mouth. He could feel it crunching between his teeth.

They searched every corner of the south pasture, but there was still no sign of the two missing goats. Julian asked everyone to dismount near a water tank so the horses could take a much-needed drink. Lekana and Felix rode up ahead and out of sight. Frankie kept an eye on the horizon for their return. He had just finished giving Shadow a few oat treats that Julian had provided when he heard the four-wheeler's return in the distance.

When she reached the group, Lekana stopped the ATV and shook her head, disappointed.

Julian's head dropped in frustration, and then he nodded. "Everyone, mount up!" he said, helping Elise onto her horse before mounting his own. Onora offered a hand up to Frankie, who took it willingly. He was hot, exhausted, and covered in dirt, and he was grateful for the help.

Everyone rode toward the hillside at a slower pace than before. Frankie reined Shadow closer to Rocky. "Elise, dial the goats up and see where they are," he suggested, with more than a hint of heat-induced impatience.

Elise straightened in her saddle, offended. "It doesn't work that way."

"Come on, Elise. At least try! It's hot out here!" Frankie whined.

Elise rolled her eyes and then closed them. She tightened her grip on Rocky's mane to steady herself and took a deep breath. Frankie studied her face for any clue that she had made contact with the goats. She suddenly opened her eyes wide and inhaled sharply.

"There!" shouted Felix. He stood up on the four-wheeler and pointed to the rocky hillside where there were two small, white dots about twenty feet up.

"Yes!" Julian called. "Good eyes, Felix!"

The horses picked up on the excitement, and they galloped closer to the hillside but stopped short. They were cut off unexpectedly by a river of rushing water. Frankie couldn't believe the massive volume of water that seemed to appear out of nowhere in the cracked, barren land. Across that eight-foot stretch of muddy rapids, on a ledge barely wide enough to set a small book, stood two bewildered goats.

"Blast it!" Julian yelled. "The rains flooded the arroyo! The goats must have been on the other side when the storm hit, and when the water overwhelmed the spring, the flash flood cut them off from the rest of the group." Julian tipped back the brim of his hat and scratched his forehead. One of the goats bleated, a sound barely heard over the rushing water. "I could construct a bridge," Julian deliberated out loud, "but I am afraid I don't have enough wood back at the shop."

Frankie observed the roiling brown water. Swimming across was out of the question.

The storm had severely damaged the landscape. A deep scar ran down the side of the hill where a mudslide had formed, swiping trees—roots and all—down with it. Debris lay at the foot of the hill, amassing into a heap of tree branches, roots, sediment, brush, and stone. An uprooted pine tree had landed close to the ravine on the opposite bank. Frankie eyed the length of rope that was looped on Julian's saddle.

"Are you any good with that lasso?" Frankie asked Julian.

"Why yes, if I do say so myself," Julian answered. "Why?"

"If you could lasso a branch and pull the tree around, we could use it as a bridge. It's long enough to cross the water," Frankie said surveying the downed pine.

"Sorry, Frankie, but the tree isn't safe for us to cross," the doctor rebutted.

"Maybe not for us, but the goats seem to have much better balance than we do." Frankie gestured to the two goats, who had scaled a steep, rocky hillside that would have taken ropes and grappling hooks for a man to climb.

"True," agreed the doctor, deep in thought, "but it might take days for them to understand that they can use the tree to cross."

"Not if you *tell* them how to use it," Frankie grinned.

"I don't speak goat, Frankie," Julian replied, unamused.

Frankie smiled smugly. Julian didn't speak goat, but Frankie knew someone who did.

"Elise, maybe you could tell the goats that we're trying to help them, but they need to climb down off that ledge first," Frankie said.

Uncertain, Elise bit her lip and nodded slowly. She stared intently at the goats. After a moment, they began to shift their weight and climb down the slope, finding seemingly impossible footholds in the rock.

Julian stared, slack-jawed, as the goat landed safely on the bank below. He scratched his head in disbelief. "I suppose we could try to move the tree, considering."

Frankie gave Elise a high five while Julian prepared his lasso. Twice, he tried to loop a branch, but the rope missed and fell into the water. On the third try, the rope caught one of the thick roots instead. Julian wound the rope around the pommel of the saddle. Blister, who was not keen on being close to the water to begin with, backed up. The tree budged but not enough. Julian urged him even more, and the stalwart palomino heaved with all his strength, his flanks rippling with effort.

Another rope cut through the air. Onora secured her loop around the same tree root on her first attempt. Lekana took the end of the rope and fixed it to the four-wheeler's bumper. She reversed the engine and, together with Blister, pulled on the felled tree. The roots skidded through the mud and then rolled into the water. Blister hopped back with the released tension. Julian eased the reins back and spoke calmly to his horse. Blister chewed on his bit and pulled back on the rope again. Finally, the rushing water released its hold on the roots, and they sprouted into view on the bank. The tree now spanned the arroyo, though the tumultuous water leapt up repeatedly in effort to reclaim it.

Julian cast a cynical eye onto Elise, who appraised the tree bridge for a few moments before focusing on the goats. They bleated, and then—with the same remarkable athleticism they used to descend the steep slope—they romped along the tree trunk like it was a game. They mocked the violent flood with their spirited steps and reached the other side, one goat hot on the other's heels. Buddy issued a warning bark to stop them from wandering too far away.

"I am absolutely amazed, Elise!" Julian exclaimed. "This is truly phenomenal!"

The heat had brought a rosy glow to her cheeks, which made Elise's blush more pronounced.

Julian dismounted and scooped up the nearest goat. It didn't put up much of a fight. "These fellows were just released into the flock. I'm willing to bet they will stay closer to the rest of them from now on." He situated the goat in front of Elise on Rocky's back. Its hooves dangled on either side of the big bay's withers. Julian put the second goat on Shadow, in front of Frankie.

The goat seemed groggy and disoriented. Frankie figured they had probably been awake all night, scared and confused in the storm. He stroked its long brown ears.

"They can rest in the shed tonight. We will release them tomorrow," Julian explained, gathering his ropes and reining Blister into a trot.

Frankie and Elise walked their horses so as not to jostle their weary hitchhikers. Onora followed close behind.

Elise gave Frankie a nervous glance. "Before Felix spotted the goats, when you asked me to talk to them, I felt something else out there. I couldn't tell what it was, what *they* were. All I could tell was they were frustrated. They were hunting two things, and they could smell the prey, but they couldn't get to them."

Onora reined Tinny up closer to Elise. "Could they have been the coyotes we encountered a few nights ago?"

"Yes, I think they could have been," Elise answered. "I've never tried to talk to an animal from that far away before, so maybe that's why this time was so confusing."

"Why was it confusing?" Frankie asked.

"The dogs and wolves I've seen in the zoo are pack animals. All their thoughts are based around their place in the pack. Like Buddy, all he thinks about is Felix, Lekana and Dr. Weyls, what they want from him, and how he should act to get what he needs from them."

Onora nodded, focused intently on Elise.

"If these things I 'dialed-up' were coyotes, they should have the same kinds of pack thoughts, but I didn't pick up anything like that. I know there was more than one of the same animal, but it felt like they didn't care about each other. Their thoughts were only about the prey, about hunting and destroying it. And they were so terribly hungry."

Suddenly, Felix let out a high-pitched giggle, interrupting the hushed discussion. Lekana revved the engine of the four-wheeler, opened the throttle, and the twosome sped off into the horizon. A cloud of dust rose in their wake.

Elise watched them ride away before speaking. "Do you wish our mother was here?" she asked Frankie.

Onora shifted uncomfortably in her saddle and then nudged Tinny so she could trot ahead of them. Frankie was uncomfortable too. Unsure of what to say, he looked forward in silence.

"I miss her," Elise sighed, and looked down at her goat, avoiding eye contact with Frankie.

Frankie scoffed inwardly. *Miss her? How could she miss her? We don't even remember her, let alone know her.*

Sure, he was curious about his mother and father. Sometimes, he even wondered what they might look like. But the truth was Frankie and Elise's parents had abandoned them. He didn't think he was missing out on a quality relationship with people who would just give up so easily. Elise thought she was missing out, and look how badly she felt. He wasn't going to let them make *him* feel that way. He was doing just fine without needing or missing anybody. He didn't need Lekana either.

He snorted audibly and shook his head. He took a sideways glance at Elise, who looked like she was about to cry again. His shoulders slumped.

"It's going to be okay," he said reassuringly. He tried reaching a comforting hand out to her, but the distance was too wide between the horses. He let his arm drop. "If I can get a portal open, maybe we can go see our parents again soon."

And give them a piece of my mind, he thought indignantly.

Elise gave him half a smile, and they walked the horses onward.

Frankie caught a wisp of movement from the corner of his eye. He looked to the hills and did a double take. A figure stood up on the ridge behind them! He squinted, thinking that maybe it was just a tree, that perhaps his mind was playing tricks on him again like it did in the saloon.

If it was actually a person, what would I do, tell someone about it? he wondered, doubtingly.

Elise would definitely freak out if he told her. He didn't quite trust Lekana, and he didn't trust Julian not to tell his own wife. Onora would certainly overreact and take them on the run again, and that would do them more harm than good, in his opinion. He glanced back once more. It was still just a tree, he was positive. He sighed heavily, wishing at that moment that he knew how to make a portal open.

Once Frankie and Elise reached the goat shed, Julian was waiting to help them unload their goats. He ushered the goats into their stall, where they went straight to the water bucket and guzzled. Onora and Elise took the horses back to the barn. Meanwhile, Frankie leaned on the top of the stall door, his chin resting on his arms, and watched the goats drink greedily.

"Why did you pick this place to live?" he asked Julian. "It's so hot and dry, and in the middle of nowhere."

"This is a place of extremes," Julian agreed, chuckling. "Parched one minute, flooded the next, hot as blazes in the summer, freezing winters. It is an unforgiving land. That's why most people don't live out here. Plus, a lot of people think the ghost town is actually full of ghosts," he laughed.

Frankie squirmed remembering the shadow in the saloon. For a moment, he considered telling Julian about what he saw, but then he thought better of it.

"That suits me well, though," Julian continued. "I needed a secluded place to keep the obluvium secret. I also required a place without neighbors who might ask questions if two children happened on my doorstep one day and stayed for a while." He clipped Frankie's shoulder. "I like it out here too. I am free to delve into my research." He grinned up at the rafters of the goat shed. Frankie was sure Julian was imagining distant galaxies instead of seeing the cobwebs that stretched from beam to beam.

Eventually, Julian refocused his attention on the goats, who continued to drink insatiably, pausing only for air. He gave Frankie a thoughtful smile, "You know? I'm quite thirsty too. Let's go see if the sun tea is ready."

Frankie followed Julian out of the shed. A glass of ice-cold tea was just the thing he needed to wash the grit from his teeth.

· Chapter Twenty-Nine ·

"**T**hank you all for your help with the goats today," Julian said laying freshly cut tomatoes on the table. "They are tough animals, but might not have survived another day in this heat without water."

Elise thought back to the goat draped over Rocky's withers. It looked so weak and exhausted. It was truly a pitiful sight.

"Have you seen my tin of saddle soap, dear?" Dr. Weyls asked Lekana, as he sat down at the dinner table. "The saddles are starting to look worn, and I can't find it anywhere in the tack room."

Lekana frowned. "I have not," she answered as she disappeared into the kitchen.

"No matter." Dr. Weyls shrugged and then peered at Elise over the rim of his iced tea glass. "I must admit, when I first heard of your talents, Elise, I didn't believe that you could actually speak to animals. Though today, you certainly demonstrated that talent quite well!"

Elise struggled to smile politely and maneuver a large piece of spinach off her fork at the same time.

"Tell me," he said touching his fingertips together, "can you also speak with insects and other invertebrates?"

Elise chewed her spinach thoroughly and swallowed before answering. "Yes, kind of."

Intrigue spread across Dr. Weyls' features, encouraging Elise to explain further.

"Insects don't have as many thoughts. They're much simpler. They don't have the same kinds of feelings that we have, and they don't see themselves as single animals."

Dr. Weyls nodded. Elise saw Frankie's eyes glaze over in boredom. She sighed, knowing that he was not interested in a conversation about bugs, but also that he was a bit jealous of her. "Sometimes it's hard to talk to just one insect. Most of the time, they don't know they're separate from their colony," she continued, resolving to ignore her brother's eye rolls.

"How interesting." Dr. Weyls set his glass down on the table and leaned forward. "My thought is that the obluvium has given you and Frankie these rare abilities. I could be wrong. Perhaps Onora is aware of others on Anwynn who have uncommon talents.

His gaze shifted to Onora who sat stoically, observing the room and its occupants like Sister Marguerite during a math exam. After a time, she finally spoke.

"There were people called Sages who could reportedly do wondrous things that seemed unnatural, but that was a long time ago. No one believes in them now, and they are viewed more as a joke or a cautionary fable."

"Oh yes! I heard this story about the Sages," Dr. Weyls responded enthusiastically. "They were persecuted and hunted down. Your temple said they were unholy, most likely because the parishioners were scared that the Sages were uncontrollable. Those that weren't killed went into hiding."

Julian paused, scratching his silvery goatee, deep in thought. He turned to focus on the twins. "I don't know how much truth there is to that story, but I do have a hypothesis regarding you two. Remember how I told you about the obluvium being programmable to intent?" Frankie and Elise nodded. "I think that the metal entered your bloodstream and went into your brain, but before it was able to create a foothold to control your mind, your brains reacted to the metal and protected themselves!"

He smiled broadly, excited for the audience. "Your subconscious mind was able to reprogram the obluvium inside of you. That newly-programmed obluvium gave you extra capacities. So, while Carvil was trying to poison your mind, he actually *expanded* it! The power of a young mind is astounding, especially before society puts limits upon it. I believe this is evidenced by the unique abilities you both have now."

"Pah!" Frankie scoffed. "An ability is something you're able to do. I am not able to open portals. They just happen to open when I'm around. Sometimes. They never happen when I try." He crossed his arms over his chest, looking simultaneously argumentative and deflated.

Onora squinted her eyes suspiciously when Frankie said the word "try".

"Oh, come now. That tells me you have the raw ability, you just have not found out how to harness it yet," Dr. Weyls chided good-naturedly. "Do you know how many experiments I have worked on that did not succeed until many, many, *many* tries later?"

Frankie waved at him dismissively and then leaned forward with his chin on his hand.

Elise felt a pang of sympathy for her brother. She wondered why her talent came so easily to her, while Frankie had to struggle. She inwardly reprimanded herself for having even talked about it. Dr. Weyls did ask though, and she had to answer him. Elise wished she could help Frankie in some way, but she had no idea how.

"Sometimes, it just takes practice," Dr. Weyls assured Frankie. "Sometimes, you simply need to try yet one more time." He grinned knowingly, and smile lines creased at the corners of his eyes. "Speaking of portals, it has been decided that we will begin searching for a new portal near here to send you back to Stromboden."

"We're going back?!!? Back to Stromboden?" Frankie sat straight up in his seat.

Elise took even more time to chew her salad. It was suddenly unpalatable.

"You'll have to wait a few weeks," Dr. Weyls continued somberly. "We have to find a portal first. This reality is no longer a safer alternative to your own, I'm afraid. Try as I might, I have not come up with a better solution. I should have been more honest with you before. I wanted you both to feel safe. I even deluded myself into thinking you were, but the evidence suggests otherwise."

"The unexplained bootprints in the sand, the perimeter alarm going off, and the tendency for portal travelers to gravitate toward each other are all factors that have forced our hand," Onora said. "Our best plan now is to risk returning to Stromboden. It's possible that Carvil has not been successful, and your father still remains on the throne."

"Perhaps they have defeated him by now," Dr. Weyls chimed in optimistically. He and Onora exchanged a glance, though, that told Elise this was unlikely.

"Regardless," Onora resumed, "they found you in this reality. They found you in Missouri. They may have already been here. We must do something, and right now our only option is to send you through the portal."

Dr. Weyls sat back in his chair. "I've met a man on one of my message boards who has a collection of antique maps. One particular map apparently illustrates various sacred sites on an ancient Native American trade route through this area. Some of these sacred sites are labeled as doorways to the spirit world. We can assume they are potential portals to a parallel universe. We're hoping to find a portal in the very mountain range that's behind the farm."

"That portal would send us to our castle?" Frankie asked.

Elise put her fork down.

"That is unknown, Frankie. Your world is definitely linked with this one in more than one place. Each door leads to different places on Anwynn, however. They might even lead to a country other than Stromboden."

Questions formed in Elise's mind, but she disliked this topic of conversation, so she stayed quiet.

"Our plan is to get this map from my friend on the Web, find the portal near here, open it, and merely see where it leads. If Onora deems it safe, you can make your journey to

Stromboden from that point." Dr. Weyls gently folded his hands and laid them on the table.

"We will consult with the king and wait for his instructions," Onora added.

"What if he's dead?" Frankie asked bluntly.

"Then I will protect you until we find a safe place," Onora answered.

Fear crept up behind Elise. It leaned over her shoulders and whispered of hostile foreign lands, sinister devils, and cold strangers masquerading as family. Clawing its bony fingers up her spine, Fear grabbed her with its cold hand and clenched her stomach tight.

"What if we just stay here!" she asked too loudly. All eyes turned to her. Even Felix, who had zero interest in the conversation, stopped building his LEGO rocket ship long enough to stare at her. "I mean, you have all these safety measures in place, and I'm sure no one actually knows where we are," she giggled uneasily. "We could be happy here!"

Dr. Weyls turned to face her. His eyes lacked their usual twinkle. "Would you truly be happy, Elise? What kind of life is that for you? Being hunted by violent men, never knowing who you can trust, or wondering if tomorrow is the day they will finally find you doesn't sound like a formula for happiness to me. Fear stunts growth," he said with conviction.

Elise withered in disappointment. She lowered her eyes and nodded.

Julian's expression softened. "Yes, you might be safe here. We would keep you clothed, fed, educated, and as secure as possible. But I can't help but think of everything you could have become if you had only left this place. What if, when you leave here, you're given a chance to grow and flourish out from under the shadow of fear? I don't think I could live with myself if I denied you the opportunity." He offered a comforting smile.

Elise considered what Dr. Weyls had said, knowing that he made sense. In fact, the way he explained their situation made her want to leave immediately. But then, she looked around the room admiring the delicate lace curtains, and the wood floors, worn from the family's daily comings and goings. Her eyes roved over the carefully-set table, with its wildflower centerpiece, freshly-baked bread, and plates of home-cooked food. She glanced at the smiling faces of

Lekana and Felix, and Buddy's lolling tongue, and listened to the comforting melody of the crickets outside. She didn't want to…couldn't give it all up. This was a *real* home and a *real* family. Here, she was only a visitor, but she treasured every moment.

"Here, Emmet will protect you," Felix said handing her a small action figure. He had finished his dinner long ago and chose to sit on the floor with Buddy to continue building the rocket. Emmet had been commissioned to ride up in the rocket ship, but now it appeared he had been assigned a new mission.

"Thank you, Felix," Elise said, clutching the figure close to her heart.

"Can we see the map?" Frankie asked.

Elise was grateful that he drew attention away from her puddling eyes.

"The map seller travels with a Renaissance festival around the South. They will be in Odessa in a few weeks, so you will have to wait until then," Dr. Weyls answered.

"We shouldn't need a map," Onora added in an even tone. "We have someone here who can show us the nearest portal."

Elise shot a glance at Frankie, waiting for him to reveal that he opened a portal nearby without telling her. Instead, he gave her a dumbfounded look and shook his head.

"Where did you come through, Lekana?" Onora asked with a sidelong glance. Lekana, who was in the midst of stacking empty plates at the table, stiffened.

"How long have you known?" Dr. Weyls asked.

"Since we arrived," Onora responded, her eyebrow arched. "What I didn't know is why you were keeping her origin a secret."

"Because I knew you would suspect her!" Dr. Weyls said slamming his hands on the table and rising from his seat.

Onora looked at him with a blank expression, not bothering to respond to Julian's instant defensiveness. Lekana gently set her stack of plates down on the table and flicked a nervous glance between Onora and Julian.

"If you knew that Lekana had come from Anwynn, you wouldn't have trusted her around Elise and Frankie. You wouldn't have seen her as I do, the most loyal, loving, and kind woman I have ever known." He grasped Lekana's hand in both of his. "You would only see trouble. Frankly, I will not let your distrust drive a wedge between me and my wife," he said with determination.

Elise didn't dare breathe, the tension in the room was so heavy. Frankie dropped his fork on his plate with a loud clatter.

"I do trust her," Onora finally said with a calm, even voice. "If I didn't, we would have been gone long ago."

"Oh," Dr. Weyls responded, and then collapsed into his chair with a sigh.

"I recognized the tattoo on your thumb immediately, Lekana. It marks you as a shaman from the Ni Ama people," Onora added.

"Yes," uttered Lekana, looking stunned.

"The *walkganko* identified you further; it's the same dessert that my teacher, Ho-Tse, used to make for me when I was little. He said his great-aunt taught him to make it."

Elise tried to imagine Onora as a small child enjoying dessert. It was difficult.

"Ho-Tse?" Lekana's eyes brightened. "He is the son of my mother's sister. He taught me to hunt!" She smiled, but her grin quickly faded. "He was lost to us long ago. There were many battles in his heart, and he left. The village made him go."

"He spoke of all his family with great honor, even though he knew he could not live among you," Onora said. "You have shown great care for Frankie and Elise since we arrived. Because of all this, Lekana of the Two Waters, I trust you."

Elise breathed a deep sigh of relief. She knew in her heart that Lekana wasn't scheming to hurt them. It still didn't explain her outdoor excursion at midnight, though.

"Do you realize what this means?" Frankie shouted, suddenly putting things together. "Lekana, you can show us to the portal you came through! We won't need a map!"

Lekana stared at the floor. "I cannot remember from where I came."

"Lekana's people were under attack from the Tanbarian clans from the west," Dr. Weyls explained. "They sent her to seek help from a neighboring tribe a few days away. When she returned, no one was left alive, and the invaders had moved on," Dr. Weyls put a comforting arm around his wife.

"I sought help from my ancestors who lived beyond the doorway in the mountain," Lekana said, her eyes distant, viewing events long past. "For one day and one night, I chanted and fasted. Then, the mountain glowed, and I stepped through the gold ring. The sun and the heat met me on the other side, but the spirits of my ancestors were silent."

"I found her wandering through the valley, dehydrated, sunburnt, and near exhaustion," Dr. Weyls said. "She likely walked in circles for days. We just can't be sure where she came from."

"I see," Onora replied flatly. "Then we will wait to secure the map. When we have done so, we'll investigate the sacred sites marked on its trade routes for potential portals to Anwynn."

Elise squeezed the Emmet action figure so tight in her hand that it hurt.

· Chapter Thirty ·

Elise held a hand to her forehead to shield her eyes from the sun's direct glare. A trio of vultures soared in lazy circles high above. Earlier, Lekana had told her that, in her language, vultures were called Peace Bringers. Elise wished they would bring her peace. Perhaps it would untangle the knot in her chest that had settled there ever since Dr. Weyls announced their plans to return to Stromboden. Though, the knot felt familiar, as if it had been there all along and simply forgotten until now.

She was anxious about Frankie's desire to open his own portal to Stromboden. Though she hated seeing him struggle with his talent, she was content with his lack of progress. His inability to open a portal meant they weren't going anywhere. But now the grown-ups were planning a journey back to Stromboden, which made it seem more of a reality. Things were getting serious.

She pulled her black baseball cap lower on her forehead. The morning was transitioning into afternoon, and their work in the garden was not yet finished. She knelt down to pull more weeds in the potato patch. Her long hair clung to the sweat on her neck.

Frankie dug a hole in the ground of the corn row behind Elise and cleared out a weed-choked strip of soil where they planned to plant more corn. "Julian says you have to plant new seeds every week or two so you'll always have fresh corn to harvest," Frankie said, grunting as he pulled a tenacious clump of native grass out of the red soil. He had yanked so hard on the deeply-rooted grass that he stumbled back, sending his hat careening to the ground.

Dr. Weyls had given it to him; it was one of his old hats. He had offered it to Frankie to prevent another sunburn like the one he got on their first ride out to count the goats. Frankie wore it everywhere, except at the dinner table, where Dr. Weyls always removed his own hat. Made of straw, and formerly white, the cowboy hat was much too large for Frankie, but his thick curls kept the brim from sinking below his eyelids.

Elise retrieved the hat from a broccoli plant, and handed it to Frankie, who received it with an exaggerated, "Thank ya, ma'am" and a tip of the hat, before continuing with his chores. Elise gathered a handful of pulled weeds. There was an existing pile by the gate waiting to be removed from the garden, and this bundle would join them. She rose from the ground, brushed off her knees, and walked toward the gate. When she passed her potato patch something seemed amiss.

"Frankie, did you just pull one of the potatoes?"

"No, I've been working over here," he responded, confused. He walked over the gravel path toward where Elise stood. Together, they examined the large chunk of freshly-disturbed dirt right in the middle of the potato patch.

"Well, the plant couldn't have just walked away by itself," she said, putting her hand on her hip. A sudden rustling of leaves to the left caught their attention. Okra stalks appeared to part and spring back together on their own. Then, the garden gate squeaked.

"Hey!" Frankie yelled, sprinting down the gravel path toward the gate.

Elise forgot about the weeds and dropped them to the ground. She ran after her brother, fully intent on catching their sneaky potato thief. As she ran past the garden, she spotted a brown-haired blur turn the corner at the house.

"It's Felix!" Frankie yelled over his shoulder.

Elise slowed her pace, suddenly confused. *Why would Felix be stealing potatoes?*

Frankie's hat fell off again, and he slowed to pick it up.

"Leave it!" Elise shrieked, sprinting forth determinedly.

Elise and Frankie turned the corner of the house, just in time to see the top of Felix's head disappear beneath the slamming wooden doors of the storm shelter.

"Aha! Got him!" Frankie yelled with glee. He flung the door open, and Elise carefully followed him down the steep, narrow metal stairs. Their footsteps echoed eerily off the concrete walls around them. The bottom of the stairs didn't open to a room, but rather to the entrance of a long hallway. Felix was nowhere in sight.

A gust of hot air swirled through the stairwell, and the storm door slammed shut. They were thrown into complete darkness. Elise stepped on both of Frankie's feet as she tried to find him in the dark. She muttered an apology after his exclamation of pain. As her eyes finally adjusted to the darkness, she saw a faint, white light glowing down the hallway.

"There!" Frankie said and charged forward.

Elise grabbed on to the back of Frankie's shirt so she wouldn't lose him in the dark tunnel. She hated to admit it, but she was frightened of the dark. She couldn't help it. The minute any light was turned off, she felt as if some invisible being stood just behind her. Elise and Frankie bumbled along together as they made their way down the dark passageway toward the light.

The hallway ended in a T. The light emitted from the right, and to the left, pitch-black nothingness. A cold breeze ghosted past them to the left, and Elise held her breath, hoping that Frankie didn't want to follow it.

"Shh!" Frankie hissed.

"I didn't say anything," murmured Elise.

"There! Do you hear it?" he asked.

Elise strained her ears and eventually heard footsteps coming from the hallway on their right. "Yes!"

"Let's go!"

She was relieved they would not tread down the darker tunnel; however, now it was directly behind her. Anything could be sneaking up on her, and she wouldn't know until it was too late!

After taking several more steps, Elise could make out a doorway from which the light was pouring.

"Hey! I know where we are!" Frankie pointed to a metal door with a slender, rectangular window and said, "That's the surveillance room where Julian keeps all the computers. We're right below the ghost town!"

The sound of running footfalls came again from farther down the hallway. It was dark past the door.

"Let's go," Frankie said, his grim expression illuminated in the flickering computer light.

Elise quickly glanced through the window at the computers before being pulled along by Frankie. She secured a firmer grip on the back of his shirt, and in the process, stepped on the back of his shoes twice. The passageway curved to the left, and all trace of light disappeared. The cool air that had rushed at them earlier was now gone, replaced by a stale, musty odor. Elise could feel the motion of Frankie's arms as he reached in front of him to avoid accidentally running into an unseen wall.

The further they walked, the more obvious it became that Felix was nowhere to be found.

"Felix! Where are you?" Frankie whisper-shouted, his voice sounding strangled and suppressed in the cramped passage.

Elise heard a flutter and a squeak. A bat flew over them, its wingbeats disrupting the air right above their heads. Frankie shrieked and curled down defensively, pulling Elise down with him.

"It's in my hair! It's in my hair!" he cried.

She patted his back with her left hand, while her right maintained a steel grip on his T-shirt. "The bat is gone now," she said shakily. "It's okay."

Wood creaked somewhere in front of them and overhead. Frankie rose, inhaled deeply, and they continued their not-so-amusing game of Blind Man's Bluff with Felix. He led his sister down the darkened hall with a determined and quickened pace.

Kwang!

Elise heard Frankie issue a shocked gasp, followed by a growl of anger.

"What happened? What's wrong?" Elise fussed.

"I hit my forehead on something metal," Frankie answered through clenched teeth. He glanced above him, rubbing his head. Light seeped through wood planks overhead, revealing a metal ladder. After a few mumbles, he began to climb.

Elise held on to his shirt until it was absolutely necessary to let go. She scrambled up behind him before the wide mouth of the dark passage could gobble her up.

Frankie reached the boards and pushed. A small, square door gave way, and he lifted it just a few inches. It was then that the knocking began. It was a hollow, rhythmic sound, coming from beyond the door.

Knock-knock-knock. Knock-knock-knock.

Frankie leapt up the last few rungs of the ladder and clambered through the trapdoor. Once he reached the other side, he took a defensive stance. "Who's there?" he yelled, his angry tone, barely masking his fear.

Elise, still midway up the ladder, held onto a rung for dear life. She was faced with the choice of braving the unknown dark beneath her or chancing an encounter with a possible poltergeist in the room above. The room, now emanating the sick smell of rot, was at least above ground...and her brother was there. She stalled for half a second before scrambling to the sunlight and closer proximity to her brother.

She entered the room where Frankie stood, fists raised, behind what looked like a long wooden counter. To Elise's left, there was a stage of some sort with tattered curtains that might have been blue once. She glanced frantically around the stuffy room, listening for a knocking ghost. It didn't take them long to realize that the sound came from behind the counter where they stood. A series of shelves were beneath the large, wood slab, and arrayed upon one of them was a collection of mechanical robots that were made from a hodgepodge of household items. One unfortunate gadget had a spork for a head and was powering its L-bracket feet and walking repeatedly into the shelf's side wall. Knock-knock-knock, it sounded as its metal body thudded against the wood frame.

Frankie's fists relaxed, and he picked up the teetering automaton in wonder. "I found Julian's missing saddle soap tin," he said tapping the robot's body. Suddenly, a wire sprung loose from the robot's back, and its movements ceased. A brown crop of hair sprouted from across the countertop. Felix peered over the splintered wood, his eyes deep with worry about the fate of his creation.

"No! You unplugged him!" Felix ran around the counter with his bottom lip protruding. He snatched the tin toy away from Frankie and searched for the electric wire.

Elise couldn't find any indication of electricity in the saloon; there were no outlets anywhere. However, when Felix hooked the alligator clip end of the wire to the robot, its legs began to move again.

"How on Earth . . ." she trailed off searching under the bar for a hidden electrical panel. She wasn't prepared to find potatoes, lined up in a row, with wire-wrapped nails poking out of them at odd angles. The potatoes were connected together by curls of colored wires.

"FrankenTaters," Frankie announced proudly. The wires tapered down to one single, black wire that plugged into the back of the robot and brought it to life. A pile of discarded and rotten potatoes lay two shelves over, stinking heavily and drawing flies.

"In here!" A shout rang outside the door. It was Onora. She opened the wooden saloon door and sheathed her curve-tipped blade. Buddy appeared at her knees panting, having enjoyed a brisk run. Lekana and Dr. Weyls showed up momentarily with worried faces.

"I heard yelling, but I could not find you," Lekana puffed.

Felix looked frantic, appearing to be caught between making a run for it and standing firm. His lower lip quivered.

"Wow, Felix," Frankie uttered in awe. "This is really awesome. You guys should see all these robots he made with vegetables."

One-by-one, the group walked behind the bar to see Felix's handiwork. Felix, meanwhile, stared at his shoes, large drops of tears splashing onto their toes.

"Astounding!" Dr. Weyls exclaimed, beaming at his son. "We made that first potato battery nearly a year ago, but I never dreamed you would take it this far! Look! You have joined them in series to increase their power!" Dr. Weyls shook his head in disbelief.

Felix remained quiet.

Elise edged her way along the bar until she was close to the boy. "Why are you so sad, Felix?" she asked.

He sniffled. "Because Mama doesn't like robots and computers. Now I'll have to turn them all off!" he cried and buried his face in his mother's skirt.

Lekana looked as puzzled as everyone else.

"Perhaps he is referring to Brunhilda," Dr. Weyls softly reminder her.

"Oh, I see," she responded, eyes lit up in understanding. She gently mussed Felix's hair.

"Brunhilda is the personality I attributed to our Smart House. The house would actually converse with us, give us weather reports, compile grocery lists, monitor our health, and so forth. She played a great game of chess! Her voice sounded almost exactly like my dear departed mother," he added wistfully.

Lekana's face lost its humor.

"Understandably," he said, reaching out and touching his wife's arm, "Lekana wasn't accustomed to such a lifestyle, and so I turned Brunhilda off a while ago. Felix must miss her."

"She did not like me," Lekana added.

"Nonsense!" Dr. Weyls waved her notion away with his hand and bent to inspect the shelf of robots.

"She always burned my toast," Lekana muttered to no one in particular. Elise stifled a giggle.

"Let's bring these marvelous creations into the sunroom. We will make a robot workshop!" Dr. Weyls declared.

Felix backed up, looking at his mother for approval. She nodded down at his tear-streaked face. "Yes!" He jumped up and down, his hands outstretched.

"Awesome!" echoed Frankie.

The boys gathered all the robotic implements, their arms full of clanging and tinkling parts. Elise didn't understand the allure of robots, but she would pick them over a malevolent spirit any day. She helped Lekana gather the rotten potatoes into Lekana's apron, and then followed her outside. The saloon was lifeless once again.

· Chapter Thirty-One ·

Sunshine streamed through the sunroom windows, filling every inch of the room with light. It glazed over the various robot parts that were strewn in front of Frankie on the laminate counter. Sunlight glinted off of metal tools and glared on the laptop screen. Frankie flicked the wand on the vertical blinds and shut the light out.

He had skipped meditation time with Onora again to build robots with Felix. Occasionally, Elise would pop in after meditation and hover around. She'd ask a few questions, then she'd lose interest and leave. Frankie, on the other hand, was enthralled, often losing track of time. Julian had taught them to enhance their potato powered robots by boiling the potatoes first. Now, they had moved on to the big leagues. At the moment, Felix was taking apart an old power drill so he could use the motor in a robot he was building.

"Robots are all about the two Ps: Power source and Purpose," Julian would often say. "What function do you want it to carry out, and how is it getting its power?"

This particular robot that Frankie was making had a function especially dear to Frankie's heart. As for the power source, he was nearly ready to position the battery.

The laptop was whirring, the soldering iron, heating. The box fan was on its laziest setting in the doorway. Frankie was surrounded by the soothing hum of quiet machinery. If he hadn't been concentrating so hard, he would have sat back and grinned in sheer bliss. The battery had to be placed just right; too far forward, and the arms wouldn't extend, too far back, and the whole machine would topple over backward.

A glow lit up the area to the right of him. At first, he thought it was the soldering iron catching something on fire, but it sat to his left, waiting to be used. Then it dawned on him.

A brilliant ring of light shimmered right next to him. An open portal.

Its golden, rippling edges reflected across his work surface. Not wanting to jinx himself, he didn't look directly at it for a minute. Eventually, he carefully set down his screwdriver and turned his whole body to face the opening between worlds.

The circle of light was about as tall as he was and floated just off the floor in the middle of the room. Within the circle, he saw a wooded area. White beams of sunlight streaked through tangled branches crowned in green. To the left, a stream tumbled over rocks and flowed out of view.

Frankie stood up from his stool and approached the circle. He had a strong urge to reach forward and touch it but had stronger suspicions that this was not a good idea. Julian said matter could only travel one way through a portal. Frankie worried that if he poked at the portal, he might not get his finger back. He took slow, deliberate steps toward the circle, observing its undulating edge. He tiptoed to the reverse side of the portal, unsure of what he would see. Curiosity getting the best of him, he peered around the side of the portal before bringing his body fully around. Astonishingly, the view from the back side was exactly the same as the front. The scenery mirrored the one he saw from the front; sunbeams streamed through the same trees, and the stream flowed on the left.

"What in the blazes!" Felix exclaimed, an expression frequently used by his father. Attracted by the glowing light, he jumped off his stool and ran over to join Frankie. "What's in there?" he asked, gazing through the portal's surface at the woods beyond. He lifted a blue cowboy boot to step in.

"Whoa, whoa, whoa!" Frankie put an arm across Felix's chest to halt him. "We can't go in there. It might not be safe." Felix's face rumpled in annoyance. Frankie's eyes searched the room for a way to explain this situation to a five-year-old. A brainy five-year-old, but a five-year-old nonetheless.

"You see, it's like…it's like outer space! Yeah. And, in space, the atmosphere might be toxic. We need to send something through first to make sure it's okay." Still frowning, Felix nodded his understanding. Frankie reached for the robot Felix had made out of the saddle soap tin. They had replaced its potato battery with two C batteries, and affectionately dubbed it "Tin Man." It could walk on its own now for a few feet before falling over.

"Tin Man will be our astronaut!" Frankie said with added enthusiasm. Felix nodded, smiling broadly. Frankie popped in the missing C battery, and the robot came to life. Its feet, made from L-brackets, moved back and forth in the air. He set the robot down a few inches from the portal, and it began to lumber forward. As it passed by, Felix touched the top of its spork head with his index finger. Frankie watched anxiously, worried that the robot might catch one of its feet on the portal's rim, but it went through smoothly.

The two boys watched in amazement as Tin Man walked into the silent new world on the other side of the portal. It made six tiny steps into the dappled sunlight before running into a rock and toppling over.

Now close, Frankie thought, narrowing his eyes and concentrating hard on the portal. Suddenly, as if someone had flipped a switch, the portal wavered and shrank down to nothing. Frankie and Felix sat staring into thin air.

"Wow!" Felix shouted, hopping up and down with glee. "Mama!" he called, running from the sunroom and through the living room. "Mama!"

Frankie heard the screen door slam, Felix's yells for his mother waning in the distance.

He sat still for a moment, absorbing what had just happened. He had closed the portal with only his mind! Or, had he? He instantly wanted to find Elise, tell her what happened, and ask what she thought about this.

He picked himself up off the floor and unplugged the soldering iron before stepping into the living room. A bright flash and a clattering noise from behind startled him.

The laptop!

He spun around, expecting to find the laptop in a hundred pieces on the floor, but it was safe and sound, whirring away on the counter. He hunted around the room for the source of the commotion and found it under the card table. It was Tin Man, dented and dirty. More interesting than the robot's sudden reappearance was the ribbon tied around his neck. The light blue velvet was tied in a bow.

"How in the world? Who did this?" Frankie wondered aloud, the hairs standing up on the back of his neck. "Okay, that's it! I'm going to open a portal right now but on purpose this time!"

Determined to discover who—or what—had sent the Tin Man back, he plopped down on the floor. He quickly worked through what he had to do. First, he would meditate, which should put him in a trance. Then, a portal should open. He squeezed his eyes shut.

"Meditate, meditate, meditate!" Frankie chanted aloud. He concentrated on imagining the portal, its golden ring shimmering around a scenic backdrop, but his mind drifted to the robot, then to Felix, then to the goats and all his chores, then back to the robot again. Mind whirring in overdrive, Frankie opened his eyes in irritation. "Ugh! This isn't working!" he shouted, pulling at his hair in frustration.

He exhaled heavily, and then took a deep breath. Feeling his aggravation cool slightly, he inhaled and exhaled deeply again. He felt better.

That's right! Breathing. Onora said to focus on the breath. Newly motivated, he closed his eyes and tried to meditate once more. At first, his breathing was fast. It sounded ragged and desperate and was completely distracting. He squeezed his eyelids tightly and tried focusing on taking deeper, slower breaths. But the more he tried, the more out of breath he felt, and the more rapid his breathing became.

Frankie leapt up with a roar of aggravation. "This is impossible!" He stormed from the sunroom and out the front door. He blew through the gate at the picket fence, leaving it rattling in his wake.

"Why is this so freaking hard?!!?" he shouted to no one as he stomped toward the old ghost town. Opening a portal would be so much easier if it was mechanical. If portals were robots, he could take them apart and understand what made them work. He paced up and down the town's avenue, trying to vent his frustration.

So far, the portals seemed to just pop up out of nowhere, and he couldn't figure out their common denominator. Somehow, some way, he should be able to open a portal, but he was running out of ideas about how to do it. Infuriated at his lack of control, he kicked a rock in the street and flopped down on the saloon's porch stairs. He lowered his head in defeat. Why couldn't portals simply work like a methodical and predictable machine? He rubbed his face and stared out at the mercantile.

"Or, a watch," he whispered. A grin crept across his face.

· Chapter Thirty-Two ·

Dust and bits of hay swirled through the rafters of the goat shed. The setting sun beamed through a crack in the wood plank wall, partially blinding Frankie and reflecting off the metal object in his arms. He moved a few inches to the right. A goat bleated for its dinner from one of the pens.

"I hear you have something to show me," came a genial voice from the doorway. Julian strolled through, with Felix in hand.

Frankie placed the bundle in his arms on the ground. "Dr. Julian Weyls and Mr. Felix, may I present to you the

Scoop-o-matic!" He bowed and displayed his freshly-made robot with a flourish of his hands.

"Oh-ho!" Julian whooped, impressed.

"Made from only the finest scraps of steel found in your machine shop, and customized to carry out the nastiest of chores. Try one in your barn today!" announced Frankie, doing his best infomercial salesman voice.

"It looks cool," said Felix, kneeling down close to the robot.

"Frankie, this is excellent! You used wheels from Felix's broken RC car, and look at how well the arms align! Are those my calipers?" Julian asked in dismay after observing the robot's hodgepodge composition.

"Let's try it out!" Frankie blurted out in his excitement.

Frankie opened a door to one of the goat pens and flipped a switch on the back of the robot's body near the battery. Using a joystick, he guided the robot forward and through the door. The two goats in the pen huddled in a corner at its approach. He wheeled the robot toward a pile of brown pebbles on the ground. "The arms are built with sifters in the scoops. The clean shavings will drop through and then back into the pen." Frankie clicked a button, and the robot arms swung up and out and circled back down to gather goat droppings into their scoops.

The goats jumped at the robot's sudden movements. They ran in a tight circle and, when they saw no way out, they tried to climb the walls of their enclosure. One clambered onto the other's back and used it as a springboard to leap over the robot and out the door. Frankie hastily switched off the robot, while Felix hauled out of the shed after the runaway goat.

Julian closed the pen after removing the robot and laid a hand on Frankie's shoulder. "It's a wonderful invention, Frankie," he said, "but you can see now why many things remain unautomated around here."

Frankie sighed and clutched his creation. "It's still pretty cool, but it's not half as cool as the portal that opened today!"

Julian frowned, looking concerned. "Oh? You opened another portal?"

"I guess so. I mean, I didn't do it on purpose. I was just making the robot here and, *poof,* there it was!"

Felix appeared in the door, winded but alone. "I put the goat in the pasture, Papa."

"That's good, that's good. We will release the rest of the goats with him in just a few minutes. It's time these fellows join the herd! But first, I want to hear more about the portal Frankie saw today."

"The wavy circle?" Felix asked. "We put Tin Man in it!"

"Did you, now?" Julian's expression turned to one of fascination.

"Yeah," Frankie answered, "he walked right through and tripped over a rock. The best part was when I realized that I could somehow close it! I just knew how automatically! So, I closed it!" He left out the part about Tin Man coming back. If he didn't tell the adults about the possible shadow on the ridge, he certainly wasn't going to tell them that someone was interacting with him through the portal.

"Well, how about that!" Julian exclaimed, amazed. He opened the door to the pen again and unlatched the gate that separated it from the main pasture. The remaining goat scampered out, eager to join its comrades. Julian watched the goat as it joined the herd, and then turned to Frankie, with a thoughtful expression. "So, you used your instincts and closed the portal with your mind. That is fascinating! Where did the portal open?" he asked while releasing the remaining two goats in the last pen. They were more timid about stepping into the wide open space but were soon grazing with the others.

"It lead to a stream in the woods somewhere. I could see the water flowing," Frankie explained.

"Absolutely fascinating," Julian whispered almost to himself. "The full moon is in two days. If we can get the map, we can try a marked location that evening and send you to Stromboden as soon as possible." Julian dropped into a more serious tone. "Frankie, you were wise to send only the robot through. Do not go through any portals without us."

Frankie nodded in agreement, but that irked him. One day soon, there wouldn't be so many people telling him what to do.

· Chapter Thirty-Three ·

Following the red carpet, Elise stepped lightly. Unsure of where she was, she gingerly walked down a dimly-lit corridor with stone walls. Chilled, she crossed her arms over her chest. She followed the red carpet around a corner and through a wide, arched doorway. She quietly padded inside. A cavernous, circular room lit by flickering torchlight opened before her. At the opposite end of the room was an elevated platform with three golden thrones arranged on top. A man and a woman dressed in regal clothing stood with their backs to her in front of the thrones. Each wore a crown on their head.

It's Mom and Dad! It just has to be!

As she drew closer, Frankie came into view just beyond, facing the king and queen. The king placed a crown on Frankie's head, and it sank down atop his curls. "Have a seat, Son." The king quietly commanded, gesturing to the ornate golden chairs. The three stepped up to the platform, each taking a seat on a throne. Frankie's legs dangled from the chair.

The queen turned mechanically to face Elise. "Oh, Elise. You're here now." Her voice was flat, loveless.

"Your seat is through there," the king uttered, his tone expressionless. The royal trio pointed in unison to an open portal at the left of the dais. The portal glowed and pulsated with an orange light; its center was pitch black.

"We only need one," the queen said with a blank stare.

Suddenly, Elise was propelled toward the portal by some invisible force.

"I don't want to go in there! I don't want to go!" she screamed, struggling in vain to kick out with her useless arms and legs. She tried to resist but was pulled steadily toward the black portal. It was so close now that it filled her whole field of vision. Blackness surrounded her. She was hurled into the center of the dark opening with no way of stopping.

"No!" she screeched as she reached forward, searching desperately for something to grab on to.

Her body gave an involuntary jerk, and she awoke. Gasping for breath, she sat up in bed and looked around the room. Frankie was still lying in his own bed, facing the wall, and lightly snoring. She breathed a sigh of relief, thankful that it was only a dream.

The room was brighter than she had expected it to be. Stepping out of bed, she shuffled to the window and sought the source of the light. She peered into the night and saw Lekana strolling through the front gate. She watched as the woman turned at the walkway and disappeared around the corner of the house.

Elise twirled a strand of hair around her finger. It took little time for her to decide that she needed to investigate. She tiptoed toward the door, slipped out of the room, and carefully turned the doorknob so she wouldn't wake Frankie. This time, she was determined to find out what the mysterious woman was doing wandering around at night.

Elise crept down the stairs and snuck across the living room floor. She was just about to open the back door, when she heard Felix's small voice in her head, saying, "Scorpions."

One evening, not long ago, she had attempted to go out barefoot, and the boy had warned her about them. Bearing this in mind, she considered Felix's tiny green slippers by the door. Not wanting to step on any scorpions, she slipped them on. Her heels stuck out the back, but it was better than nothing.

Thank you, Felix.

Buddy poked his head out from the stairwell, looking at her curiously.

"It's ok. I'll be back," she whispered. He shook his head vigorously and moseyed back to his bed.

The moon was low and full and seemed to rest on the mountain tops. Its brightness painted the landscape in hues of blues and greys. Elise didn't have to look far to see Lekana who stood in the pasture. She was a wild thing in a vast stretch of land. An unfelt breeze stirred the woman's skirts and hair as the moon held her in its cool radiance. She tilted her head to the right as if she were listening to a story. Elise observed the scene in quiet reverence until Lekana turned around and beckoned her forward.

"You are awake," the moonlit woman observed.

Elise nodded. "I had a bad dream. I saw you from the window, and wondered where you were going."

Lekana gestured to the split rail fence. "Let us sit a while."

They climbed the fence together and sat atop the highest rail. Elise adjusted her nightgown, making sure it was between the fence and her legs to avoid splinters.

"I can't believe I got out here without Onora seeing me," she remarked.

"I am sure she is watching us now," Lekana smiled.

Elise nodded, thinking this was probably true, but she didn't care.

"I come out here to talk with Grandmother Moon sometimes."

Elise looked at the moon and searched for a face. A lot of people talked about the Man in the Moon, but Elise could never see him. All she could ever see was a rabbit. She grinned, and then looked at Lekana. "Does Grandmother Moon talk to you like the goats and horses talk to me?"

Lekana thought for a moment. "She doesn't use words or pictures. She soothes and comforts with her soft light. From her great height, she tells us our worries are very small. She sees the bigger picture." Lekana paused, the quietness emphasizing the crickets' song. Somewhere an owl called out and was answered. The warm summer air wrapped around them like a blanket. "She has seen so much, and she still shines," Lekana softly explained.

Elise lifted her face to the bright orb in the night sky and listened. Basking in the brilliance of the moon, she smiled peacefully, and the dark shadows of her nightmare melted away.

· Chapter Thirty-Four ·

Elise rose early the next morning, doubly surprised to see Frankie's bed empty and already made. She followed suit, and then went downstairs, where she found her brother sitting alone at the table in a state of eerie calmness.

"What are you doing?" she asked, her voice dripping with trepidation.

Onora breezed in, having completed her morning jog of the property's perimeter. Buddy trailed behind her and collapsed on the cool floor, panting. His tongue made a pink pile on the wood planks. Onora headed straight for the kitchen, where Elise assumed she would get a glass of ice-cold water, but she poured herself a cup of steaming, hot coffee instead. Without adding cream or sugar, she leaned against the kitchen counter and sipped from her mug.

"It's Fair day!" Frankie nearly yelled. "I've been waiting *forever* for everyone to get up." He looked at the grandfather clock, which had not yet struck 7:00.

Elise rolled her eyes as she poured herself a bowl of cereal. She carefully carried her breakfast to the table and took a seat next to her brother. His excitement was barely contained. It was like sitting next to a crate of dynamite.

Dr. Weyls and Felix soon descended the stairs. Dr. Weyls was in the midst of explaining jousting to his son. "…knights in armor riding toward each other on horseback with long lances pointed at each other," he described animatedly. Seeing Felix's underwhelmed expression, Dr. Weyls smiled in amusement. "It's called a jousting tournament, and we will have the chance to see one today!"

"Yes! I can't wait!" Frankie shouted as he sprang from his chair.

Elise pretended not to notice the awkward squawk in his voice as he shouted. She stifled a giggle when she saw the color rise in his cheeks at the sound.

"When do we leave?" Frankie asked, trying to act nonchalant.

"We aren't going," Onora replied flatly, taking another sip of coffee.

"WHAT?!!?" Frankie and Elise bellowed in unison. They had been looking forward to the Renaissance fair all week. The thought of not being able to go was crushing. When living at the St. Dominic's, they used to see advertisements on the public broadcasting system for the Renaissance fairs in New York. Lively commercials showed horses, fancy costumes, face painting, tournaments, and glass blowing. All the children had begged to go, but the Sisters had never taken them.

"Dr. Weyls is merely retrieving a map. He does not need our assistance."

"Oh come *on*!" Frankie whined. "Who's going to look for us at a Renaissance festival anyway?"

"We thought no one would look for you in another reality," Onora reminded him in a reproachful tone, "but they did."

"Yeah, I guess," Frankie responded, deflated. "But, nothing has happened in two whole weeks! No alarms, no more bootprints, nothing! If they did find us, then they probably gave up and left a long time ago." He crossed his arms over his chest in defiance.

His short rant was met with silence. Dr. Weyls stood stoically in the corner while Onora took a long drink of coffee and fixed Frankie with a firm stare. Felix blinked several times, looking nervously at Frankie and Onora.

Frustrated, Frankie shouted, "We can't hide forever! What if that map doesn't lead anywhere? What if I never learn how to make portals? Are you going to keep us locked in this goat ranch for the rest of our lives?"

"He's right, Onora," Dr. Weyls agreed softly. "Psychologically speaking, they need to get out and have cultural experiences amongst other people. It might be difficult for us, but we have to find a way to let them have fun while also keeping them safe."

Felix ambled over to a chair and sat down, bleary-eyed.

"Plus *you'll* be with us, right Onora?" Elise offered.

"Yeah! What she said," Frankie implored.

Onora lifted her chin and stared at the ceiling in contemplation. A few seconds passed before she set her coffee mug down and gave them a stony gaze. "We can go."

The twins rejoiced by jumping from their chairs and giving each other a high-five. Dr. Weyls beamed broadly.

"*But*," Onora cautioned, an index finger pointed right at Frankie, "if I say run, you run. No questions. You do what I say, when I say. I mean it."

"Yes ma'am," the twins chorused. Frankie saluted.

⏷

The ride to the fairgrounds was lengthy, and all three kids grew restless in the back seat of the truck. During the entire ride, Felix sat between Elise and Frankie fiddling with one of his robots, which now sat motionless because its battery had run down. Onora sat in the passenger seat while Dr. Weyls drove. Lekana elected to stay at home, looking after a hen that had not laid eggs recently. Elise suspected Lekana's real reason to remain behind was because she wanted the house to herself for a change.

Dr. Weyls had his truck radio tuned into a crackling country station, where the singers crooned and yodeled about hard work, family traditions, and unstable relationships. Elise didn't particularly care for the genre but found it incredibly amusing when Dr. Weyls would sing along, his peculiar accent echoing the singer's laments with skinny vowels and hard consonants.

They arrived in Odessa, and wove their way through the town's flat, brown buildings to a sports complex that had been converted into a "Realm of Renaissance Revelry!" Bleachers and concession stands were thrown hastily back in time with colorful banners, the smell of roasting meats, and the plywood façade of a castle that hung regally over the ticket counter.

The man who sold them their tickets addressed Elise as "Mi'lady" and kissed her hand. Elise blushed and smiled. Onora fixed the man with a gaze that would have melted iron, but he just winked at her and moved on to the next customer. Highly amused at the scene, Frankie laughed heartily.

They entered under plywood arches painted to look like weathered stone and then headed straight to the first shop to their right, a costumer.

Onora chose outfits for the kids that would offer the best disguise. For Elise, she decided on a green-and-gold brocade gown with puffed shoulders and long, angel sleeves. Elise thought the dress was pretty, but Elise was secretly disappointed that the skirt didn't twirl when she spun around. The matching cap was like a crown but made of green and gold fabric. The net attached to it held the length of her hair, reminding her of the hairnets that the nuns wore in St. Dominic's cafeteria.

Onora picked out an archer's costume for Frankie because it had a hood to hide his distinctive brown curls. Frankie protested, insisting to be a knight with a sword instead. However, the only costume left in his size that came with a sword was a guardsman, which included tights and a Shakespearean ruffled collar.

"No way am I wearing tights," he declared with disgust. In the end, he opted for the Robin Hood outfit.

Felix came out of his dressing room in full, clanking knight regalia, complete with a child-sized plastic sword. Frankie hid his jealousy, but just barely. Dr. Weyls emerged wearing long, flowing, brown robes tied at the waist with a length of cord. His silver hair fell at a white starched collar. A black cap fit snug against the crown of his head.

"Well, what do you think?" he asked, with a slow turn. The tips of his cowboy boots poked out beneath the robes.

"Are you a rabbi?" Frankie asked, clueless. Elise thought it was a good guess.

"I'm Galileo!" he said with considerable enthusiasm. No one else shared in his excitement.

"I. AM. A. ROBOT." Felix walked around the main room of the shop as if the elbows and knees of his knight costume needed oiling.

"And what'll ye wear, Mistress?" the costumer, a boisterous woman with a hump in the middle of her long nose, asked Onora.

"No."

"Thou wilt be as out of place as a pig in a hen house. You'll surely stand out ye will," the woman remarked with a knowing nod.

"You don't want us to stand out, do you?" Frankie asked, chortling.

"Very well," Onora agreed as if she had just consented to being tarred and feathered.

The costumer presented dress after dress in lavenders, pinks, and yellows, and was a relentless font of Renaissance dialogue. Elise tried to discern whether the mole on the woman's face was real or painted on. Until that is, she saw a short wiry hair growing out of it. She grimaced despite herself. Onora selected a dress off the rack in a velvet of such a deep wine color that it was almost black.

"Goest thou to the dressing room, Mistress, where I shall help thee with thine corsets anon."

"I'm no stranger to corsets," Onora countered, her jaw set firmly. The costumer raised an appraising eyebrow while she watched Onora march straight to the dressing room alone.

"But, Mistress, it laces in the back!"

Onora ignored her and flung the dressing room curtain closed.

"Suit thyself!" the woman yelled across the shop, snorting at her unintentional joke. She shook her head in amusement and then disappeared behind the counter.

After a moment, Onora poked her head out of the curtain and gestured for Elise. Mystified, Elise entered the dressing room and shut the curtain behind her.

The shop was well-planned, with fitting rooms spacious enough to fit large petticoats, piles of fabrics, and at least two people. Onora hung her dress and petticoats and kicked off her boots, which Elise quickly set aside. Onora removed her standard uniform of jeans and a long-sleeved, black tee. She left her larger falchion swords, which typically hung at her belt, concealed in the truck. Regardless, she was still covered with hidden weaponry, and, Elise noted, several scars. She folded Onora's clothes, trying not to stare at the thick, silvery scars that slashed haphazardly across the woman's arms, legs, and torso.

Onora caught her in the mirror's reflection. Embarrassed, Elise looked away too quickly, a flush of crimson spreading across her face. Onora slipped on her petticoat. "No one gets out of this life without a few scars," she confided while tying the petticoat at the waist in a tidy bow. "The ones that hurt the most are the ones we inflict on other people."

She pulled the dress over her head and smoothed it down the length of her body. The scars were hidden away once more, except one hairline mark on the left side of her chest. Elise tied the laces that zigged and zagged across the back of Onora's dress. A cream-colored inset flared out from her waist, matching the cream-lined sleeves that draped from her elbows. The costume reeked of the previous occupant's powdery perfume. Elise sneezed.

"You're nice to do this...go to the fair, and dress up, I mean," Elise said sniffling.

Onora answered with a displeased grunt as she hurriedly donned a headpiece similar to the one Elise wore.

"You look really pretty," Elise added tentatively.

Onora stared blankly at Elise a moment, her mouth twitching as if she fought a smile. "So do you, Princess," she uttered, adjusted the dagger-wielding garter around her leg. Without pausing to check her reflection, she threw back the fitting room curtain and left in a rush of fabric.

"Oh, merry be!" the costumer gasped dramatically. "Thy dress makes thine golden eyes shimmer like the sun!"

"You look lovely, Onora," Dr. Weyls said with a gentlemanly nod.

Onora ignored both of them and left the shop with haste.

As Onora made her way into the courtyard, she yanked the hood of Frankie's costume up. "Stay concealed," she ordered.

He flipped his hood back in defiance just as a trio of belly dancers traipsed across their path. What little costumes they had jingled and sparkled in the sunlight. Frankie ogled uncontrollably. Elise shook her head. Life among a bevy of nuns had left him ill-prepared for the number of low-cut necklines they encountered that day.

"According to the directory, Ye Olde Cartography Shoppe should be this way," Dr. Weyls announced, pointing past a mime standing in front of the stadium's center bleachers.

The group wound their way through the lane, dodging bustles and ducking feathered hats. Lively fiddle and lute music wove through the air, which was periodically peppered with the sound of peddlers hawking their wares. Their path was lined with stained glass artisans, swordsmiths, fletchers, incense makers, wood carvers, potters, painters, and candle makers. Roving entertainers performed in the lanes, promising more delights later at their scheduled show times. A juggler amazed them by throwing six flaming torches! Vendors enticed them with their candied pecans and almonds, pretzels, fruit tarts, smoothies, and anything on a stick, including roasted corn, which Dr. Weyls bought for all three children.

As the kids munched on their buttery corn, they happened upon a face-painting booth. A jovial, olive-skinned woman in gypsy garb was painting a pink cat on the cheek of a little girl dressed as a fairy. Excited to give it a try, Elise chewed her fresh bite of corn comically fast, and then gulped it down.

"May I please get my face painted?" she asked, looking up at Onora, and then hastily down to the ground.

"Good idea," Onora replied, leading the way to the booth.

Surprised and elated, Elise skipped after her.

The kitty-faced girl hopped out of the seat and bounded away with her mother. Elise approached the chair.

"Good day!" the face painter greeted amiably with a bow. "How now on this fine day, young mistress?"

"I want to get my face painted, please!" Elise responded, hoping she answered the gypsy's question correctly.

"Huzzah! Would a kitty-cat please thee, like yonder wee girl?"

"Sure!" Elise blurted and climbed onto the chair. She didn't really care what she got, as long as it was purple.

"I will take the boys to watch the chess tournament over there," Dr. Weyls informed Onora, pointing toward the field beside them. In the middle were the festival's king and queen, who sat under a red canopy and ordered human chess pieces around a giant board painted in the grass. The scant crowd groaned and laughed as the black knight on his hobby horse violently slew the white bishop, the scene complete with mock blood and dramatic death.

Onora nodded once, and Dr. Weyls walked away with the boys. Elise noticed that Onora repositioned herself so she could watch them and Elise at the same time. While the painter readied her palette, Onora thumbed through a portfolio of face painting options, and then stopped the gypsy right before the first brush stroke.

"This one," she said, holding the book open to a picture of a girl's face nearly covered with an exquisitely vivid design.

"Ooh! Yes!" Elise clapped. She then sat statue-still while the gypsy painted rapidly.

"Thou art an enchanting mistress of mystery!" the gypsy announced, handing Elise a mirror. Elise beamed at the beautifully-painted butterfly on her face, its purple-and-gold wings stretched across both eyes and flowed elegantly down her cheeks like a masquerade mask.

Onora paid the gypsy, who bowed again, and they set off toward the chess board. Onora greeted Frankie by flicking his hood on his head once more.

"Keep it up. You might be recognized," she cautioned.

Frankie made a mutinous grunt and flipped it back. "But it's hot!"

"You agreed to do what I said. If you do not, we will wait in the parking lot until the map is retrieved." Her face wore its usual impassiveness. Frankie didn't call her bluff, and he pulled the hood up again. They departed the chess game just as the murderous black knight dispatched the white king and bowed to the applauding spectators.

Underneath the stadium bleachers was a complex of buildings that typically housed T-shirt and snack vendors during sporting events. Now, they featured fairy art galleries, hat shops, a leather-bound book store, and various other places of interest for the period. At the end of the row of shops was another grassy field, which was full of wagons and kiosks.

They found Ye Olde Cartography Shoppe toward the end of the row. The store's façade looked like it was carved out of an enormous fallen tree trunk. Elise was curious to see if the inside of the shop continued the log theme as well, but she couldn't tell. It was closed. The sign on the door said:

Charting a New Course.

Back in 1 Hour!

Onora exhaled irritably.

"He's probably having lunch," Dr. Weyls guessed. Attempting to pacify Onora's annoyance, he smiled broadly. "Surely we can find something to do for an hour!" he said with cheer. Hot and tired, Felix made a noise mimicking the sound of a robot shutting down. "Oh, come now. We could learn a court dance."

"Pass," Frankie proclaimed, tugging at his hood and crossing his arms.

"Well, we missed the joust. There's not another until this evening." Julian unfolded the fair brochure and scanned the schedule of events. "There's dressing the maypole... there's a maze. Oh, look! There's an archery competition, Frankie!"

"Yeah, I could get behind that," Frankie approved. They started walking toward the archery range, but not before Onora gave the cartography shop one last glare.

· Chapter Thirty-Five ·

The archery contest started with twenty competitors. Frankie didn't make it past the first round, completely missing his entire target. Elise wasn't surprised he lost; he had never even held a bow before that day. She figured his costume must have given him an added boost of confidence to enter the competition.

He moped around for a bit but was ultimately captivated by the drama of the final draw between three people. One finalist was a woman dressed similarly to Elise and Onora. The next was a teenaged boy dressed as William Wallace, and the final competitor resembled a wizard in a grey cloak and fake white beard. Elise rooted for the William Wallace character to win. Not only was he a talented archer, but he was also kind of cute. The three lined up, knocked their arrows, and pulled back.

The contest announcer shouted "Loose thy arrows!" into his megaphone. All three contestants hit the red center of their targets, but the arrow that struck dead center belonged to the woman. To Elise's great surprise, Frankie sprang up and hollered in celebration. Elise clapped politely, of course.

Afterward, Dr. Weyls bought everyone candied almonds and pecans at a booth directly beside the glassblowing workshop. A glassblowing demonstration had just begun, so they decided to sit down on a long bench to watch while enjoying their treats. A woman emerged, wearing brown pants with a colorful sash around her waist, and narrated while the glass artist went about his work. Elise thought the glassblower looked a lot like Mr. Smee from Peter Pan. He dabbed sand of different colors at the end of a long pole and heated it. As the man blew into the hollow pole, the sand ballooned out to form a glass bubble. The bubble changed shape as he spun the tube. Elise was transfixed in the twisting and whirling of the bubble as the man swung it effortlessly through the air. It was just beginning to look like a vase when someone tapped on her shoulder. She looked to find the bench empty and Frankie pointing toward the exit.

"It's time. Onora wants to get the map now," Frankie said.

Of course she does. Elise thought resentfully as she rose from the bench, saddened that she wouldn't see the finished vase.

Arriving at the shop, Elise was disenchanted to find that the inside was just a regular, square room. However, the walls were covered in framed, brown-tinged maps of all manner and type. She saw maps of America and Europe, and a map of ancient Istanbul streets hung next to a map of Middle Earth. Globes of various sizes and materials were clustered into corners, and even the carpet was a giant map of Africa.

A man with stringy brown hair and a pointy goatee leaned against the counter. A ridiculously long and fluffy feather protruded from his wide-brimmed hat. He touched its brim in greeting as they entered.

"Good day, travelers! How now?"

Elise noticed his eyes lingered on Onora.

"Are you Mr. Bautista, the map collector?" Dr. Weyls asked stepping forward.

"No, m'Lord. I am Sir Brandon of Eastbury," he announced, removing his hat, waving it about, and then flourishing a bow, "Sword Maker and Sword Master at Wicked Weaponry, at thy service. We build custom blades and teach combat lessons." Elise discreetly covered her nose. Apparently, he was committed to his character, because he certainly smelled like he was observing the bathing practices of the period too. "I am minding the shop for Señor Bautista, whilst he hath journeyed to meet good friends in the square."

Onora's eyebrow arched slowly upward, and she narrowed her eyes in suspicion.

"There must have been some misunderstanding," Julian said. "Perhaps he thinks we're meeting him elsewhere." After seeing Onora's displeased gaze, Dr. Weyls offered an apologetic smile. "Felix and I will go to the square to search for him. You three stay here in case he comes back."

Onora gave no response but pursed her lips tightly in disapproval.

Dr. Weyls then turned to Sir Brandon. "How might we recognize Señor Bautista? What is he dressed as?"

"The gent is wearing brown traveling robes similar to thine own, Sir. Though he hast a hood and is known for his most wondrous white beard."

"Thank you," Dr. Weyls said, nodding at the man. He then faced Onora and the twins. "Felix and I will hurry along, and will meet you back here, regardless." He held the door with infinite patience as Felix powered his robot-knight arms and legs out of the shop.

"Please take a look 'round the shop. I wilt be hither if thee needeth assistance." Brandon leaned back against the counter. He retrieved a knife from his belt and picked the dirt out from under his nails.

Onora leaned close between Frankie and Elise, putting her arms around them conspiratorially. "Scan the walls and display cases. See if you can find anything that resembles Texas or the Southwest."

The three disbursed on their separate searches, Frankie spinning all the globes while Elise dutifully scoured the hanging maps and the bargain bins. Onora took a calculated turn around the shop, scrutinizing every nook and cranny. After several minutes, Onora gestured for the twins to join her in the center of the shop.

"Anything?" she asked in a hushed tone. The twins shook their heads in unison. Onora nodded. "Okay. You two go ahead and wander around. Pay close attention to everything you see. I'll ask the man a few questions."

Frankie and Elise began browsing together through various trinkets on a display shelf, while Onora found a box near the counter to rifle through.

"If I were interested in a map of the ancient cities of Cambodia," Onora spoke while flipping through a box of posters, "where might I start looking?"

"Such a map would not be on display. Tis a rare map, and Señor Bautista wouldst keepeth it with his collection upstairs," he answered, thumbing over his shoulder toward a brown sheet that hung in front of a doorway.

"I see. Might we browse the collection upstairs?

"Nay, I am afraid travelers may not venture upstairs. That is his private office." He made a gesture of finality with his hand.

"I understand," Onora said politely. "Thank you."

They loitered a while longer. Elise busied herself by perusing the maps once more and deciding which places she would most like to visit. She quickly discovered that a majority of her dream destinations were mythological. As the sun hastened its journey across the sky, Elise perceived that Frankie became restless with boredom, and Onora seemed tense.

Onora meandered around the shop at a slow pace and maneuvered the twins into a far corner. She leaned in close and whispered, "The fair will be over soon, and they will pack up this place and leave town. Our window of opportunity to get you out of this reality is closing. If we wait too much longer, it might be too late." She took a cautious look over her shoulder. "We need that map *now*. I will draw his attention. You two go upstairs and find it." She straightened up, and in a louder tone, said, "How about you both go buy some sodas, and meet me back here in a few minutes? Here," she handed Frankie a twenty dollar bill, "I will see you in a little while, and I expect to see change from that twenty." She gave them a feigned look of reproach.

Elise was impressed with Onora's added reprimand; it sounded like something a mom would say. She felt a wishful pang in her stomach, as she wondered about her own mother. Before she could dwell on her feelings, Frankie grabbed Elise by the hand and led her out of the shop.

Elise ambled along behind Frankie, unsure if he really planned on buying a soda before stealing the map. He led her toward the field at the end of the row of shops. The swordsmith's was just a few paces away, but they turned right, skirting the edge of the buildings. Elise mimicked Frankie's slink and crouch. He seemed to be an expert at sneaking around. She wondered how much practice he had acquired at St. Dominic's, creeping into the Sisters' quarters to play pranks.

Finally, they reached the back of the shops without being noticed and stopped three doors down from the swordsmith's. The cartographer shop's back entrance was covered in a brown sheet. Frankie flung it aside, finding the real door standing open to allow air flow into the building. A few feet ahead was the other brown sheet leading into the shop. Elise could hear Brandon's voice as he answered Onora's questions.

To their left was a set of stairs. With a stealth that troubled Elise, Frankie ascended the stairs. She crept up behind him, being careful not to make a sound. At the top, was a miniscule room—more of a storage closet—that was crammed full of boxes and strewn with papers. The walls were covered, from ceiling to floor, in maps framed and under glass. On a stool in one corner sat a closed laptop, its power light blinking.

Frankie flipped his hood back and stared agape at Elise. "What are you doing here? You're supposed to be my lookout!"

"Oh!" Elise quietly exclaimed, and then paused, taken aback at how her brother sounded like Onora did when she was the librarian at the orphanage, scolding them in her hallowed library. She scuttled downstairs, stopping halfway down, and then tiptoeing back to the top. "What do I do if someone is coming?" she softly inquired.

Frankie threw his hands in the air. "I don't know, make a bird noise or something!"

"Bird noise. Got it."

Elise snuck back to the bottom of the stairs, situating herself between the back door and the brown curtain leading to the shop. She waited to catch her breath before braving a look. She quietly crept to the curtain and peered through a slit on the side. From her vantage point, she could see that Sir Brandon had trapped Onora in conversation. His voice grew louder and more animated the longer he spoke, the feather on his hat ruffling in his excitement. She glanced at Onora, who was forcing a grin. Elise stifled a giggle, thinking that perhaps Onora wasn't grinning, but baring her teeth. Sir Brandon offered Onora his sword, which she took clumsily in two fists like a child with a toppling ice cream cone.

"I could teach you some moves," he said with an eyebrow wiggle. "Free of charge."

"Splendid," Onora responded, baring her teeth again.

He moved his sword at her in a slow-motion thrust. Grasping her sword arm, he pulled it in a small circular motion to block his thrust. "This is called a parry," he explained slowly in a tone that Elise knew must infuriate Onora, who merely nodded politely. They began a slow and measured parry and thrust action.

Elise glanced behind her shoulder as she heard papers shuffling upstairs. She winced, and then took a hurried look through the curtain, hoping that the sound didn't carry through to the shop. She breathed a silent sigh of relief when it appeared as if the two on the other side hadn't heard a thing. They were too distracted by their swordplay. Elise wondered how long Onora would let it go on before she'd had enough pretending.

She didn't have long to wait for an answer, because Onora suddenly disarmed Brandon, his sword clanking to the ground and skidding across the floor. Visibly stunned, he offered bewildered congratulations before going to retrieve his weapon. Onora primly covered her mouth with the tips of her fingers.

While Sir Brandon was sidetracked, Onora glanced toward the back entrance. Elise thrust her hand past the sheet, gave a quick wave, and pulled it back again. Onora nodded once in acknowledgement and then quickly refocused on Sir Brandon as he returned with his sword. He struck a pose and challenged her once more. Onora immediately disarmed him again, smiling demurely.

Elise was startled by louder shuffling sounds from upstairs. Figuring that Frankie must have been moving boxes around, she flicked a worried glance at the shop and then wilted when she noticed Sir Brandon look over his shoulder at the noise. Abruptly, Onora rushed at him with a thrust. His focus regained, he blocked her, but she disarmed him, regardless.

Retrieving his sword yet again, Sir Brandon laughed despite himself. "Tis excellent to have such an apt pupil. Shall we try something new?" Sir Brandon asked with a smile. "Tis a technique called Advance and Retreat. First, ye must assume the correct stance." He circled around to stand directly behind her and put one hand on Onora's sword hand. His other hand rested at her waist. Elise twisted her face in disgust. Sir Brandon looked way too close for comfort.

Onora kept her grin plastered on but Elise saw her fist clench. Correct stance achieved, Sir Brandon walked around to face Onora and brandished his sword. "Now, take a large step toward me with thine front foot, and attack," he said.

A loud thud came from upstairs. Elise cringed.

"Like this?" Onora said loudly, throwing her arms wide, and knocking over a tall spinning rack of postcards. Sir Brandon reached to pick up the rack, but Onora thrust her sword toward his outstretched hand. He parried instinctively as another hollow thud echoed through the stairwell.

What is Frankie doing up there? Elise thought, sweat dripping down her forehead. She risked a glance up the stairs but saw nothing except moving shadows.

Returning to the curtain, Elise discovered that the situation in the shop had escalated. Sir Brandon and Onora were now fencing in earnest, the former looking confused and amazed at his student's sudden progress. Receiving several taps to the arm and one to the face with the broad side of Onora's blade, Sir Brandon appeared newly determined, a fire lit in his eyes. He took his fighting skills up a notch, coaxing an amused look from Onora. Their energetic sparring caused globes to spin and career to the floor, posters were slashed on the walls, a glass case cracked, and books cascaded to the ground in their wake.

Elise was glad for the noise because it diverted attention away from Frankie's rummaging upstairs. He was making enough noise to drown out an army.

The battle drew nearer to the brown sheet, where Elise stood. Eventually, they were close enough that Elise could smell Sir Brandon's pungent body odor. She had to warn Frankie.

"Bawk-bawk!" she called out.

Sir Brandon, looking even more confused, glanced toward the curtain in the midst of the melee. Thinking quickly, Onora redirected his attention by stomping hard on his boot. Elise heard him groan in pain.

Frankie peered around the corner of the stairwell and loudly whispered, "A chicken? *That's* your bird noise?" As he leaned forward, something dark and round fell out of his pocket, noisily bounced down the stairs, and landed at Elise's feet. She picked the object up, examined it, and instantly dropped it back on the floor. It was the obluvium pocket watch from the mercantile!

"I can't believe you brought that thing here," she hissed.

"I thought it'd be authentic," Frankie muttered defensively as he carefully trod down the stairs. He adjusted a framed map into the crook of his arm, and then he picked up the watch and re-pocketed it

"They didn't have pocket watches during the Renaissance," Elise whispered, keeping her eye on the curtain.

"How was I supposed to know that?"

Annoyed, Elise balled her fists. She stepped to the curtain and peeped out to ensure they weren't heard. She turned again to Frankie. "Never mind, not important."

"Why aren't you whispering?" Frankie asked, registering her change in tone.

"Because they took the sword fight outside."

A grin spread across Frankie's face. "Let's go!" he said enthusiastically, grabbing his sister's arm.

The twins dashed out the back door and rushed around the buildings. They ducked under the bleachers and blended into the edge of the crowd that had assembled around Onora and Sir Brandon. Frankie tucked the map under his arm as best he could. Elise pulled up his hood.

The fight had moved out the front door, which hung askew by one hinge. The crowd continued to grow, chanting for Onora's victory. Elise could tell that Onora was holding back, while Sir Brandon appeared red-faced, determined, and exhausted. A lock of Onora's hair had come loose and dangled over her forehead while she skillfully parried.

During a slight lull in the duel, Frankie whistled. It was a particular whistle that Dr. Weyls used to call Buddy, the sound low, high, then low again.

Onora, recognizing Frankie's signal, pirouetted, and then slapped Sir Brandon on his rear-end with the flat of her blade, knocking him to his knees. "What a stupendous teacher! Three cheers for Sir Brandon of Eastbury!" she shouted with gusto.

The crowd broke into raucous applause, and Sir Brandon glanced around with a baffled smile shakily playing on his face. Elise spotted Dr. Weyls and Felix, who had just arrived, looking puzzled. They joined the spectators, clapping slowly as they looked for the cause of the excitement. Meanwhile, Onora melted into the crowd as Sir Brandon rose and took several deep bows on wobbly legs.

Elise caught movement in her periphery and turned slightly to see Frankie, who was looking around as if he was making sure no one saw him. He slipped the pocket watch into the tall mouth of his high-top sneaker. Elise's eyes narrowed. "I don't want to be a tattle-tale, but that's dangerous, Frankie!"

He sighed, tucking the map under his arm again. "I wanted to see if it would help me make a portal. I thought that if I held the watch and concentrated hard enough, a portal might open up."

Elise's jaw dropped. *How could he even think about touching that thing?*

"Relax," he said. "It didn't work. Nothing happened. I guess Julian was right when he said it's just a watch now. I'll put it back tonight."

Clearly, he was dejected that his scheme hadn't worked. However, Elise was still angry at him for doing something so stupid. Handling that evil, poisonous metal was just asking for trouble. Regardless, she was overwhelmed with relief that he was unharmed. She couldn't think of anything to say to help him feel better about his disappointment, so when Onora found them in the crowd and led them away, she dropped the matter entirely.

The five travelers convened behind a wine-tasting tent to study Frankie's plunder. Dr. Weyls explained that he had searched the entire square, and asked around for anyone matching Señor Bautista's description. No one had seen him, and he finally gave up once a parade marched through the square, making the search impossible.

Dr. Weyls surveyed the framed map. "Yes, yes!" he exclaimed with satisfaction, pointing to a section of the map. "See, way over here is Mount Livermore, there is the Knife Ridge, or what I call it, anyway. Here is the spring, so that means our home is…here." He pointed to the lower left area of the map. "These spirals indicate sacred sites, and this one is outside our property. But it's not too far away. We could try it out this evening if you're not too tired."

"The sooner, the better," Onora answered. Elise's heart caught in her throat.

· Chapter Thirty-Six ·

On the drive home, Felix fell asleep on Frankie's shoulder. A large bump in the road made his head bounce down painfully on Frankie's shoulder bone, but the boy still didn't wake.

Impressive, Frankie thought as he gazed out the car window, surveying the landscape. Evening sun had turned the horizon golden, the sky above it shifting into a gradient of bold orange, magenta, and finally, deep purples. The sunset cast stark shadows behind the sagebrush, making them seem longer and leaner than they really were. The world seemed still for that moment. As they neared the ranch,

Frankie sat straighter as he noticed a strange mass growing alongside the mountains on the horizon.

"What's that?" Frankie asked.

Julian didn't answer but gunned the engine. The truck moved at an alarming speed, and the closer they got, the more recognizable the mass became. A wide column of black smoke rose high into the air, tainting the golden sky with an ominous haze. The truck flew over the gravel road, fishtailing when it hit the sandy ground at the turn-off. Julian never hit the brake. The smoke grew thicker and blacker.

Julian furiously pushed the buttons on his watch, calling Lekana's name at his wrist. He received no answer.

Felix awoke, looking confused at the commotion. His eyes widened in fear, and Frankie cast a pleading glance at Elise, who immediately took action to distract the boy with his robot.

"She should have had time," Julian murmured. "She should have had time."

Onora leaned forward in her seat, clinging to the bar at the top of her window as they bounced over the rugged terrain. "She should have had time for what, Doctor?" she asked, her brow knitting.

"I put a fire suppression system in the perimeter fence," he said between gritted teeth. "It's designed to hold off wildfires long enough for us to round up the herds and get out to safety. There is a passageway past the spring that leads between the mountains. We have a small cabin there; it is not fenced though. Maybe the fire didn't burn it," he said more to himself than to anyone else.

They approached the perimeter fence, which had small tongues of flame licking through the posts. Julian pressed a button to open the gate, but nothing happened.

Onora faced the kids in the backseat and yelled, "Hang on!"

Frankie met Elise's eye just before the truck barreled through the iron gate. Scared out of her mind, Elise screamed. Though the behemoth truck barely slowed, its occupants were slammed around in their seats like rag dolls. Frankie could see the fire spreading across the plain that surrounded the ghost town, flames hopping from one clump of grass to another, fanned by a hot wind that swirled about their alcove in the hills.

"Come on, come on, come on!" Julian growled as he steered the truck at high speed. The cloud of dust behind them rivaled the roiling smoke before them. Everyone gasped loudly when they nearly clipped the mercantile's porch as they turned the sharp corner at the end of the old pioneer town.

They safely cleared the corner, and Julian punched the gas. The truck barreled toward the farmhouse at breakneck speed. Frankie clenched his jaw and peered around the driver's seat, worried about what they would find. As they rolled down the gravel drive, the house came into view, still standing, and covered in a fine mist from Julian's fire suppression system. The front door stood wide open.

Julian barely stopped the truck before throwing open his door and running toward the house. Onora unbelted herself and instructed the children to stay put. She slid out the driver's side, pushing the auto lock button before closing the door. Frankie heard a clunk as all the truck's doors locked.

Onora looked toward the house. She drew one of her longer dragonfly blades from her belt.

As if that's going to help put out the fire, Frankie thought, shaking his head.

"Lekana!" Julian shouted toward the house, his voice sounding muffled through the truck's closed doors. Julian ran inside, returning a few seconds later, alone. Suddenly, a loud groan and a tremendous shriek sounded, and they turned to see the barn collapse under the fire.

Frankie knew it was only a matter of time before the house went up. The mist couldn't keep the fire away forever. It had crossed the alleyway and was nearing the old ghost town.

"Mama?" Felix called, his voice hitching in his chest.

"It's okay" Elise soothed, putting an arm around the frightened little boy.

Frankie glanced sympathetically at Felix and then exchanged worried looks with Elise. He was just about to ask if she sensed any of the farm animals when her eyes suddenly seemed to lose focus. She stared forward, appearing as if she could see through the back of the seat in front of her.

"I can hear Buddy," she uttered dreamily. "He's with Lekana…and a lot of goats and horses. There is no fire where they are. I can…" she trailed off, a look of perplexity on her face. "I can hear those other animals," she shuddered involuntarily, "the ones I heard when we found the goats after the flood."

Just then, Frankie saw something move out of the side of his eye. He turned to see a man stepping out of the thick smoke. The man was tall, wore a long black trench coat, and had a Mohawk.

"Holy hash! It's him!" Frankie shouted. He and Elise ducked out of view behind the front seats. Elise pulled Felix along with her. Frankie edged closer to the window and rolled it down a crack so he could hear. He inched his body toward the center of the truck and peered through the space between the front seats.

Frankie saw Julian backing away from the man, his arms held out protectively in front of Onora. He thought that was particularly brave of Julian, considering Onora was the one wielding a sword and dagger.

"Where are the children?" the man asked, his voice like wet gravel.

Julian and Onora held their ground and their tongues.

"I've tracked you across thousands of miles. We couldn't get to you through your fancy security system," he said with contempt, kicking the picket fence, "so we thought we could climb in over the mountains. That failed too. Then, we thought we'd smoke you out. You know, it's so dry here. Everything goes up like wildfire!" He raised his arms to the burning world around him and laughed scornfully. "But again, the children were not to be found. So," he said, his tone ominous, "I'll not ask nicely again. *Where* are the children?"

Onora smoldered. Julian said nothing.

"Oh, come now. You're smarter than that, Dr. Julian Weyls. You, of all people, should know what happens when we don't get answers." He knocked Julian's hat to the ground with the back of his hand. "How are your feet, by the way? Are there any toes left for me to cut off, or shall we start with the fingers?"

Frankie met Elise's panicked gaze. She held a now whimpering Felix tighter and began quietly shushing him, saying that everything was going to be all right. Frankie didn't share her optimism, if that's what it really was. He had no idea that was how Julian lost his toes. He swallowed hard as he strained to hear the exchange outside the truck.

A dark-hooded figure emerged from the thickening smoke. In his hand was a long rope, the end of which was tied around the neck of another man, who shuffled on his hands and feet, his nose to the ground like a hound. The knees of the Hound Man's robe were threadbare and muddy, and he drooled heavily as if he'd caught the scent of food.

The Handler threw back his hood revealing his bald head and pale white skin. He sniffed at the air. "No sign of them here," he affirmed, as eight more men in black robes slunk in from all sides, some behind Onora.

The Hound Man tugged at his neck rope, dragging the Handler toward the truck. Frankie stiffened and held his breath, hearing the odious drooling creature snuffling at the ground around them.

Ignoring the dog-like creature's sudden interest in the truck, Mohawk Man strode to Julian and mashed one of his heavy boots into the toe of Julian's until he winced in pain. He grabbed the scientist by the shirt, and then flicked out a wicked-looking round blade that inched close to Julian's throat. "Now, you were just telling me where to find the children, weren't you?"

Frankie's heart pounded in his chest, and sweat trickled down his forehead as he sat helplessly watching Julian's life being threatened. He looked at Elise, who was now silently crying, the tears flowing freely down her face.

"Frankie, what do we do?" she asked, her lips quivering.

"I don't know," he whispered. "But, we can't let them know we're here," he finished, guessing that Elise thought of jumping out of the truck, just to get the man away from Julian. He'd thought the same thing, but knew it was a disastrous plan.

"We can't let anything happen to…" she trailed off, mouthing Dr. Weyls' name so Felix wouldn't hear.

"We need to trust Onora," Frankie said, fixing her with a firm gaze before peering out the windows again.

Mohawk Man still held Julian hostage, the knife cutting into his throat, blood trickling down his neck. "Tell me!" he yelled, twisting his boot into Julian, pushing the knife closer.

"Never!" Julian shouted, right before giving Mohawk Man a solid right hook to the jaw.

His battle cry seemed to set off a chain reaction. The robed men drew their swords and crossbows. Onora dispatched two and managed to deflect the crossbow bolts as she dove for cover. More men in robes materialized from the smoky shadows, brandishing weapons. Mohawk Man threw Julian to the ground, forced his left arm behind his back, and yanked at his pinky finger. He put Julian's pinky against the blade and prepared to slice.

"Wait! They're here!" the Handler yelled. "The twins are in the truck!"

All heads turned, watching as the Hound Man put his head and hands against the back window and snarled. Onora leapt to action, jumping across the hood, and sending two men flying to the ground. Four others followed her, whom she held off while putting herself between them and the truck.

The Hound Man growled, and drove his fist into Elise's window, shattering it. Elise and Felix screamed as glass flew everywhere in the cab. She put her arms over Felix's head and huddled closer to protect him from the glass.

Onora struck at the Hound Man's fist with her blade but was hit in the arm by an arrow. Two hooded men grabbed Onora, and pulled her away, as two more circled around her, reached through the shattered window, unlocked the truck door, and pulled the children out. Frankie grabbed hold of Elise's legs but couldn't keep his grip. They pulled her loose, and then wrenched free a kicking and screaming Felix.

Suddenly, the window on Frankie's side was smashed. He ducked, covering his face and head from the shattered glass that flew around him. He heard the door being unlocked and then opened before a hand grabbed at his ankle and forcibly dragged him from the truck. Glass scraped against his back as he was drug across the floor, and he cried out in pain.

Being struck by an arrow only seemed to motivate Onora, as she intensified her assault on the robed men. She spun and dropped one with a high back kick, then whirled to finish another with a jab to the throat. Two men closed in on her left and right. Undaunted, she crouched low, kicking out the feet from under one, and then lunged forward with her blade on the right. She seemed unstoppable, dropping one assailant after another until the Mohawk Man stopped them all.

"Enough!" he shouted. He picked up Julian by his hair and handed him off to another robed man. "Mingus!" he called to the Hound Man, who snarled and yanked Elise's hair back.

Elise yelped as the creature put his pointy teeth against her throat. Struggling for breath, she stared wide-eyed up at the orange sky.

Onora looked up from her current adversary. She had the man by the neck and had forced him to his knees. She held her sword aloft, poised for a killing blow, but she didn't move a muscle.

"Unless you want to see her precious throat ripped out here and now, Onora," Mohawk Man spat, "you will desist your onslaught of my men. After all," he grinned evilly, "Count Carvil only needs one of them."

Mingus growled, his thick slobber dribbling down Elise's shirt. She whimpered in disgust and fear, tears streaming down her face.

Enraged, Frankie fought against his robed captor's grip, but couldn't escape to help his sister. "Leave her alone!" he yelled into the scorching air.

Onora took two breaths, her eyes scanning the scene around her, before dropping her sword. The man she previously held in a death grip rose, picked up her sword, and then pushed her to her knees, a calculating grin spreading across his face.

"That's better," Mohawk Man said.

"Carvil's calling himself a Count now?" Julian asked, out of breath.

"Yes, and soon, he will be much more than that."

The security system's mist finally failed, and the house began to catch fire. Felix wriggled out from his captor's grip and ran toward the house, screaming, "Mama! Mama!"

"Felix, no!" Julian cried, but Felix ran on unhindered. Julian wrestled from the man that held him, elbowing him once in the ribs and in the face. Once free he ran for his son. Both disappeared into the house. Three robed men attempted to follow them, but Mohawk Man ordered them to halt.

"They're extra baggage. We have what we came for."

One of the men rifled through the truck and found the framed map. He smashed the glass, removed the map, and handed it to Mohawk Man. "General, look."

With a laugh, Mohawk Man said, "I have you all to thank! It appears our job to find a nearby portal has been made easier. We can have you back to the Count tonight!" he rubbed his gloved hands together in anticipation.

"How do you know that portal leads to Carvil?" Frankie inquired, genuinely interested despite his dire circumstances. "It could lead anywhere."

"Ha, ha, dear boy. It *would* lead anywhere…if you didn't have a key, that is. But we have Mingus, our portal navigator."

Recognizing his name, Mingus snarled, his jaw still firmly set on Elise's neck. On all fours, his face was eye level with the children, his hulking presence making Frankie worry for his sister's life.

Mohawk Man's eyes glinted at the fear in Frankie's face. He grinned. "Mingus' mind has been specially…adjusted, shall we say, to open a portal wherever we want to go. On your feet now, Onora." He gestured forward with his knife, prodding the group along the road past the mercantile.

Mingus released Elise from his hold but crawled menacingly beside her, his face just inches away from hers.

Mohawk Man kept a close watch on Onora as they walked. "It took months of tweaking to develop our portal navigator. Many of Mingus' predecessors died, but he had what it took. We need to use him quickly, though; he's only got one more portal in him before he loses it completely. Just look at him!"

A string of Mingus' drool spattered in the dusty ground as he glowered at Elise, who breathed shallowly from having her neck clutched so tightly in his jaws. She slowly reached a hand up to touch her neck, cringing when running her fingertips over the tooth marks embedded in her skin.

Fire ravaged part of the mercantile, and as the group walked past, glass shattered forcefully under the stress of the heat. Onora used the distraction to launch another attack, sweeping the Mohawk general off his feet and into the dirt. She caught a crossbow bolt in the back for her effort. She fell to the ground, and two robed men hoisted her and helped her stand.

General Mohawk rose, dusted himself off, and punched her in the face. Blood gushed from her lip. He pinched her ear and jerked her forward. "This way. I want to have a conversation with you, Onora, without you trying to kill me." He dragged Onora up the plank steps and into the old jail. "Mingus! Open!"

Mingus scampered forward. He looked at the locked cell door and cocked his head. Frankie heard a clink, and the door swung open.

General Mohawk, with the assistance of another robed man, chucked Onora through the door and slammed it shut. He stood back a few paces and regarded her for a moment. Then, he chuckled. His chuckle grew, turning into a full-blown, doubled-over, belly laugh.

"Just look at her!" he screamed through guffaws. "Look at her *face!*"

No one else seemed to find the humor. Frankie could tell Onora was angry, but her current expression wasn't all that different from her usual one.

"Look how utterly furious she is!" General Mohawk chortled. "All because she failed to protect the king's twin children. Again."

Frankie hated him.

"Oh you can't see it?" he asked, eyes gleaming with amusement over Frankie's visible hatred. "It's the same look her mother had on her face before she died. Grim determination right to the end."

Onora's eyes narrowed.

General Mohawk wiped a tear of mirth from his eye and sighed. Heat rose in the small room, and flames licked through gaps at the ceiling as if the hungry flames sensed a fresh fuel source. Most of the roof was alight faster than Frankie could have imagined.

"But, that's a story for another time!" General Mohawk continued, glancing at the growing flames. He turned to Onora, feigning a look of sorrow. "Unfortunately, we won't get to have that chat, Onora. Perhaps in another life. Ta!" He waggled his gloved fingers at her, an evil smile on his face as he closed the door behind him.

One last glance showed Onora in the middle of the cell, her jaw set, and her face a hellish orange hue from the flames that enveloped her. She followed General Mohawk with her eyes until he was out of sight.

"Move. Now. It's nearly dark." General Mohawk led his captives outside what remained of the entry gate. Minutes later, a colossal moan of stressed timber sounded from behind them.

Frankie turned to see the entire ghost town collapse into a pile of rubble and a cloud of smoke. From somewhere in the smoke, a sharp wail broke out that sent a shiver up his spine. It grew in intensity, and then abruptly stopped.

Onora. Frankie thought, his heart dropping. He looked at his sister. Her eyes widened in terror, and her breath hitched in short bursts as if she couldn't take a full breath.

General Mohawk sneered at Frankie and shoved them along.

· Chapter Thirty-Seven ·

I t took everything in Elise's power to put one foot in front of the other. The chaos and emotion were overwhelming. Terror seemed to have opened a floodgate in Elise's brain; images and thoughts of the desert animals around her flowed through her mind, rarely stopping long enough to make sense. A coyote smelled smoke and danger, and then, in her mind, Elise saw the coyote begin to move her pups from their den. Elise could sense mice and jackrabbits scampering in panic from the smoke and flames. A bat caught an insect mid-flight, and for the briefest of moments, she felt the reverberating clicks of echolocation resonating in her head. She grew dizzy. The strange feeling was interrupted by the image of a goat, its body pressed tight as the herd squeezed together in fright. Then, a hawk—no it was an owl—soared into her thoughts as it flew high above them. Through its eyes, Elise could see herself, stumbling along on the ground below. She seemed small and insignificant in the owl's sight.

Elise couldn't tell how long they had been walking. An hour? Maybe more? The sun had set, but the sky was still alight from the burning ranch. She struggled to regain control of her senses, to feel the ground beneath her, and the hot air on her skin. However, she would unintentionally connect with another animal before long, which would break her concentration.

Somewhere in her mind, Elise understood that Onora was dead. Dr. Weyls had vanished into the fire, chasing after his son. She and Frankie had no one left to count on. No one could protect them now.

Elise couldn't grasp how she could hear the thoughts of the hooded men around her. They were people, not animals. Yet, she could hear them both in her ears and her mind, frantic, hungry, tired, and driven by palpable anger. Most clearly, she could hear the thoughts of Mingus, the crazed

Hound Man who drooled at her side. His thoughts rattled away in an incessant chatter about doors and portals, hunting children, how slow the little girl was, and how delicious she smelled. He had fixated his anger and frustration on Elise, and when it reached a fever pitch, his thoughts cycled back around and repeated. Beneath his chatter was a primal desire to give chase and pounce on something, to rip its heart out and eat its flesh. Elise could hear and feel all of this emanating from Mingus. She heard a growl coming from within him, not from his throat, but from his very being. She had to stay calm. If she made any exaggerated movement or sound, she knew he would pounce on her.

Just when she thought she was in control of herself again, she was bombarded with the image of a tarantula skittering into its hole, and then she was aware of a moth finding a yucca flower in the moonlight. She tried to steady her breathing, but she caught her toe on a rock and stumbled slightly. Mingus growled audibly now, sending a wave of gooseflesh up Elise's arms and legs.

A lizard had made its home for the evening underneath the rock Elise had stumbled on. The lizard remained unseen by everyone, but Elise knew it curled in on itself when the rock moved. She felt its fear mingle with her own, and she struggled to breathe. She forced another foot forward anyhow, to keep some kind of control over herself.

She had never heard so many animals at one time before. Every now and then, she would recognize Buddy's thoughts and see Lekana's silhouette through his eyes. Lekana paced and looked to the moon.

Elise wished Grandmother Moon would erase her nightmares like the night before when she and Lekana sat in the pasture together. That time seemed like a distant memory to her, and now her nightmares were too real to be washed away in the moonlight. As the group continued their laborious march toward the mountains, all Elise could hope for was to keep control of her senses, or at least for the animals' thoughts to drown out Mingus' horrifying and deranged mind.

· Chapter Thirty-Eight ·

What am I going to do? Frankie wondered with dread. He couldn't fight like Onora. He wasn't smart like Julian. He and his sister were alone.

Maybe I could try to reason with the General.

Taking a gulp of smoky air to muster his courage, he stammered, "W-why does Carvil want us anyway? We're just two kids. We didn't do anything to him. It's not like we can do anything *for* him. What does he want with us?"

"Count Carvil has worked exhaustively using the obluvium metal to alter people's minds. For example, the men here were redesigned with the ability to hunt you two.

Obluvium entered the men's brains, and gave them enhanced senses of smell and hearing."

Frankie glanced over his shoulder at Mingus, who lumbered behind Elise, scowling and snarling, thick drool oozing from his mouth. Frankie grimaced in disgust.

"Mingus is a unique experiment," the General said, seeing Frankie's repulsed expression. He smirked in amusement and then continued. "Every one of our obluvium experiments was successful, and if it wasn't, the subjects died as a result. You two were different." He put a surprisingly gentle hand on Elise and Frankie's shoulders. "You weren't affected by the obluvium at all. You two are the missing link in the Count's otherwise impervious armor. He wants to know why. Plus, he absolutely loathes the king, so toying with his children is icing on the cake." He laughed and elbowed Frankie hard in the arm, sending him back a few steps.

Frankie clutched at his arm and pressed forward. "But, how were you doing experiments? Julian, said that he brought all the metal with him here."

"Clever Dr. Weyls brought the obluvium to Anwynn from his own alternate reality. He wasn't clever enough to realize that as a parallel universe, of course, Anwynn would probably hold an identical metal. It took some digging, but once I found it, Count Carvil had a nearly limitless supply of obluvium to experiment with."

"Wow. This guy's kind of a jerk, making you do all his dirty work while he sits back and does nothing." Frankie hoped he sounded casual.

"Nice one," the General chuckled, looking mildly impressed. "Trying to manipulate me into turning on him, eh? I like you kid," he said, ruffling Frankie's hair forcefully. It hurt. "It's too bad that he's probably going to kill you. He might not, that's possible. But you'll die eventually from whatever exploratory surgery he performs on you. At the very least, you'll end up like Mingus here." General Mohawk gave another grin, his teeth glistening in the moonlight.

Frankie frantically searched his surroundings; he was out of ideas. He and Elise could try running for it, but where would they go? They would only be hunted down again, swiftly this time, and the men would probably hurt or kill one of them at that point.

They walked westward for what felt like hours. Frankie's feet hurt. His arm ached. His back stung where the glass had scraped him. His face felt like he had a sunburn, likely from being too close to the flames. Gradually, the mountains blotted out the firelight. Elise remained quiet next to him, only issuing small grunts now and again as her feet found a stray rock. Frankie internally wilted; he was letting his sister down. He was a fool to think he could get them out of this. They would probably both die, and he would have done nothing except make conversation with a psychopath.

The moon continued its ascent in the sky; it was full and round and gleaming white. Like a mini sun, it illuminated the landscape around them. The robed men—Frankie counted ten of them now—and General Mohawk periodically stopped along the way to consult the map. He caught snippets of their conversation and concluded that the portal was in a cave halfway up a mountainside.

He glanced at his sister, she was visibly tired and her walk had slowed. Her increasing weariness worried him. He didn't trust Mingus, who never took his hateful glare off her, and The Handler constantly griped about how long it was taking them because of the children's dead weight. He didn't know what either of them was capable of—what they might do to her—if she were to drop in exhaustion.

Well, maybe I am a useless, poor excuse for a brother, but I can help her walk. Resolutely, Frankie put his arm out for Elise to hold. She nodded at him with a look of desperate gratitude and clung to his arm, squeezing it painfully.

Finally, they reached the base of the mountain, where General Mohawk determined the portal to be. He ordered his company to a halt. "According to the map, the portal should be up this mountain, but it could also be up the next slope." He looked at the Handler and the Hound Man. "Pernio, Mingus. You take the twits and head up this slope. We're running out of moon time, so if it is the right place, open the portal and send them through. We can't wait another month. Send a signal of what you find back here to me." The General turned to his other men. "Corrincio, Schlatter, Quincy. You three go around to the next slope, just in case the portal is there, and signal of your status. Go."

At his order, each team went in their commanded direction. Pernio and Mingus led the twins to the rocky hillside, which was covered in a film of slippery dust. The climb was slow and the terrain difficult; it took little time for Elise and Frankie to grow weary. With each wobbly step over jagged rocks, and each painstaking stride over steep, uneven ground, Frankie noticed Elise becoming frailer, her breath rasping, her face pale. Whenever she stumbled or tried catching her breath, Pernio would shove her, hard, in her back, while Mingus snarled at her, as if he waited for one misstep so he could finish her off.

Frankie hated both of them.

Eventually, they reached a point where Frankie thought he could see the cave. It was a black spot on the hillside in the moonlight. As they climbed to a steeper part of the hill, Frankie helped Elise navigate and balance on the treacherous terrain. He felt deceitful, like his helpful actions were treacherous themselves, as he guided her toward her doom. At one point, he even entertained the idea that it might be better for both of them if they just died right there on the hillside. He didn't know what to do but cling to some small hope that whatever lay beyond that portal was actually friendly, or if not, they would have some chance to escape on the other side.

When the steep incline leveled out, Elise took one step and fell solidly to her knees. Mingus, aggravated by the sudden movement, pounced on her. He knocked her flat to the ground, and then stood atop her back, baring his teeth, issuing a low, bone-chilling growl.

"Hey!" Frankie yelled before kicking Mingus hard in the thigh like he was going for a fifty-yard punt. Unscathed, Mingus rounded on Frankie, who hadn't considered his next move. Frankie backed up with his hands in the air.

"Ah! I've had enough!" Pernio screamed in angry disgust. He loosed the rope around the Hound Man's neck. "Have at it, Mingus. But remember, we need to keep one alive."

Mingus' pupils dilated, his eyes turning a menacing, milky black. He opened his jaws unnervingly wide and lunged straight for Elise's throat. Frankie frantically rushed toward his sister to do something...anything. He closed in on Mingus and jumped, grabbing at the Hound Man's boot with the tips of his fingers. Elise screamed as she saw Mingus jerk his foot free from Frankie's grasp, and lurch toward her. Frankie scrambled forward, scraping his knees on sharp rocks, as he tried desperately to stop Mingus from killing his sister.

Just then, and from out of nowhere, an arrow point blossomed in the middle of Mingus' forehead. A figure sprang over the crest of the hill, knocking Pernio in the jaw with the butt of a crossbow, and slapping the sword from his hand. The figure then used the sword to dispatch Pernio with one swift cut of the blade. Pernio dropped to the ground in a silent heap.

Relieved, Frankie let out the breath he had been holding. He glanced with disbelief from Pernio to Mingus, who lay quiet and still at his feet. Then, he looked up.

Standing over the vanquished Pernio was Onora, who breathed heavily, holding a wet sword that dripped red onto the ground below. Her clothes and hair were singed, and her brow looked bloody and burned.

"How did you get out?" Frankie asked, stunned. "We thought you were dead!"

"The building and floor collapsed, and I fell through to one of Dr. Weyls' tunnels. I followed it as far as I could, and then ran the rest of the way." She passed her gaze over Frankie, and then over Elise, who was frantically gulping for air.

Suddenly aware of his surroundings, Frankie rushed to his sister. "Elise!" Frankie shouted, gently shaking her shoulders. Her eyes remained wide and unfocused as if they searched the sky for the air her lungs could not find to breathe.

Angry shouts from below startled Frankie, and he glanced at Onora.

"They know I'm here," Onora said, kneeling down next to Elise. "Elise?" Onora quietly urged, her expression betraying deep concern, which scared Frankie. She tugged at her remaining sleeve and wiped the spattered blood from Elise's face. "I need you to take deep breaths as we practiced. Can you do that?" Elise barely nodded. Onora counted the breaths. "In, two-three-four. Out, two-three-four."

At first, Elise struggled, but after a few tries, she breathed more steadily.

As shouts from the men below drew nearer, Onora noticeably tensed. "Elise, there is a brave girl who lives inside here." She tapped the girl's chest. "Take one more breath, and bring her out." Elise breathed deeply. Onora smiled. "There she is."

Her smile dimmed as she peered up at the summit behind Frankie. "We have to move. Now." She glanced at Elise. "Take my hand." Onora offered her blackened and scraped hand to Elise. She helped the girl to her feet and led them onward.

Together, the trio pushed ahead, up another steep slope, and then stopped so Onora could scan the terrain ahead. To the left was thick and thorny scrub brush. To the right was a sheer drop-off down a blank rock face. The cave was about twenty paces ahead, up a gentle grade.

Onora rested her hand on Frankie's shoulder. He met her firm gaze.

"Open the portal," she commanded.

"But I don't know h—"

"Yes, you do," she asserted firmly. "I'll give you the time you need to go into that cave, and quiet your mind. The portal *will* open. Take this." She unsheathed the remaining dragonfly dagger hidden in her sleeve, handing it hilt first to Frankie.

Frankie noticed her knuckles were raw and swollen, as he took the knife from her. He turned it over in his hands; it was heavier than he expected.

"When you get to the other side, tell whomever you meet that you have diplomatic immunity and that the Black Wolf is watching them.

"Black Wolf?" Frankie echoed.

Onora nodded. She brushed a strand of hair from Elise's face and then offered Frankie a thin smile. The moonlight shimmered in her eyes, reflecting her hardened determination. The voices grew louder, and Frankie could hear growling and barking as well. Elise began to cry quietly.

"Go," Onora ordered, her marbled expression returning. She crouched behind the brush's natural bottleneck, deadly sword poised to strike. The twins hesitated. Onora gestured stiffly toward the cave, her eyes focused in the direction of the approaching voices.

Frankie forced the dagger through his belt loop, slicing it through, so carefully inserted it into the next one. He took Elise by the hand, and they both jogged to the cave. Surprisingly, Elise only stumbled once, considering her vision was obscured by tears. Somewhere in the back of his mind, Frankie was truly proud of her bravery, but he mostly wracked his brain on how to open a portal.

They reached the cave entrance and dashed in. The cave was shallow—about twenty feet across and ten feet deep— and had a wide mouth. On the ground immediately in front of them was a black spot, where ancient man had built multiple campfires centuries ago. Frankie heard water dripping down the wall to his left. Instead of pooling on the ground, the water had found tiny spaces in the rock to trickle through and continue its journey underground. He also heard a stream rushing somewhere down below. "This must be where Julian's spring comes from," he said aloud.

"Where is the portal supposed to be?" Elise asked, ignoring her brother's trivial details.

"I don't know." He heard the weakness in his own voice. He needed to find a portal soon. The clash of steel on steel, and the sound of men shouting and dying came from outside. He didn't hear Onora, but she fought silently. He knew that now. His mind raced.

What do we do now? he wondered, feeling powerless. *There's nowhere to go. I've failed. I've failed us all.*

It was then that Frankie noticed moonlight illuminated a large pictograph that stretched from the ground to the ceiling inside the cave. The painting looked to be twice as tall as any man, and Frankie wondered how whoever created it was able to paint something so large. It was a towering geometric drawing of thin lines, some with square shaped heads at their tops. A horizontal line cut across the midsection of all of them.

What the heck are those supposed to be, snakes?

The intersection of the horizontal line and the snakes began to glow faintly in the exact center. The glow then exploded out into a brilliant circle of white light rimmed in gold. The light glimmered and danced along the outer edge, and the center surface undulated with ripples.

"Holy cow! It's open!" he shouted, pointing excitedly at the wall.

The portal hovered in the center of the rock wall, well over six feet off the ground. The ripples rapidly calmed until the portal was smooth as glass. It was dark on the other side, but Frankie could see a few flickering torches on what looked like a stone wall beyond. He hoped this opened to a good place. For a split second, he feared that Mingus had opened a portal leading straight to Carvil, but then calmed when he recalled that Mingus was lying dead at the bottom of the slope.

"But how do we get up there?" Elise asked, casting a wary eye toward the approaching skirmish, and then again at the lofty expanse in front of them.

"We'll have to climb. I'll give you a boost. Are you ready?"

"No," she replied while marching purposely forward toward the ring of light.

Frankie glanced at the cave entrance and saw Onora, who was very close now. The robed men had driven her back toward the cave, but she had managed to reclaim one of her own dragonfly swords. Now, with a sword in each hand, she dove and spun, attacked and countered, fighting the only two men left. One was an exhausted-looking man in black robes, who was huffing breath to keep up. Frankie knew the man would be dead soon. The other assailant was General Mohawk. He was an extraordinary fighter and a formidable opponent for Onora.

Knowing they were running out of time, Frankie laced his fingers together to help boost Elise to the portal. Elise raised a foot and stepped into his waiting hands. Frankie lunged, lifting her upward where she searched for crevices in the rock that she could grip with her fingers.

Frankie heard a guttural moan to his right, signifying the demise of the last robed man. He risked a peek over his shoulder, panicking when he saw the fight had moved closer to the cave. He saw General Mohawk snatch the dead man's sword. It was just he and Onora now, both armed with two blades, circling and eyeing each other.

"Do I just walk through?" Elise asked with a frightened voice, staring eye level at the portal.

"I guess so," he grunted, pushing her up the wall a few more inches. He steadied her as she put her elbows in place, and then she heaved herself up. She gathered herself onto a skinny ledge that wasn't wide enough for an average person, took one last fearful glance at Frankie, and then walked through.

Frankie watched his sister walk to the other side. She looked around and then turned back to face the portal. She mouthed something to Frankie that he couldn't make out. He remembered then that sound waves don't travel through portals. He glanced over his shoulder at the battle outside.

Onora and General Mohawk fought with intensity now. The battle seemed more of an acrobatic dance involving failed attacks and successful dodges. They ducked, sidestepped, and flipped, and rarely did a hit land its mark.

Frankie had to move quickly. He began to climb in earnest, his fingers feeling around for holes or cracks in the rock face. He slipped once, but caught himself, wincing in pain as he skinned his fingertips. He held his grip, catching his breath, and looked out at Onora. General Mohawk had pushed her closer to the mouth of the cave. Frankie saw that she favored her left leg, but she still out-maneuvered her opponent at times.

Frankie scrambled to the ledge where Elise had stood earlier just before walking through the portal. He hoisted himself up by his elbows. Seeing there wasn't enough width for him to stand, he decided to crawl. He lifted his right knee up and used his right foot for balance as he extended his left hand through the portal's glassy surface. Unable to feel his hand, he tried removing it, but it wouldn't come back out. It was too late; the portal had its hold on him and he had to go through. As he pushed himself through, he glanced back in time to see General Mohawk leaping for him.

· Chapter Thirty-Nine ·

"**H**alt!" **shouted a** deep voice out of the darkness.

Elise held her hands up in surrender, glancing nervously at her brother, who had halted. His body was halfway through the portal.

"I'm not alone here," she said in a high-pitched tone that echoed off the rock walls. The voice didn't sound like her own.

"Halt in the name of the king!" the voice commanded.

Elise suddenly saw four guards in clanking armor, who quickly closed in, their lances pointing threateningly at the twins.

"I *did* halt!" Frankie yelled at the guard. "I can't feel my legs!"

"That man is hanging on by your leg!" Elise shouted at her brother, though she still faced the guard.

Frankie attempted to crawl forward with just his arms, but it was as if he was frozen in place. "Elise! Help! Pull me!"

Elise made a move toward her brother, but the guards jabbed their lances forward in a halting motion.

"I said, don't move!" the head guard warned.

Elise thrust her hands in the air again but shuffled toward Frankie anyway. *They don't seem like the type of men to stab a child,* she thought. They were nothing like the robed men on the other side of the portal. She eyed the lead guard, daring him to try stopping her from saving her brother.

As she neared Frankie, she had a better view of his situation. General Mohawk was hanging in the air, clinging to Frankie's leg with his left hand, and with his right, was struggling to hold off Onora. Elise grabbed Frankie's hands and pulled with all her might. He didn't shift an inch.

She heard footsteps outside an opening in the rock wall. A man appeared. He was so tall that he had to duck to avoid hitting his head on entry. He silently commanded the guards' attention, who straightened but kept their lances pointed toward the kids.

"Why is the portal already opened? Report."

"We were waiting for you, Prince Sigurd, but the portal opened on its own. Then, this girl walked through. Not long after, the boy came through too…well, half of him. He seems to be stuck, Sir."

"Elise? Francis? Is that you?" The prince swept forward through the cave-like room. His dark hair fell just below the shoulders of his black leather tunic. "Stand down, men!"

Lances promptly pointed toward the sky.

"It's Frankie," Frankie answered, "and I could use some help here."

The prince peered out of the portal, and Elise stepped with him. She could see Onora limping on her injured leg, but she still forged on determinedly. Onora blocked General

Mohawk's sword blow, and then vaulted up, grasping the man's belt. She used his belt to pull herself upward as she clambered up the man's torso.

After a struggle, the two were in a contorted grapple that left her blade at his throat and his blade at hers. She wound her arm around the man's left arm. They wrestled stiffly for a moment until Onora looked up toward the portal. Her mask fell for a second time that day. A ray of hope shone briefly in her eyes, before being drowned out in a blink by a wash of despair, and as the sun broke free of the mountains behind her, it glowed faintly on her familiar marble façade once more.

"Close it," she mouthed to Frankie.

Frankie's eyes widened in a brief moment of anguish, and then he nodded hesitantly.

With one slight move, she disabled General Mohawk's elbow. His face contorted in pain, and the two of them fell.

Prince Sigurd and the guard quickly pulled Frankie free as the portal dissolved. Everyone stood staring at a blank stone wall in disbelief.

"Where did they go?" Elise gasped. "Where are they? Where's Onora?" She frantically looked around the room for any sign of hope.

Prince Sigurd shook his head, his jaw clenched tightly.

Sounds echoed off the rock room's walls, wrapping around them. Elise heard waves crashing somewhere not far away. Frankie explored the room and then leaned around a corner where a bright shaft of light had begun to stream through. The prince pulled him back by the shoulder.

"Careful there," he said. His voice sounded a bit British, but not.

"Whoa, we're on a cliff," Frankie said in a rush as he was pulled back around.

Elise held on to Frankie's arm and tiptoed closer to the light source. It was coming from a large hole in the rock, where the sunrise could be seen displaying colors of bright blues and golds. She teetered a bit internally when she saw the sheer drop at her feet, which led to a torrent of waves some ten stories down.

The pit-pat of slippered feet on stairs sounded from outside the entrance to the cave room. A lady stopped in the archway. Morning light shone on yellow curls that peeked out from a white lace head covering. Her alabaster dress trailed the floor. She wasn't just any lady.

"The Lady in White," Elise whispered.

As the guards bowed, Elise's jaw dropped, and Frankie appeared befuddled.

Prince Sigurd cleared his throat. "Prince Francis, Princess Elise, may I present Genevieve of Lowland, Queen of Stromboden."

Disbelief was etched onto the lady's face. She stepped forward timidly with her hand outstretched as if she wanted to touch the children but was afraid they would disappear.

"Queen?" Elise asked. "Then you're our...our..."

"I am your mother," the Queen replied, her voice trembling. She reached forward and fell to her knees wrapping both children in a tight embrace.

"I thought I was too late! The sunrise!" she wept.

Elise was crushed against her shoulder, barely able to breathe. She loved it.

The woman sobbed tears of joy into Elise's hair. Eventually, she leaned back to put a hand on each of the children's cheeks. "There hasn't been one moment since you left that I have not felt the ache of your absence! My heart shattered to let you go, my darlings." She wiped at a tear, sniffled, and continued. "Though I was warned not to, I secretly passed through to see you every time the portal opened. I had to see if my children were alright. However, tonight when I went through, you weren't in your beds! I searched everywhere! I was nearly caught by the Sisters. I begged Prince Sigurd to come and help me find you. But now, here you are, and my heart is whole again!" She caught them in her arms again and squeezed tight.

Elise felt the knot around her own heart fall away. She was lighter. She was home. Tears streamed from her eyes, and she even saw Frankie hurriedly brush a drop from his flushed face.

"Enough of these tears," the queen said, removing a crisp white handkerchief from her sleeve and wiping Elise's face. The cloth came back streaked with dirt and a small amount of blood that was not her own. The queen smiled softly. "We have many happy times ahead."

Elise noticed that Prince Sigurd looked dubious, but he said nothing as the queen tenderly put her hands on the children's backs and guided them toward the cave exit.

Elise hesitated. "But Onora...Dr. Weyls..."

The queen looked to Prince Sigurd, who merely shook his head. Her countenance fell, but when she laid eyes on her children again, they gleamed. "They returned you to me, and I am forever grateful. We shall tell your father, the King, and they will be honored!" She stroked Elise's cheek once before continuing toward the door. A slight man in long white robes peered around the opening.

"Father Fritz!"

"Forgive me, my Lady. I did not wish to disturb a private family moment."

"Of course, not Father. Francis, Elise, this is Father Fritz. He helped you escape before, and has kept the cave entrance a secret for many years."

"Hello," Frankie muttered.

"Pleased to meet you," Elise whispered, offering an awkward curtsy for reasons she didn't know, other than it seemed the right thing to do. Frankie gave her a sidelong glance and grinned incredulously.

"My Lady, I am so pleased for you. Thank Heaven they are safe." The Father continued his discussion with the queen, commenting on the children's happy return and how fit and well they looked.

Elise felt he was being too kind about their appearance. She knew full well they looked like they had been dragged through a pit of rocks. Elise's hair was tangled and matted, and her jeans were torn. Frankie's shins and hands were bloodied and scraped, and he was missing a shoe. The queen beamed at them and resumed their conversation.

"We can't just leave her," Elise whispered to Frankie. She knew Dr. Weyls and Felix would be alright. She could hear Buddy at random times throughout the night, and though he seemed far away, she was fairly certain that he had finally met up with his favorite little boy and Dr. Weyls. However, Onora was alone and in trouble. "What if she needs our help?" Elise asked, tilting her head back to look the tall prince in the eyes, eyes that were a deep blue, just like hers and Frankie's.

"What if she's dead?" Frankie asked.

Prince Sigurd stared straight ahead for a moment. "There is nothing we can do for her now," he said and resolutely strode forward.

Around the corner of the cave's opening there was a series of stone stairs which they began to climb. Despite the stairwell being too narrow for three, the queen held both the children's hands. She kissed their knuckles repeatedly, occasionally gushing her delight to the priest, who seemed genuinely happy in return. Gradually, the stairwell narrowed even more, and they were forced to climb in single file. The queen followed Father Fritz, talking all the while.

"Frankie, you did it!" Elise whispered over her shoulder. "You opened a portal on your own!"

"Yeah, I did! I think."

"Of course you did! It didn't just send us anywhere, it sent us to our mother!"

"Hmm. That's true. I have no idea how I did it, though. I should have been more focused, but I got distracted by some snake drawings." He chewed the inside of his lip. "And then, it just opened right when we needed it to, exactly where we needed it to go."

"Maybe it worked because you didn't force it; you just let it happen," Elise offered.

"Maybe. How long is this staircase, anyway?" he asked wearily. They climbed in silence for a time before he spoke again, this time softer. "Elise?"

"What?"

"I saw Julian's dark matter. In the portal. Did you?"

"I was scared. I had my eyes closed," Elise said, embarrassed.

"Oh. Well, when I put my head through, for a fraction of a second, nothing made sense. There were two circles, which must have been the portals. All around them were hundreds of dark shapes holding them open and filling the space between."

"That's scary!" Elise said, out of breath from her climb.

"But, it wasn't! It was awesome! I think Julian's dark matter is what holds the portals open. I just wish I could tell him." He fell silent.

Elise's legs were on fire from the endless, winding stair climb. Just when she thought her legs would either give out or burn off, they came to a ladder at the top of the stairs. Trembling with exertion, she ascended the ladder. Father Fritz helped her up. She emerged from underneath an altar in a lofty church building. Instinctively, Elise crossed herself, as did the queen. Sunlight glowed colorfully through the stained glass set in the thick cathedral doors.

The group proceeded down the blue carpet in the center aisle between dark wooden pews, Frankie with his one sock, Elise with her ripped denim jeans. She tried to smooth down her matted hair, but it was a hopeless task. She blushed.

Prince Sigurd pushed at the massive entry door and held it open for them. Light streamed over their faces. Elise squinted in the flooding rays of the morning sun, and then she reached into her pocket to clutch Felix's LEGO astronaut.

"Welcome back," the queen said.

More by R. Dawn Hutchinson

Wayfarer: Book Two of the Obluvium Series

Frankie and Elise are safe in their original reality, but the portal closed taking their cherished guardian with it. The twins expect a homecoming, but they're greeted with suspicion instead. In Stromboden, sages are seen as evil, and those with supernatural abilities aren't welcome in the kingdom regardless of their royalty.

The twins' rapidly expanding abilities reveal startling aspects of themselves. Can their powers grow enough to save their guardian cast adrift across space and time? Or will their abilities spiral out of control and change them into the monsters their own people condemn to chains?

Rift: Book Three of the Obluvium Series

Elise and Frankie are on the run as the supernatural sages are hunted down and put to death. The tyrannical king of Stromboden is out for blood, and the twins aren't safe even if they are his children. But the mad Count Carvil is after them too, bent on taking the kingdom as his own and using the mysterious mind-poisoning metal, Obluvium, to enact his revenge. As danger closes in around them, Elise doesn't even feel safe in her own skin, haunted by how dark her own talents can become. Frankie desires nothing more than to let his rising anger out in battle, a battle their small band is proved ill-prepared to fight.

But when Elise is kidnapped, an uneasy alliance is formed. Elise finds herself diving ever deeper into the dark depths of her sage gifts in hopes of controlling an army, and Frankie must use all his power to bring peace to his people instead of the war he had longed for, even if it means changing the course of time.

Caught up in a tempest of vengeance, blood-ties, and powers beyond their control, the twins must discover what is truly worth fighting for and make the ultimate sacrifice to save an entire world.

Thank you, dear reader, for spending time in my world. If you enjoyed this book, I encourage you to sign up to my mailing list at RDawnHutchinson.com, and to leave a review wherever you bought it. There are more books on the way. In the meantime, you can listen to my audio fiction podcast, *The Future History of Newburg*, at RDawnHutchinson.com/podcast. I also invite you to connect with me on social media.

Facebook—https://www.facebook.com/R-Dawn-Hutchinson-Author

Acknowledgements

This book would not be in existence without the help and guidance from some cherished people.

Three cheers to my editor, M.L. Harveland, who graced these pages with her grammatical prowess and who graced me with sincere advice and many needed pats on the back. I am truly grateful.

Special thanks to Kristen for pointing the way. Also, thank you to Anastasia and Aubrielle for being my early book readers. Warm hugs to all of my family and friends who welcomed primitive copies and supported me throughout the entire process.

Finally, to my husband James. Without your unshakeable faith in me, this book would still be merely an idea. My profound thanks and love to you.

About the Author

R. Dawn Hutchinson is a former landscape designer turned professional daydreamer. She still loves spending time outdoors during nature walks around her central Texas home which she shares with her husband, an exuberant dog, and two old-lady cats.